Acclaim fo

"Shuman has the talent to put . . . evil on the page and make it specific and real. . . . "

—*The Washington Post*

"Shuman, who has worked for more than twenty years with the Washington, D.C., metropolitan police, brings a chilling realism to his depiction of crime scenes and has a real gift for conveying fear. . . ."

—*Publishers Weekly*

"Shuman's experience as a veteran cop is evident in his protagonist's carefully worked investigation."

—*Library Journal*

LAST BREATH

"Mesmerizing."

—*Publishers Weekly*

"A story that is intricate, shocking and terrifying. . . . "

—*Tucson Citizen* (AZ)

"Part police procedural, part psychological thriller . . . engrossing."

—*Kirkus Reviews*

"A mesmerizing, gritty, gut-wrenching, gruesome tale that's distinctly not for the weak at heart."

—*Lansing State Journal* (MI)

Last Breath is also available as an eBook

"Shuman does an excellent job . . . the details of the investigation ring true. . . . A gripping, fast-paced and extremely creepy thriller. . . ."

—Bookreporter.com

". . . a unique novel, with a very different protagonist. . . ."

—Iloveamysterynewsletter.com

18 SECONDS

"Excellently paced. . . . Surprising and affecting conclusion."

—*The Baltimore Sun*

"The book is memorable . . . for the pace of the action."

—*The Washington Times*

"Fans of the television series *Medium* should enjoy this novel's combination of parapsychology and real-world detective work, and should also appeal to fans of twisted psychological thrillers (Jeffery Deaver, or say, Thomas Harris)."

—*Booklist*

"Suspenseful . . . Like a John Sanford novel—with a psychic twist."

—*Library Journal*

"Vividly drawn central figures and [an] authoritative voice . . ."

—*Publishers Weekly*

"Moves like a bat out of hell. . . .Fascinating characters, nonstop storytelling, and an explosive ending."

—Robert Crais, author of *The Forgotten Man* and *The Two Minute Rule*

"At turns lyrical, horrifying, and—dare I say—poignant, *18 Seconds* takes an ingenious notion and spins it into a killer yarn."

—Gregg Hurwitz, author of *The Program* and *Troubleshooter*

"Fast-paced, compulsively readable . . . This book's crackling sense of menace pulls you in from the first page. . . ."

—Denise Hamilton, author of *Prisoner of Memory*

"A convincing, perfectly paced novel. You won't be able to look away."

—Paul Lindsay, author of *The Big Scam* and *The Führer's Reserve*

"[An] explosive thriller—brutally authentic in detail and absorbing from beginning to end."

—Robert K. Tanenbaum, author of *Counterplay*

"With a brilliant concept, truly human characters, and a *Sixth Sense* sensibility, *18 Seconds* is terrifyingly authentic."

—Brad Meltzer, author of *The Zero Game* and *The Tenth Justice*

"Intricate, compelling, and real, *18 Seconds* is suspense at its up-all-night best. . . . Welcome to a new and substantial talent to your bookshelf."

—John J. Nance, author of *Pandora's Box* and *Orbit*

"A thrill ride, no doubt about it. From page one, Shuman grabs you and pulls you into his chilling, twisty plot,never letting you go until you finally close the book."

—Jillian P. Hoffman, author of *Last Witness* and *Retribution*

By George D. Shuman

Last Breath

18 Seconds

LAST BREATH

A SHERRY MOORE NOVEL

GEORGE D. SHUMAN

POCKET STAR BOOKS
NEW YORK LONDON TORONTO SYDNEY

Pocket Star Books
A Division of Simon & Schuster, Inc.
1230 Avenue of the Americas
New York, NY 10020

First Pocket Star Books paperback edition July 2008

Cover design by Jae Song

Manufactured in the United States of America

10 9 8 7 6 5 4 3 2 1

ISBN-13: 978-1-4165-3491-4
ISBN-10: 1-4165-3491-1

For Melissa and Daniel

My reasons for everything . . .

1

September 28, 1984
Norwich, Connecticut

She didn't feel quite right about the red dress; it wasn't a red dress kind of day. The blue one was nice. She'd tried on the blue one twice already, but the more she thought about it, the more she knew it had to be green. Yes, green would be best for today.

"Green," she said, satisfied, laying it out neatly on the bed. She put nylons, panties, and jewelry next to it and went downstairs in her slip to vacuum the living room for the third time this morning.

By nine she was at the kitchen table, stirring a cup of tea that she had no intention of drinking. She got up twice—once to search for cigarettes, then forgot what she was looking for and came back empty-handed; once to answer the doorbell, but as usual there was no one there.

She chewed the skin on her knuckles, studying the refrigerator, conscious of the passing time. The rubber seals on the sides of the doors were dappled with mold, a job for Mr. Clean or Clorox or Natural Citrus, she could never remember which.

Her nerves were shot, she thought, laughing out loud. "Silly, silly me." She pinched her wrist until it hurt, glanced up at the second hand sweeping the yellow sunburst wall clock. "One," she said out loud, and then "two," but by "eight" she couldn't get the words out anymore, and the first tear of the day plunked into her tea.

She stared at the murky ripples in the cup, looking for a sign. Why couldn't she feel anything? Why couldn't she remember anything? What was she missing that the rest of the world seemed to have?

She breathed in the warmth rising from the cup, the sweet cinnamon and sassafras collecting around her nostrils, and formed a crooked smile. She would like to have had people think of her as eccentric—eccentric was fashionable these days—but in truth she had a screw loose. That was the problem and everyone knew it.

The ripples in the tea went still; she watched her reflection transforming into a gingerbread girl, silver candied beads thumb-pressed into a tiara. She smiled at the memory of rolling dough with her grandmother, but only for a second. There was a shadow behind the woman, and it portended bad things.

The image of the gingerbread girl began to soak up the tea and then an arm broke away, a leg, and at last the head sank into the murky liquid and the girl with the tiara was no more.

The noon bell tolled from Our Lady of Joy on Madison Street. Her eyes snapped up to the clock, then to the telephone on the wall, then to the grocery list on the refrigerator. She had been thinking about the refrigerator off and on all morning, but she didn't know why.

She took a deep breath. Where had the morning gone? she wondered. It seemed as if there was never enough time to get anything done.

"Groceries and green," she said evenly, "groceries and green." That's why she'd picked the green dress for today. It was to remind her of something, but what?

Maybe John knew? John knew everything. She wanted to call John, but they would only tell her he was at work. That's what they always told her. Work, work, work, couldn't they understand that she needed to talk to him?

She shivered. The house suddenly felt cold.

She looked at the telephone again, then the door to the living room. Maybe she should turn on the television and check the weather. Maybe she would need a raincoat when she went out. "No, no, silly girl. It's not supposed to rain all week. You're just trying to think of excuses not to go upstairs."

She put a hand on her chest, took a deep breath, and slid her fingers beneath the silk slip. She closed her eyes and massaged her breast, thumb exciting the nipple until it was hard, tears running down both cheeks now, and slowly she stood. With her hand still on her breast, she started for the stairs.

The mask was in a bottom drawer under a yellow sweat suit she had bought at Neiman Marcus. What she planned to do with a sweat suit, she had no idea. She'd never worn anything but knee-length dresses all her life. That was about the only thing she was allowed to wear as a child. That was all she cared to wear as an adult.

Besides, she was the same weight now that she had been in high school. Sweatpants were for women who either were trying to lose weight or had accepted the fact that they weren't going to. That's what her neighbor Celia was always saying.

That's why she'd never put on the yellow sweatpants.

Celia? Why did she just think of Celia? Why did Celia make her think about the grocery list?

It was Friday. They needed everything—milk, eggs, bread—even though she had just been to the store on Tuesday. Why in God's name hadn't she remembered to get them on Tuesday? It must have been one of those senior moments, like Celia was always joking about.

She closed her eyes and pursed her lips. "Concentrate, concentrate," she told herself. "John says you never concentrate enough. That's why you never get anything done."

A moment later she sighed, pushed Celia from her thoughts, and looked down at the mask, not unlike the way a junkie looks at a tourniquet: wanting it, repulsed by it, repulsed by herself. She lifted her hair and pinned it behind her ears. Then she picked up the mask and held it in both hands, thumbs kneading the rubber collar, tracing the molded cast of the rubber face piece.

It was Soviet made and as obsolete as its designers, but then almost everything John handled was obsolete, from dated survival gear to archaic uniforms, things that could be qualified for sale only as novelties. In fact the only thing he handled that was new were the medical kits he took to restock nursing homes.

The mask had a frightening quality, she thought. She remembered the first time she had seen the boxes in the basement. The cartons were labeled Red Army-SchM-1 M38—1941. Someone had written HELMET across the box in Magic Marker. It wasn't a helmet, of course, more of a hood, and the face was made to look like that of a giant insect or one of the aliens you see in vintage comic books. It was black and smooth, with a broad forehead and a triangular chin. Its eyes were round glass panes, and over its mouth there was a respirator hose attached, which was supposed to match up to a filter canister, but canisters would be in other boxes that weren't in the house and you didn't need one anyhow unless you were trying not to breathe contaminated air.

She couldn't explain why she had to put it on, but she knew the moment she saw it that she had to. That was almost a year ago. By now she had gotten very good at it.

She tilted her chin and slipped the hood over her head, pressed the face piece against her cheeks, and sucked the air out of the mask until it was snug.

She grasped the footlong hose that protruded from the mouthpiece, took a deep breath, and heard the rushing of air through the intake hose. Then she cupped off the open end of the hose with her hand and felt the stifling discomfort of a vacuum. This was a world where you couldn't bring your little problems, your little idiosyncrasies. This was a place of the present, of focus, where you thought about yourself and nothing else. This was the amateur walking the high wire.

Things looked different when the senses were ratcheted up to the nth degree; the world looked unfamiliar through the lenses of the round glass eye portals. She was on the other side of the continuum, anonymous and looking back in. She was no longer naughty Mary Dentin.

She put her hand on her face, caressing the slick black rubber. Her husband handled the masks all the time, but John would never have appreciated the beauty, would never have considered putting one on. Poor dismal John in his world of gray. He saw no good, no bad; no happy, no sad. She knew she was to blame. She knew that she weighed heavily on his mind. John, who worked three menial jobs to support her and all the while she was forgetting or burning his dinner, spending like she was out of control, having no interest in his hands, his lips, unable to respond to his slightest attempts at affection. She knew all that.

She knew too that he loved her, even though he understood there was no love inside of her to give back. It wasn't that she didn't love *him* in particular. She had no love for anyone. She was devoid of the feeling and there was nothing he could do, no matter how hard he tried, to make her happy. They had come to terms with that long ago.

He would be horrified to look at her now. He knew that she had secrets. He knew there were nights she walked the streets alone, was not at the movies with friends.

He knew she drank and she did, but only to anesthetize her racing mind. She used the mask when she was home alone, because when she put it on, she wasn't responsible anymore. She wasn't the disgraceful wife and mother. She wasn't a bad girl anymore.

She pushed off the straps of her slip and let it fall to the floor. She took a terry-cloth belt from one of John's old bathrobes and walked mechanically to the bathroom, where she closed the door and pulled the old wicker clothes hamper to the middle of the floor and stepped on it.

One end of the belt had been fashioned into a noose, and this she slipped over her head, pulling it snug around the collar of the gas mask. The other end was knotted around a large S hook she'd bought at a Home Depot. She slipped the S hook through the antique iron ring that held the light fixture, stuffed a small washcloth into the hose, and let her knees bend until the fixture took the weight of her body.

Slowly she picked up her feet and put her hands down, closing her eyes to a faint field of stars, nerve endings prickling. She put her hands on her breasts, then on her stomach, and goose bumps began to rise on her arms and thighs. She felt her head begin to clear, the clutter of her craziness dissipating into the vacuum of space.

She groaned at the pleasure, put a foot on the hamper, and pushed to take the weight off the noose. She found the slightest bit of oxygen in the air she sucked through the plugged hose, prolonging the experience; then she dropped again, and again, until she was nearing climax. One more minute, one more breath; she arched her foot, toes on the hamper, pushing off one last time, when she heard a loud snap and a leg of the hamper skidded across the bathroom floor and under the space beneath the closed door.

She fell five inches fast and jerked to a stop, arms shooting upward to grab the light fixture, legs kicking frantically to find the hamper again. She couldn't die like this, she couldn't be here; she couldn't let them see how pathetic she was. She swiped up at the hook above her head, breaking lightbulbs. Glass rained down over her.

She began to get dizzy, the glass eye windows fogged, she thrashed about some more, then her arms fell to her sides, muscles contracting, spasms contorting her back. Her fingers were clenched into fists, legs swinging over the broken hamper, feet trying to catch the edge, and then suddenly she managed to touch a corner of the hamper with a big toe.

The doorbell rang.

She hung there as still as possible, arms at her side, one leg out in space, the other supported by her big toe on the hamper now leaning precariously to one side.

The doorbell rang again.

Celia?

She put pressure on the toe, managing to rise gently a quarter of an inch. The old wicker groaned under her weight. It was enough to relieve the pressure on her neck, but she was panicking and there was little oxygen to be had through the plugged tube. She tried to calm herself, to hold off as long as she dared without breathing, then put pressure on the toe again to rise and catch another breath, letting herself down again.

Someone was knocking now, knocking persistently on the door, and no one but Celia ever came to her door anymore. What had she forgotten this time? Was she supposed to do something for Celia?

Suddenly she thought of the grocery list on the refrigerator. Was she supposed to go to the store with Celia to buy something?

The doorbell quieted. The knocking stopped. Whoever it was had given up. Green and Greg's mom and groceries. . . .

She raised herself an inch on her toe and took a careful breath.

How many more could she get before the hamper broke?

It was Friday and the end of a week of school. The first hint of orange tinged the leaves around the old brick schoolhouse. The sun was low on the horizon, casting long shadows of the maple trees onto the city streets. He ran his hand along the iron picket fence that went around the playground, kicked a tennis ball lost by a dog, and jumped over a fire hydrant. Horns persisted on distant Fremont, where people rushed home from work to the suburbs.

His father would be at work until midnight at his second job, stocking nursing homes with medical supplies. He was never at home to take him anywhere. They had never played ball together or gone to a game. The family had never taken a vacation together. It seemed there were always bills to be paid, groceries to buy. He couldn't understand why the other boys' fathers were able to do things his father couldn't.

He stopped in his tracks.

The newspaper was still rolled and stuck in the door. The old blue Nova was still parked at the curb. His mother must not have gone shopping. His heart sank in a long moment of wretched disappointment.

He started for the house again, crossed the street, and tried not to doubt her. The windows looked dark at Greg's. Greg's mom's little white Toyota was not in front of her house either.

Stop it, he told himself. She won't forget. She wouldn't forget this time.

He took the steps two at a time. "Home," he yelled, letting the screen door bang.

He opened the fridge and grabbed a Pepsi, snapped the can, and climbed on the counter, looking in the space above the kitchen cabinets for something to eat.

His mother often bought junk food and hid it from herself. She was forever buying things and forgetting about them. He knew most of her hiding places—candy in the well on top of the kitchen cabinets, new clothes under the basement stairs, shoes under the twin beds in the extra bedroom. She had a way of acting as if there were different people inside of her, all fighting for her attention at the same time, all disagreeing. She'd buy a television for the kitchen and put it in the attic. She'd light cigarettes only to stamp them out. She'd fix a drink and pour it down the sink, open a savings account and close it in the same day. She never wore the same clothes all day long, never returned clothes that didn't fit, never read the books she purchased or watched the movies she rented. It was as if she were guided by opposing voices.

"Mom?" he yelled, grabbing a handful of Oreos from an open package, guzzling the soda. "I'm going next door to Greg's."

He was only kidding, of course. He couldn't go next door until everything was ready. Until his friends got home from school and changed and picked up their presents and got rides back to Greg's.

He knew about the surprise birthday party two weeks ago. Greg had heard his mother suggest it to Greg's mom, Celia, who offered to have it at her house so it would be a surprise.

She would make him clean his room or do homework or something to take up the time.

"Mom?"

No answer.

Maybe she was still over at Celia's? Maybe she was putting candles on the cake or tying a ribbon on a new bicycle? Maybe she was hiding in the dining room with the blue eighteen-speed, waiting to yell surprise? She had a hard time keeping things to herself. Sometimes she would give Christmas presents to people at Thanksgiving.

It wasn't really his birthday, not until tomorrow, but Greg was going to Six Flags with his parents in the morning, so it was the only time he could be there, and Greg was his very best friend.

He knew he'd be getting the blue bike he saw in the window of City Cycles, because his mother felt so bad about last year. She promised she would never forget one of his birthdays again. She'd go overboard on Nintendo cartridges and other things too, as she was prone to do. Never able to make up her mind, she ended up buying everything she looked at rather than selecting one thing.

He looked in the laundry room, walked into the living room, then back through the dining room into the kitchen.

"Mom?" He looked up the stairs.

He grabbed the handrail. "Mom?" he said a little less loudly, a little less enthusiastically.

He took the steps two at a time, walked the hall toward the bedrooms. Her door was open and a green dress was laid out on the bed. He saw nylons and jewelry lying next to it. Her purse was hanging on the doorknob, an envelope with one of his father's paychecks sticking out of it. She should have gone to the bank to deposit the checks before she went shopping.

He checked the other bedrooms, all empty, looked down the hall, and saw the bathroom door was closed. He walked toward it, frowned as he bent over to pick up a piece of broken white cane protruding from under it.

"Mom?" He opened the door slowly.

He screamed.

She was hanging from the old light fixture, naked, her face and hair covered by a black rubber mask with glass eyes and a respirator hose for a mouth. There was something stuck in the end of the hose, a rag perhaps or a kerchief.

The clothes hamper was on its side beneath her feet, spilling yesterday's underwear and towels on the floor. She had a toe on it; he could see her foot arched like a ballerina's, muscles quivering to hold her weight up.

He stepped into the room and could see her eyes now through the round glass windows. She was looking down at him, eyes wide, wild, intense.

The phone rang.

He heard the wicker groaning beneath her trembling foot as she tried to raise herself up again.

He looked at her eyes for the longest time. Then he backed up and sat on the toilet seat and stared at her.

The telephone rang again. It would be Greg, calling to tell him the bad news. That his mother hadn't come through, once again.

And for what?

He knew very well what this was, knew from exploring every inch of the house and his mother's hiding places, her so-called diary that she managed to write in fewer than a dozen times a year. She had done this to herself. This was the meaning of her "other place," her "dark world, the only place I can feel pleasure without pain." It was just one more of her fucking peculiarities, the crazy side of her that everyone was always pretending not to see.

This mask, this noose, this thing she was doing to her body was more important than his birthday. This was the kind of shit she woke up thinking about rather than him. He wondered what she was thinking now.

The telephone continued, the doorbell rang, someone knocked, and he ignored it all.

He could still see her eyes from where he was sitting. She was watching him, eyes never blinking, toe trembling on the corner of that hamper. Finally he got up, walked over to the hamper, and kicked it out from under her.

She dropped fast; their eyes locked together as she bounced. He stood there a few feet away, eyes never leaving hers, until he was sure she was dead, until there was no more soul looking back.

He heard knocking at the door, persistent now. He walked to the window and looked out to see Celia. She would have known all along it wouldn't happen. Just like all the other mothers would have known. There never was going to be a birthday party. There never was going to be an eighteen-speed bicycle. She'd forgotten about him again. Just like the times she forgot to pick him up at school, or when she was supposed to take him to a movie or come to parents' day or the soccer game or the school play. He had all but stopped saying it. That his mother was going to be somewhere or she was going to do this or that. He couldn't stand that look on the other kids' faces.

"You didn't forget to do this, did you?" he said to his dead mother, his chin trembling. "How in the fuck did you remember to do this?" He wiped angry tears from his eyes with the heels of his hands. "Was this more important than me?"

He went to his room, got his pocketknife, and came back and cut her down. She collapsed in a heap at his feet. He grabbed her under the armpits and dragged her down the hall, where he put her on her bed.

It took thirty minutes to get her into the clothes she had laid out, then he brushed her hair and cleaned the mucus and the smeared lipstick from her face.

He put the noose back around her neck, then took the mask to his room, where he hid it under his mattress.

Back in the bedroom he sat in a corner chair and looked at her until his father got home.

It was nearly midnight.

The newspapers called it suicide and no one seriously questioned the fact. Mary Dentin had a screw loose, the neighbors told police. Mary was just like her own crazy mother, who stepped in front of a metro bus one Christmas morning.

Mary's grandfather was the only next of kin she

had, save husband and son, and he looked less than happy to be drawn into a funeral. That didn't really surprise the boy; his mother was always uncomfortable around the old man and it seemed there was no love lost between them. When he left after the service that day, the boy never saw him again.

His own father was an outsider, even to his mother. He lived with her and he loved her, but he knew less about her than anyone in the world.

Life changed after that. His father quit all three of his jobs. He would sit in his threadbare recliner all day with a newspaper in his lap and a pen in his hand. He had taken up his wife's erratic habits of smoking Pall Malls and drinking Maker's Mark bourbon. He filled the borders around the printed articles with random words like ROOM ROAD AUTOMOBILE BREACH GERMANY KOREA COLD. He would write the words in bold print, turning the paper sideways and upside-down, until there was no more room in which to write. Then he would fall asleep in his chair. He would still be there in the morning, staring vacantly at the paper as he bade him good-bye for school.

For weeks it went on. The house remained silent, the lamps sparely lit. The phone never rang; friends never came to visit. It was as if they had all had died together.

One day his father showed up at school, the station wagon packed tight with boxes, and they drove west.

2

March 1, 2007
Cumberland Gap, Maryland

The big sedan rolled to a stop. Sherry could hear the creak of metal gates being pulled back on their hinges. An electric window lowered and cold March air filled the cab. The driver exchanged words with a policeman, and the window closed again as the car lurched forward, dipping in and out of large washouts in the road.

She rolled against the play of her shoulder harness, her mind on a conversation she had had with Glenn Schiff that morning. Schiff was now the attorney general for the State of Maryland, but Sherry remembered him as a much younger man, a young Justice Department attorney assigned to an organized crime task force out of Philadelphia when she was only twenty-one.

Their meeting had been a watershed moment in Sherry's life. It was the result of an incident that had begun on a busy Philadelphia street corner, when a man having a fatal heart attack happened to grab Sherry's hand and pull her to the sidewalk with him. "She went down hard, white cane and all," pedestrians told police. "Man wouldn't let go of her hand, it took the ambulance crew to pry his fingers from her."

Sherry's version of what happened was little different except that between the time the man died and the time her hand was removed from his, she saw something in her mind's eye that she couldn't explain. She saw a man being murdered.

She first told her story to a young homicide detective, John Payne. Payne discovered there was a man missing who fit the description she had given him: a teamster boss who was supposed to testify before a government grand jury—prosecutor Glenn Schiff's grand jury—about pension fund fraud and the Mob.

United States Attorney Schiff had the blind, would-be psychic brought before him, thinking she was part of some elaborate scheme of the Mafia's to dupe the government into believing their witness had died.

He grilled Sherry Moore for hours until he was sure that she really had never heard of the man who grabbed her hand or the murdered teamster or any other organized crime figure before the day she recounted her story to Detective Payne. But how could he explain Moore's paranormal abilities to a jury? Schiff had lost the testimony of his murdered star witness, a murder Sherry could describe in alarming detail, but he sure as hell couldn't use her in court.

In the end, he decided to strike all reference to her from the official record and settle for a prosecution built around the hard evidence in the case. Sherry wasn't upset in the least. Sherry, young and unnerved, had had enough excitement.

Or so she thought at the time.

A government stenographer, who recorded the Sherry Moore interrogation by Schiff, later leaked the story about Sherry's vision to the press, and neither the Philadelphia Police Department's homicide division nor the United States Attorney's Office could deny it.

Sherry Moore became an overnight sensation. Everyone was suddenly interested in the blind orphan who lived in the projects of Philadelphia.

That was in 1992, the last time she spoke to Glenn Schiff.

Things had changed considerably for both of them since those days. For Sherry, notoriety brought financial freedom among other things. When she was first able to afford a private education, she decided against a formal academic curriculum in favor of martial arts training. There was a sensei in Philadelphia who was famous for teaching karate to blind children.

As it turned out, the sensei agreed to come to her house twice weekly and give her private lessons, and though initially it was to have been a short-term arrangement, the sensei was so impressed by Sherry's dedication that the lessons continued for more than a decade. Sherry worked her way through the belts like a virtuoso in the making. Her dream was to transform sound and instinct into vision. She was determined to interpret what was around her. Was the hand coming at her a greeting or a threat? Should she meet it with a kick or a block or simply take it and shake?

Becoming physically sharp wasn't so much a choice in her mind as a necessity. She could read and listen and learn at her leisure. But to feel and appear confident in a world of darkness, she knew she needed an edge. She needed some kind of training to heighten her remaining four senses. That was what the fighting arts did for her. It was a marriage of mind and body, bringing balance, composure, confidence, and a perceptible inner calm. Sherry credited the martial arts with getting her through the worst emotional days of her life. Until now. Now she was faltering, and badly. And she knew it.

If Sherry had been surprised to hear Glenn Schiff's voice, she was not in the least surprised by the purpose of his call. A major news story had been unfolding out of western Maryland over the past twenty-four hours. Police in the mountains of Cumberland Valley had been called to the grounds of a defunct meat-processing plant, where someone had discovered three bodies in a refrigeration container. Police wouldn't confirm the identities of the victims, but reporters were speculating they might be the remains of three women abducted along rural I-70 almost two years before.

The story of the missing women was familiar to anyone who was living in the Northeast at the time. Two of the women were last seen in the office buildings they worked in. One, a caterer and the wife of a Washington County police lieutenant, was delivering hors d'oeuvres to an after-hours meeting of health care executives nearby.

All three buildings were just off a forty-mile stretch of the interstate highway between Hagerstown and Frederick, Maryland.

The kidnappings spanned an eleven-week period between June 10 and August 27, 2005.

Sherry remembered the cases well enough. The cable news anchors had dubbed them the Office Park Kidnappings and they were headlined throughout the remainder of that year. The usual experts came out of the woodwork to talk on TV. There were private detectives and former police chiefs, FBI agents and forensic psychologists. There were the profilers as well, but profilers were getting to be too predictable when it came to suspected serial killers, as they were still blaming that same twenty-five- to thirty-five-year-old white male with a history of women issues.

One crotchety old psychiatrist told Fox News, "He will appear normal to the rest of society, but not to the women he has tried to be intimate with. Those women," the psychiatrist said, "would remember something wrong about him, something a little off-key, a bizarre tendency, a hint of hostility"—she raised a painted eyebrow—". . . red flags, the women who knew him would have seen red flags."

They found other experts who made much ado over the design of the employee parking lots where two of the women's cars were parked. They were modern "office park" settings, with grounds meant to complement the ebony glass and stucco buildings, esthetically pleasing mazes of asphalt landscaped with flowering trees and shrubs, but failing in the most basic of crime prevention tenets. They violated the line of sight.

To security experts and cops the world over, ground cover was a bad thing. Police believed that whoever abducted the women was waiting behind the trees and bushes.

A columnist for the Hagerstown *Herald-Mail* responded to the expert the following week using the headline: DUH?

If the killer was waiting behind bushes in the parking lots, nothing of substance was ever found. There was nothing to indicate that the women had even made it to their cars. In fact two of the women's purses and car keys were found at their desks, as if they had left momentarily and intended to return.

If anything could be assumed at all, it was that the kidnapper had a vehicle and was using the interstate to make his getaways. But experts thought it curious that none of the various security cameras that panned loading docks and rear entry doors picked up anything unusual. None of the abductions was ever in view of workers in adjacent office buildings or on access roads, where a passenger in a car might casually see a woman being forced into a car. None was ever in a parking lot that had been seeded—after the second woman's kidnapping—with policewomen acting as decoys.

There had been a theory that the victims knew their abductor. Perhaps he was a security guard who rotated between the buildings or someone from a contract cleaning company or a copy machine repairman or the man who exchanged watercooler containers.

They studied lists of every agency that did contract work with any of the buildings, but none of the vendors interviewed overlapped between the various organizations, and the theory was eventually dismissed.

The fact that two of the women left personal items behind suggested that the women had exited the buildings suddenly. Though all three buildings were alarmed with infrared, none had needed security entrances or cameras trained on employees, so if the women walked out the front door willingly and agreed to meet someone off the property, no one would have been the wiser. They could have gone almost anywhere.

In August the FBI joined the investigation, which by then included police officers from Washington and

Frederick Counties, Maryland State Police, and the City of Hagerstown, all of them amassing hundreds of hours of overtime. They set up night vision surveillances on rooftops and checkpoints on main thoroughfares, and used policewomen dressed as office workers strolling to their cars in parking lots at late and unusual hours.

And nothing ever happened.

Then came the night of August 27, 2005, when a maroon van with a broken taillight was spotted driving erratically on I-70 west of Frederick, Maryland. A trooper attempted to pull the van over and a high-speed pursuit ensued, ending when the van flipped over the side wall of an overpass. It fell fifty feet to the four-lane highway beneath it and the fuel tank exploded. The occupants, two teenage boys from Ellicott City, a town on the fringes of Baltimore, were killed instantly. So was the young woman they had just kidnapped from a downtown Frederick office building.

Unlike the first three kidnappings, there was plenty of evidence in the Frederick parking lot. A witness saw the woman being pushed into the back of the van. The victim dropped her car keys on the sidewalk next to her car. Police found a full five-finger handprint left by one of the teens on the victim's car window. The whole incident was caught on videotape from a loading dock cam.

It was, Attorney General Glenn Schiff said, everything the first three kidnappings were not.

The FBI agreed with that assessment. The acne-faced teens weren't at all the white male, twenty-five to thirty-five, with a history of abuse and women issues that their profilers typed.

Whoever he was, Glenn Schiff told the press, he was not one of the boys from Ellicott City. Good or lucky, he was also far more complex. Even a seasoned convict would have trouble pulling off three successful abductions without leaving some trace of evidence, Schiff said. The Ellicott City teens had criminal histories for petty thefts from Wal-Mart and larcenies from rural filling stations where they had driven off without paying for gas. This was the first felony either of them had committed, and three successful kidnappings by the Ellicott City teenagers would have been tantamount to shoplifting the Hope Diamond.

But the hot button with the victims' families wasn't whether the suspects fit the FBI's profile. It was that the police had managed to kill, rather than capture, the only two people who might have been able to tell them where their loved ones had been taken.

If ever there was a lose-lose scenario, it was one in which the perpetrators of a string of unsolved crimes were killed. How stupid could the police be? And need anyone remind them what was foremost on everyone's mind? It had only been a matter of weeks. What if the first three victims were still alive somewhere?

There were other problems too.

An off-duty postal employee, driving home from a bar the night of the fatal crash, managed to film the burning van with her cell phone before police backup could arrive to set up a perimeter. Graphic shots of the burned Ellicott City teenagers trapped behind the wheel and the kidnapped woman's fractured face partially ejected through a glass moon roof made the evening news before police could release the names of the victims to relatives.

Family members railed against the television station. Arguments escalated on the Sunday-morning talk shows, and those ill-advised press conferences so popular in times of tragedy began to flourish. Experts popped up everywhere. Cops and small-town politicians began to revel in self-importance, their ambition enlarging in proportion to a conspicuous loss of perspective.

Police preferred to believe they had done the job. The Ellicott City teens had been responsible. The brief spate of terror was behind everyone. It was safe to go outside at night once more. And soon they would find the remains of the earlier victims and bring them home to rest.

And so the somber search for three women turned into a stage for self-aggrandizement and profit. Gun clubs were offering ladies' night rates on handgun training. A citizens' group wanted to ban advertising depicting women in provocative states of undress—

including swimsuits and underwear. A Maryland congresswoman wanted to sponsor a bill to replace Labor Day, which she proclaimed obsolete, with Women's Day; *The Washington Post* had a field day over a politician suggesting to the world that America's working class was now obsolete.

So morphed the tragedy into comedy, and the media were all buying tickets. What no one was doing, at least successfully, was explaining how two high school dropouts had been able to lure, kidnap, and hide three professional women from the combined forces of three modern police agencies and the FBI, a fact that was very much on the minds of the state's attorney general and some skeptical professionals in the more senior ranks of law enforcement.

Investigators literally took apart the boys' lives. News shows depicted the boys' homes, the schools they attended, their neighborhood haunts, even the bedrooms they slept in.

Every relative who would talk was interviewed; every acquaintance, schoolteacher, and friend, no matter how long or short the connection, no matter how important or trivial, took a turn in front of the camera.

One of the boys had grandparents living on a dirt farm in Goldsboro, North Carolina. Police there searched nearby cotton fields and a swampland canal with cadaver dogs. The other boy had done time in a juvenile facility in rural Savage, Maryland, where inmates were required to pick up litter along state roads. He would have known the backwoods routes between the city and there. Police searched the surrounding woods using infrared heat-sensitive equipment, but found nothing.

How and where the boys managed to hide the women remained a mystery, but as the days went on without any new kidnappings, police grew more confident in their rhetoric and the fact that two unremarkable teens managed a most remarkable vanishing trick slid off everyone's radar. Resources were released until only a handful of cops was devoted to the search for the missing women.

Attorney General Schiff was asked to evaluate the cumulative evidence from all three jurisdictions in Maryland where the kidnappings took place and to determine from a prosecutorial point of view whether the government could conclude that the teenage boys killed in the fatal police pursuit were responsible for all four kidnappings. In short, the police wanted to close their three other open kidnapping cases.

Glenn Schiff's opinion, written only a week after the deaths of the suspects, stated emphatically not. "Investigators have failed to connect even one of the prior kidnappings to the suspects. Not a hair, not a tire track, not a witness," he wrote. Neither the boys nor their badly burned van bore evidence of the earlier victims, and while it was theoretically possible that the boys or the fire or a combination of both had obliterated all traces of previous victims, Schiff had his doubts. He believed the teenagers planned a copycat abduction of the woman from Frederick and, in keeping with their immaturity and inexperience, were discovered within minutes of their first big-time crime.

If Schiff was correct, the real kidnapper was still out there and police should still be looking for him.

But state police commissioner Sue Blackman countered the opinion, stating the AG's people were investigating the case from an air-conditioned suite overlooking Baltimore Harbor. "Come on down to the hot streets of Hagerstown," she challenged Schiff on a broadcast of CNN news. "Come on down to the real world."

The police commissioner began appearing on morning talk shows, telling the public that the brave actions of "her" troopers saved untold lives. And with every day that passed without another kidnapping, her bravado grew.

"It is time for the armchair warriors to stop badmouthing the real heroes of law enforcement and stop wasting the working taxpayers' money. Law enforcement officials need to get on with the business of protecting their public."

The smaller agencies, Hagerstown City and Frederick and Washington Counties, held on for another month, but the impetus of the search was lost and it would never again be regained. Not until yesterday.

A car door slammed and Sherry winced. *Damn, she tried not to do that anymore.*

Someone on the police radio had been trying to raise a Sergeant Ellerbee and the request droned on every few minutes. They all sounded tired, she thought. Two days of this would wear on anyone.

"Sorry about the ride, ma'am," the driver said. "No one's been up here in years."

Three years, she knew. That's when the plant closed down. Two years ago someone drove away from here with the hopes and dreams of three young women.

The driver was young, in his early twenties, not much younger than Detective John Payne would have been when she first met him. She'd been thinking of Payne all day. The conversation with Glenn Schiff had stirred the memory, but that wasn't so tough. Payne never was very far from her conscious mind. Any excuse at all could bring him to the surface and with him came the usual tears.

But not tonight, not now, she thought. First she had to perform; then she could wallow in self-pity. She reached into her jacket pocket and felt the loose pills she kept ready. She would take one as soon as she was done. It would be the second—or possibly third—since morning, but nothing else seemed to calm her nerves.

She touched the glass of the window with her fingertips. The temperature was falling. The driver had said a storm was producing hail in Ohio; heading east it would catch up with them on the return trip to Philadelphia.

She felt the driver's eyes on her in the rearview mirror. The sensation wasn't new to her. She was used to being observed in public. Having people zero in on her. Payne used to kid that it was her looks. That she was a "hottie." But Sherry knew it was her eyes. That's what would draw people to look at her initially, the fact that she was blind. Most people, like the driver, didn't think that blind people were aware that you were looking at them, but they knew. They always knew.

Being sightless wasn't always apparent in her case. Her eyes articulated light; her blindness was cerebral, not the result of optical failures. One began to notice something was different about her only when she needed to take an untried step or had to reach for something unfamiliar. That's when you began zeroing in.

Neurologically, Sherry was reconstructed at age five when she fell down icy concrete steps; blindness and retrograde amnesia—the inability to remember events prior to the trauma—were partners in her new design. Until the events of last summer, no one knew where she came from or who she was before her fall in front of a city hospital. And certainly no one could definitively explain the third consequence of her unfortunate accident: Sherry could touch the dead and literally see their last eighteen seconds of memory.

The most recent scientific explanation of her gift, as many in law enforcement circles called it, was that Sherry, when touching a corpse, was completing an electrical connection between the neurological receptors in the corpse's outer layer of skin and the front door to the brain, the short-term or working memory. The conduit of the connection was the deceased person's central nervous system. Of course, this works only on someone who is already dead, someone whose brain is not generating its own power and whose electrical system, therefore, is open to invasion. But such a gift, as do most, has its price.

Once Sherry's mind captured another's remaining memory, it became part of her own. Over the years, she had become the repository of final memories of countless people—many of whom were victims of the most heinous crimes. There were days that the monsters rattled their cages in Sherry's mind, days when her emotional reserves were not up to the task of keeping the monsters in check. So many hands she had held, so many final memories she had seen. She could describe the terror and the tragedy of death to anyone interested, but not the other stuff, the stuff that no one asked about. These were the things that haunted her most. The poignant last memories of those who knew they were dying. A man pinned under a truck, a woman caught in a riptide, a prisoner about to be electrocuted, a pilot nose-diving into a mountainside. People anxiously trying to organize the thoughts of what they were leaving behind. The heartache was palpable, the images playing out like words that would form the final paragraph in a real-time autobiography.

It was the eighteen-second summation of one's life. What would anyone's look like?

Heartaches and monsters were the memories mingling with Sherry's own, constantly trying to rise from her subconscious mind to drive her insane. And the memories of last summer's tragedy in Wildwood, New Jersey, went into the cage too and stirred them all into a frenzy.

What entered her mind last summer? A toxic waste pit full of bodies. The lost memory of her mother's murder and revelations about her abandonment on the steps of the city hospital. A mystery father. John Payne, best friend and love of her life, dead at thirty-seven while trying to protect her.

It was more than a lot of stress. She was a ticking time bomb; of that there could be no doubt. The energies devoted to suppressing it all were sapping her vital defenses. Too many things were not dealt with, or at least not dealt with well. By the holidays she was utterly exhausted. Old ghosts were knocking at her door.

Someone on the radio spoke her name and the driver picked up the microphone.

"ETA, cruiser 264?" a woman asked.

"Thirty seconds," her driver said. "We just got through the gates."

"Copy that."

Her driver replaced the microphone and randomly patted his pockets. He needed a cigarette, she thought. He'd been fidgeting most of the last hour. People never quite appreciate how much blind people can sense their surroundings. She could read thoughts, for sure. She could always tell when people were holding back, when they had something they were afraid to say. Payne once said she caught vibes like spiders caught insects. She'd laughed at him at the time. "Everyone can do that, John," she'd said, but she knew she was better than most.

She wished now that they had been less coy with each other, more candid. John was married to Angie and not the type of man to dishonor a commitment. And Sherry was not the kind of woman who would place herself between a man and his wife.

Angie Payne told Sherry at John's funeral that their marriage had become a prison that left them both trapped but unwilling to speak the truth. She knew that John had remained faithful to her, but loyalty without love was less than she had bargained for. They finally talked about divorce the morning he left to work the Wildwood case. She encouraged him to tell Sherry about his feelings for her; they deserved to be happy and so did she. But by that evening, John was dead. And what he could not say in life, Sherry discovered when she held his hand before the funeral. The last eighteen seconds of John's memory were filled with thoughts of Sherry.

Thinking about him now, replaying in her mind his final memories, made sweet and sad feel the same. And not a day went by that she didn't blame herself for his death and grieve. Sherry sighed. She knew she wasn't in a good place right now. She fingered the loose pills in her pocket and unwillingly remembered.

Throughout last fall, she ate little, slept late, and ignored phone calls, her mail, and human contact. Her mind's music was the funeral sounds of heartrending bagpipes and bolt-action rifles. Then one day in November she woke up feeling lighthearted. She was unable to account for it. Was she dreaming? She waited, then she tested, touching the things around her, and the longer she was able to sustain the feeling, the more she believed she was awake.

Winds were pelting the windows with ice. She rolled over and put her feet on the floor. The oppressive gloom was gone. She felt lighter. Was she approaching the end of her struggle? She went about the business of showering and making breakfast. It was as if someone had lifted a yoke from her shoulders for no earthly reason she could fathom, except that today was not yesterday.

She tried all that day to rationalize the new feeling.

She had done nothing differently from the day before. No pills, no drink, no religious experience. She must have simply weathered the storm. The longer the feeling remained, the more convinced she became that she had finally accepted her loss. And acceptance, as everyone knows, is the first step in the healing process.

It was a giddy feeling the longer it was faithful. That afternoon she began to wonder if she might be ready to get on with experiencing life once more, if it wasn't too early to get back into the game.

She threw back the curtains in the living room and put her hands against the glass, delighting in the cold vibrations of ice. She was going to be okay. She would emerge from her self-imposed exile in hell.

She called her service and had her mail forwarded to her home. She called the grocer and then the liquor store, and she invited her neighbor and confidant, Garland Brigham, to dinner.

Garland, a widower and no spring chicken at seventy-one, still taught classes at a local university, but only twice a week and only in the afternoons. Like Sherry he was a night owl at heart, and since Sherry had moved into the neighborhood, she and Brigham had whiled away the evenings, sharing a drink as Brigham read the day's influx of letters entreating Sherry for help.

Brigham later admitted how curious he thought it was that she never mentioned John Payne anymore, how suddenly she had seemed to change that week in

November. But at the time change was encouraging and, like Sherry, he mistook the absence of sorrow for improvement. Brigham, a retired admiral of the United States Navy, was all for helping her back up on the horse.

Sherry deeply believed in what she was feeling, believed it was an ending to the suffering, and she certainly gave no thought that it could be the beginning of something worse.

Sherry's partitioned mind was actually beginning to work at cross-purposes with her, one part choreographing a life of normalcy to hide the other, which was spiraling into a depression as subtle and deadly as carbon monoxide in the night. She was about to learn how intensely cruel the mind can be, one day your friend, the next day your enemy. That nothing handled was nothing healed.

If she had been more like other people, Brigham might have seen what was coming. Brigham was no fool. But Sherry was skilled at hiding her emotions. She always had been. And Brigham, ever a man of action, was encouraged by her desire to work. He only cautioned that she should start slowly and stay away from the business of life and death until she was back on her feet. There were less stressful things to do, he told her, than to go to the scene of a murder.

They decided in late November to act on a request from the Historical Society in New London,

Connecticut, where salvage divers, looking for copper under an overturned barge, had found a cast-iron submarine from the nineteenth century. The vessel, shaped like a football and called a "turtle" in its day, was an obscure artifact of the War of 1812. History recorded the secretive plan for this experimental vessel to tow barrels laden with gunpowder beneath a British 74 blockading the harbor. No one knew if the mission was actually attempted, no one knew exactly if the craft ever managed to work or what happened to the prototype, but such plans were logged in a naval commander's journal, and here for all the world to see was the turtle in the harbor.

When opened, the early submarine contained nothing, however. The vessel had been either abandoned by its pilot or captured by British forces before it was sealed and allowed to sink to the bottom of the harbor.

Sherry was sent back home, disappointed.

The first week of December, Oshawan Eskimos unearthed the body of a man believed to be John Franklin, an English explorer whose ship was caught in the ice in 1845. Franklin's doomed expedition was sullied by rumors of cannibalism, as later told by local Indians. Sherry, eager to test her powers, rushed there on a night flight to Oshawa, where Canadian historical archaeologists were waiting with Franklin's frozen cadaver.

The body, which remained packed in ice, might

well have been made of the stuff, for what little Sherry could get from touching it. So she wasn't quite out of the woods. What had been a summer of loss was now a winter of failure.

On December 7, Pearl Harbor Day, frustrated and nervous, Sherry flew to Atlanta over Brigham's strong objections. Police there had been baffled by a serial killer stalking elderly men. Brigham was afraid that the stress of homicide work would cause Sherry to relapse into the state of despair he had seen her in before her miraculous recovery around Thanksgiving.

He was right.

In one old man's bittersweet final memory, Sherry saw a most startling sunset over an ocean. There was no way to describe the sadness that sunset brought to her, the heart-wrenching melancholy. She had known that it must have replicated a real memory of her own, a similar sunset, on a similar beach. It would have had to have been from a time before she was five, when her mother would have been with her and when she still had the ability to see.

That simple, tranquil, would-be pleasant memory of an ocean sunset turned out to be the straw that broke the camel's back. The inner choreographer had dropped her cold. The facade of normalcy began to crumble. She flew home in a cold sweat, wondering how long she could go on. She didn't know she needed help, but that was part of the illness.

She told Brigham it was a virus, blaming it on airborne germs caught in the confinement of a commercial airliner. That kept him at bay for a week, a week during which she lay in bed twenty-four hours a day, uninterested in moving, eating, getting dressed, brushing her teeth, or combing her hair.

When Brigham finally insisted she call a doctor, the inner choreographer rose to the occasion. Sherry knew more neurologists than you could shake a stick at. One man, whom she hadn't seen in years, was familiar with her tragic summer, and he wrote her a prescription for Xanax.

Sherry had long told another doctor of her dark winter moods—had insisted she suffered from light deprivation, in spite of the fact she was blind. Summers felt good; winters did not. It was that simple in her mind. It had nothing whatsoever to do, she told people, with being able to see—and the doctor, knowing her to be a health nut not prone to exaggeration, prescribed an antidepressant and pills to help her sleep. After all, she had managed to survive an orphanage and being blind to boot. Since he knew nothing of last summer's trauma and personal losses, he considered her no risk.

At home again the inner choreographer took over, only this time she was armed with pills. She managed to say the kinds of things that would satisfy Brigham's questions. She was simply recuperating, she said, while taking fewer and fewer of his calls. She began stacking the mail in a guest bedroom, all the while increasing the dosage and mixing medications that she had now begun to wash down with alcohol.

Just a few more hours, she would tell herself each day. That was all she needed. One more pill, one more drink, and she could put an end to another painful day. And then another and another and who knew what the next might bring? Maybe something would change. Maybe someone would intervene. Or maybe she'd fall asleep and never wake up again. That would have been all right too.

A car door slammed again, but this time she did not react. This time it was real.

The meat-processing plant where the bodies had been found had once been owned by a man named Lionel Hauck, a lifelong resident of the Cumberland Valley. Hauck died of a heart attack in the mid-nineties and his heirs promptly ran the family business into the ground. When they attempted to sell off the assets in 2004, they ran headlong into creditors who were seeking millions in debts and had their eyes on convertible equipment and valuable real estate. A court ordered the doors of Hauck's Meat Processors sealed in anticipation of protracted legal battles.

Protracted they were. The corporation was placed in receivership and the estate was ordered to provide maintenance to the plant's chattels throughout litigation. This went on until the last week of February 2007, when a decision was finally handed down and a judge ordered the assets inventoried in anticipation of disposal.

It started around nine o'clock yesterday morning. A man from Buckley and Buckley, an accounting firm in Hagerstown, arrived at the gates of Hauck's Meat Processors with a ring of keys and an order to inventory assets with due diligence.

Mid-morning the auditor came across a padlocked storage container within the main warehouse. When none of the keys he had been given opened the lock, he called for a deputy sheriff, who brought bolt cutters, and together they snapped off the lock.

The deputy was later quoted as saying it looked like a scene from a horror movie set. The bodies were in a ten-by-thirty steel container. The first of the women was hanging from a noose that had been fashioned around a meat hook on the ceiling.

Two others were found behind a screened cage in the back of the container—both dead with V-shaped ligature marks around their necks. They too had spent time hanging from the meat hook.

It was apparent that at least one of them had been kept alive for some time, though how long that might have been, no one knew. The floor was covered with human waste, waxed drinking cups, and tinfoil wrappers. Their captor had been feeding them fast food hamburgers until he eventually killed them.

The biggest surprise to everyone was how a low ambient refrigeration compressor in an interior storage container managed to chug on for two years without anyone's noticing it.

The police knew at once who the women were. Even in death, the faces made famous on the evening news would have been recognizable to most of the general public.

It wasn't good news for the state police commissioner, Sue Blackman. No one in the exhaustive investigation of 2005 had ever put either of the Ellicott City teenagers near Cumberland, Maryland. Nor could they.

Attorney General Schiff was more certain than ever that the state police commissioner had been wrong about the Ellicott City boys, and he wanted Sherry Moore taken to the crime scene to tell him what these women last saw or remembered.

No one knew the evidence of the 2005 abductions better than he did. Forensics teams had sifted through the ashes of the Ellicott teenagers' van before looking for evidence of the missing victims: earrings, buttons, wedding or engagement rings, anything to prove that one of the other three women missing from the Hagerstown area had been in that van. But there was nothing, and of the three keys found still hanging in the ignition, two matched the vehicle and the third was to the front door of the driver's home in Ellicott City.

Schiff knew that the key to the padlocked refrigeration container would have been the single most important thing in the kidnapper's life. It was the one thing he wouldn't let out of his sight, not even for a moment. The teens, he was sure, could not have been responsible for putting those women in the container.

Schiff didn't try to sugarcoat the situation when telling Sherry Moore what he wanted her to do. The story of her visit was certain to leak, and when it did, the critics would be brutal. There would be challenges to everything they did. There was a component of danger to consider as well, but then, Sherry was used to being a vulnerable witness when the media exposed her identity to the murderers of her victims.

If Sherry was apprehensive about anything, it was that she would be making her first appearance in public since before the holidays. She felt better now that she was taking her assortment of pills, though she realized it was a fine wire she was walking. A not so carefully constructed regimen of pills and alcohol kept her going.

Still, she could have said no. No one would blame her if she opted out. No one was ever going to point a finger at her and say she had done something wrong. There wasn't a civic or moral obligation attached to what she did. Her options were simply yes or no, or, more realistically, what she could live with if she said no.

In the case of these three women, she knew right away she couldn't live with a no, so an hour after her conversation with Schiff, a Maryland state trooper arrived at her home in Philadelphia to pick her up. That afternoon she was driven the four hours to an interchange at Bedford, then south into Maryland and the Cumberland Valley.

The car hit another rut and she was thrown sideways, stirring her back to the moment.

If it hadn't been the Ellicott City teenagers who killed those three women, who was it and what had he been doing for the past two years? What was he doing now? Was he in some prison or psychiatric facility, perhaps a halfway house or a work-release program? Was he reading newspapers and wondering if he left clues, if he'd made some fatal mistake? Or was he out there killing more women?

The car slowed again. Sherry heard muffled shouts and sensed the heightened activity around them. The driver lowered his window and yelled something unintelligible, a nickname perhaps. Knuckles rapped the rooftop and they moved on.

"We're behind the perimeter now," the driver called over his shoulder.

The car rolled to a stop. The driver put it in park and she heard the clip of his seat belt release. Sherry pushed the button on her own belt and leaned forward.

"Is Captain Medina here?" she asked.

"She's standing out in front of us, talking to a lady in a suit. We're about ten minutes early."

Captain Medina would be her contact, she'd been

told by Glenn Schiff. Sherry lifted the hinged glass on her Seiko and traced the raised numbers to 7:48. It was still dark this time of year, though it was often dark when she was brought to touch a body. Sherry's clients seldom wanted publicity.

She closed the crystal and rested her hands on her knees, trying not to hear car doors slam or to consider what she was undertaking. She knew she wasn't any stronger than she'd been in Atlanta when she fell apart at the sight of a sunset. Take things slowly, she reminded herself, focus instead on what the surroundings might look like.

They were in the foothills of the Alleghenies. That much she knew. Eight rugged miles from the Pennsylvania border, twenty from the jagged line that separated Maryland and West Virginia. Sherry was raised a city girl, but she wasn't altogether unfamiliar with the kinds of people that lived here. She had been to rural homes in the backwoods of other mountain states. She had attended a covered-dish dinner in a cinder-block church basement outside Bowling Green, Kentucky. She had visited the open-casket funeral of a minister laid out in the living room of his double-wide trailer. He had been "caretaking" the life savings of an elderly congregation when he died suddenly of a stroke. No one knew where the money was hidden.

She had been to Luray in the Blue Ridge Mountains, where a man beat his son to death with a chain saw.

She had visited the Ozarks in western Arkansas, where a down-on-his-luck estate attorney poisoned his clients. She had been to South Park, Colorado, where a doomsday cult sacrificed a hitchhiker at midnight on the millennium, December 31, 1999.

Not that Cumberland was wilderness. Cumberland was a city of 20,000, hardly backwoods by mountain standards, but the distinction would have been lost on a city dweller. The mountains surrounding the city were dark and silent and the presence or absence of noise and light was a barometer city folk understood. Here there were no sounds to hint of the existence of modern civilization. There were no lights to illuminate the dark highways at night.

It reminded her of her first trip to Minnesota, when she was twenty years old, her first trip anywhere for that matter. She had never before been beyond the city streets of Philadelphia and the silence she'd encountered was disconcerting. In the city you had a reassuring thrum of progress. Sirens wailing, garbage trucks backing up, vendors hawking their wares. You embraced the angry horns and jumbo jets accelerating over the river.

She didn't feel that way anymore. Now she loved silence. It was the noisy world of slamming car doors and rattling cages that frightened her most.

"She's coming," the driver said.

Sherry nodded and took a deep breath, exhaling slowly.

She didn't know Captain Medina. She didn't know what Captain Medina knew about her or her visit. Introductions to police officials at crime scenes didn't always go well for Sherry. It was a fact she had long ago come to terms with.

She wasn't one of them and she never under any circumstances pretended to be. Quite often the police took offense at her presence, and she knew that above all else, you couldn't take any of it personally. This was not covered in anyone's procedural manual. There was no right or wrong way to feel about what she did.

Sherry herself often thought about what it was that drove her to do it and decided it was purpose. That was what mattered most at the end of the day. She wanted to be among the counted. She wanted to show up and contribute. But there was even more than that, she had learned. She had become a voice for those who could not speak. She could say the words that were caught on the lips of the dead. Sometimes it was to convey a secret, sometimes a tender message to a loved one. Sometimes it was to describe a killer's face for those who might avenge their death. If all that seemed a little altruistic, it was no secret that Sherry was compensated by a number of her patrons. The treasure hunters, foreign governments, archaeologists; there were millions of unspoken secrets on the lips of the departed.

"I think they're about done," the driver said.

Not all of the people who came to this crime scene yesterday would have been cops. In fact, not all would have been professionals of any kind. In the country there wasn't always time to wait for professionals. Cops and firefighters needed to be augmented by volunteers. Volunteers—throughout history—were the men and women who were willing and available to take a risk and get their hands dirty. They were carpenters and grocery store clerks and auto mechanics, farmers, welders, and stonemasons. These were the people who raced to burning homes or pulled teenagers from twisted car wrecks. They gave CPR to heart attack victims at the bank or the Handy Dandy Market, delivered babies in cars or in house trailers while cats and dogs looked on.

The blue-light people, John Payne liked to call them. Half of them would not have gone beyond high school or moved more than twenty miles from where they were born. But you had to give them credit, John said, because no one was giving them any money for what they were doing. Sherry often wondered how well the volunteer system would work in present-day cities.

"It looks like they're finishing up now," the driver said.

According to the records of the Cumberland County clerk, four different local businesses had been contracted to care for the Hauck's processing plant over the three years it was in receivership. Two of the companies, both general contractors owned by local families, were no longer in existence. A third, which had expanded to branches in Morgantown, West Virginia, and Bedford, Pennsylvania, claimed that no fewer than seven employees, mostly temps, had been given access to the grounds over a span of two years. Another kept no temporary employee records whatsoever. In short, it was a crapshoot learning who had been given keys in the past two years.

Could they at least narrow their list to tradespeople such as electricians? The answer was no.

The thrust of the court order had been to ensure uninterrupted power to heating systems in the winter. At times caretakers might only have needed to do such ordinary things as clearing fallen tree limbs from power lines or checking main panel boxes to see that none of the breakers was thrown. So keys were entrusted to subcontractors and handymen with no particular skills.

In short, the list of people who had visited the plant over a decade would turn out to be substantial and never all-inclusive. Some might even be the blue-light people who were standing around them right now.

Sherry heard muffled voices. The driver's window was being lowered again. Someone was approaching the car, shoes crunching lightly across the frozen earth.

"Captain Medina's coming," the driver whispered.

A moment later Sherry's car door opened just a

few inches and a hand touched her shoulder. "Sit tight," a woman said softly. "I'll be just another minute."

The hand withdrew, the door closed, and footsteps padded away.

Sherry slouched back against the headrest, feeling butterflies let loose in her stomach.

Thank God, she thought, it was approaching spring, which preceded summer, which brought the healing sun to the Northeast. She had thought lately about moving to sunnier climates, but Philadelphia had been the only home she'd ever known and there was still something hard about leaving the good memories of it. She wasn't quite ready to put them away. Not yet.

The car door suddenly opened again. "I'm sorry, Miss Moore. The FBI showed up out of nowhere and it's getting a little dicey between Washington and our commissioner. I'm Sally Medina." She took Sherry's hand.

Sherry nodded, shook the hand, and forced a smile.

The captain's voice had the throaty suggestion of tidewater. The accent was familiar, she thought, perhaps from one of her cases around Chesapeake Bay.

The air was chilly and she patted the seat next to her, looking for her gloves. She found them, pulled them on, and slid out into the night. The cane she left behind, finding it distracting and cumbersome when she was on a crime scene and had a set of eyes available to direct her.

"Keep the car running, Terry," the captain told the driver.

She took a step across the unforgiving earth and a car door slammed with a bittersweet pang. She heard the wheel of a cigarette lighter spin. The driver was lighting up.

Medina touched the back of Sherry's arm. "I'm supposed to get you in and out without a whole lot of fuss. This is a favor to Glenn Schiff and way beyond my authority. I was in charge of his security detail for a year. Commissioner Blackman would have my bars if she knew about it. You'll have to let me know how I can help you in there. Do you know what happened to the victims?"

"Only what Schiff told me," Sherry said.

"Well, I can't add much more until the forensics work comes back, but there are three bodies inside. All appear to have died by hanging. One is still on the noose; two are on the floor deeper into the room. It's a refrigeration unit, not a freezer, so the bodies have been at thirty-eight degrees for the past two years. They're not in bad shape, but they're not frozen. Got it?"

"Uh-huh," Sherry said.

"We're twenty feet from the warehouse," Medina said. "All of our personnel have been pulled behind the perimeter. I told them you're a special prosecutor. The FBI might not believe that, so neither of us wants to be around when they return."

"Lead the way," Sherry encouraged.

They crossed what felt like a grassy field. The noise fell away behind them and the air was dry, having the bite of mountain elevations. Sherry could feel the texture of winter frost heaves crunching under her feet, could smell the decay of dead leaves in the forest. That, and there was rain in the air. Soon the storm would be upon them. For now she imagined stars framed by shadowy mountains.

"There are five steps up to a loading platform. Five with a handrail. I'll stay to your left and pull open the door. Fifty feet across an open floor before we get to the refrigeration unit." She paused.

"Mr. Schiff said you'd want it exactly like we found it. It's tight inside the container, Miss Moore, so we can't go in together. You'll need me to tell you where you're at and from there you will have to feel your way along."

"Are you from the Chesapeake area?" Sherry asked.

Medina turned and studied the blind woman. "Annapolis," she answered. "Easton, actually, it's just across the river."

"You sparred with Mary Black from Edinburgh. You won your class."

The captain looked confused. "I'm sorry?"

"The International Martial Arts Tournament in Wilmington, two, three years ago."

"You were there?"

"Yes." Sherry nodded.

"You watched . . . wait, don't tell me you were fighting."

"Kiko Messon's dojo from Philadelphia."

"Oh, my God, I saw you guys," Medina said in wonder. "It was amazing. I didn't even know such things were possible."

Sherry's outstretched hand found the handrail and she took the first step.

"I couldn't believe what I was seeing until it was over. Kiko hammering sixth-degree black belts blindfolded. I mean it. I never saw anything like it."

"She was my sensei for ten years," Sherry said.

Medina mounted the stairs to Sherry's left, following a step behind her. "Then you know what you're doing and I take back what I was thinking earlier," the captain said.

"What was that?" Sherry asked.

"That you didn't belong here." The police captain put a hand lightly on Sherry's back. "Just two more steps," she said. "There's the door."

Medina reached around her and opened the latch. "I was surprised when Mr. Schiff told me who I was meeting this afternoon. I don't believe in paranormals."

Sherry smiled. "Can't fault you for that."

"Some politicians will do anything to help their careers. I didn't want to see Schiff on a soapbox using the murder of those poor women to launch a political career. I like him a lot—like I said, I was on his security for two years—but you never know. People get crazy over power."

"What changed your mind about me? You said you took back what you were thinking."

Medina looked up at the stars and laughed. She shrugged. "I don't know. Respect, I guess. I worked wicked hard for my belts and degrees, but I couldn't compare that with what you had to do."

Sherry thought about that for a moment. "We all do what we have to do," she said simply.

Medina grunted, unconvinced, and reached around her to pull the door.

Sherry felt the warmth of the interior of the building. She stepped over the threshold and breathed in the musty air.

"We're going across a concrete floor. There's nothing in your way."

Their footsteps were hollow across the empty warehouse. Sherry sensed the extent of the room, the ceiling high above them.

"The room is just ahead. I'll pull the door again and you work around my left side. I'll tell you what I'm seeing and then you'll have to let me know when you want me to shut up. You okay with that?"

Sherry nodded. "Don't leave anything out." She

reached for Medina's arm and gave her a reassuring squeeze.

Medina gave one back. She reached around her again and grasped the handle of the refrigeration container. Sherry could almost feel the captain's sense of apprehension as she pulled at the door.

The room smelled of meat. That was her first thought, human meat for those who know the difference. Otherwise it stank of dried waste, wood mold, and decay.

Those who saw the crime scene said later it was particularly gruesome because you knew that it hadn't changed in all that time. It was exactly as the killer had left it.

It was remarkable, everyone said, that no one had ever wanted to know what was in that windowless container in Building C. Not for two long years.

"The first body is in front of you, Miss Moore. She's hanging next to a stainless steel table. There is a noose around her neck suspended from a meat hook on the ceiling. She is a redhead, in her early thirties." She hesitated. "Petite," she added, feeling foolish suddenly, not knowing what else to add, what else was pertinent, if anything at all was pertinent.

One corner of Sherry's mouth involuntarily twitched. She reached out, taking small steps, until she touched flesh.

"Right thigh," Medina said. She felt oddly nauseated, though she hadn't been sick on a crime scene in her career.

Sherry pulled off her gloves and tucked them into her jacket pocket. Her hand returned to the leg. Her fingers traced it up to the woman's waist.

Sherry's face took on a concentrated look as she traced the torso around the back to the hands that were bound behind the body. A small guttural sound escaped her lips as she clasped one of them in her own. It was so small. . . . She squeezed.

"If you need—" Medina started to say.

"Shhhhhh!" Sherry shook her head rapidly. *She was in a building, a commercial setting, perhaps office space. She saw tile floors in a long corridor of doors, she was looking out a door, a man was down the hall, white jacket, she couldn't make out his face from the distance.*

She is in the back of a vehicle, lying on her back, looking up at the torn green upholstery. The dome light is taped over with masking tape. It is a station wagon and the back windows are covered with inky purple cellophane. . . . Her hands are tied, there are boxes all around her, white and red boxes . . . brown cardboard, some bore a red cross, a medical insignia stitched in red . . . a black Corvette, two blond boys in swimming trunks. . . . She saw a freckled child crying on a park bench, a golden dog, a Quaker Oats carton in a cabinet, a telephone answering machine. The red light on the machine is blinking. A house trailer surrounded by palm trees . . . She is being lifted off her feet, placed on a table . . . a restaurant, candlelight reflecting on silverware, white linen napkins, there is an engagement ring on her plate. She stares at it and then there is darkness. Suddenly she is looking through fog, her vision is restricted, she is in a building, looking out a window, no, not a building, but there is glass and something in front of her eyes, obstructing her vision . . . a brilliant white light and then only darkness.

Medina watched Sherry carefully, concerned about how rapidly the little puffs of condensation were coming from her mouth.

Sherry released the hand, just realizing how cold it was in the room. She seemed to falter for a moment, then backed away from the woman and turned toward the rear of the compartment.

Medina held her breath, her own heart beating rapidly. "Are you okay?" she whispered.

Sherry nodded.

"You want to stop?" Somehow Medina hoped she would.

Sherry shook her head.

"Go straight ahead. You can feel your way around the edge of the table. Just a few steps beyond it is heavy-gauge wire. You're almost there. Okay, now move your hand to the right. Follow it to the pipe. Now down to the latch and lift. Okay, you're doing great. Pull and kneel, Sherry; they're both to your left. Reach out, straight out from your body. You're touching a shoulder. Trace it to the left, down to the arm, and you'll find a second arm lying across it. They were found like that, together."

Sherry nodded sadly.

She felt for and found the hand, took it in her own, and squeezed . . . and saw *a baby in a high chair, there were people around a table, a holiday feast perhaps. A school, something elementary, a Barbie doll, a young boy in a bright red bathing suit is running circles around her. She is in a confessional, her fingers touching an old brass screen, it is green with oxidation, the boy in the bathing suit is back, but this time he is wearing a suit and lying in a silk-lined casket. There is a naked woman in front of her, ribs exposed, she is staring blankly at a place between her feet. A hamburger wrapper is caught under her heel. . . .*

The third woman's memory disturbed Sherry the most. She saw . . . *a face, not human, not animal, black and slick, no ears, no eyelids, no mouth . . . a man's picture in a frame on a desk . . . a green station wagon . . . large glassy eyes . . . the face again but its nose was a snake . . . hard rain beyond the porch of a cottage . . . a woman with red hair, naked, hanging from a noose . . . yellow daffodils . . . a gray-green pond . . . her reflection, in the eyes of the creature . . . a man in a white jacket . . . a black dog with yellow eyes . . . she's in a small boat . . . it's foggy . . . someone's in front of her . . . a hand reaching out of the fog . . . it was the snake . . . it was touching her breasts.*

Sherry left the mountains of Cumberland in buffeting winds that fronted thunderstorms raging across the Appalachians. The trooper who drove Sherry home told his wife that she didn't speak a word in nearly four hours.

Sherry Moore's visit to Cumberland leaked to the press in a single day. The wife of the state trooper who escorted Sherry home told her best friend, whose daughter was dating a Baltimore newspaper reporter.

A blind woman had been taken to Cumberland, where those three bodies were found, a blind woman who lived in a big home on the shore of the Delaware outside Philadelphia.

It didn't take a genius to figure out who that was.

Police weren't yet confirming the identities of the victims, though they were admitting it was an old scene. The women had been murdered some time ago. All appeared to have been in the container for months, if not years.

Police weren't talking about the strange welts on one of the women's bodies or the large number of ligature scars around their necks either. As hard as it was to believe, these women had been hung more than once. Someone had taken them to the brink of death a number of times. They had all taken more than one turn at the noose before he finally killed them.

The container had been fogged and all identifiable fingerprints had been eliminated, those being the victims' own and two Hauck employees' who just happened to have prints on file, one a Navy reservist and the other a former school bus driver with an S class permit from Missouri. DNA samples found in abundance had been expedited to a Washington lab, processed, and run through CODIS—the FBI's genetic code database of fifty million people—with no match results.

The press began to dispense with the obvious. How the hell had cops missed the connection between two slipshod Ellicott City teenagers and this remote meat-processing plant in the mountains of Cumberland?

There had to be a connection, didn't there? And if there wasn't, they must have let the real killer run loose for the past two years. Commissioner Sue Blackman didn't even try to defend the state police position on the Ellicott City teens. She went straight on the offense, attacking the attorney general for contaminating her crime scene. What the hell was Glenn Schiff thinking? Who had ever heard of a high-ranking politician bringing civilians, let alone psychics, to an active crime scene before the bodies had been removed?

To be sure, the reality was that Sue Blackman and Maryland no longer had a crime scene to contend with. The FBI had now taken possession of every shred of evidence from Cumberland.

3

Allegheny County, Pennsylvania

"We haven't seen you in a year." The woman tossed her red-framed reading glasses aside. She reached for an ultra-slim cigarillo, then a yellow-and-green Bic lighter bearing the likeness of Bob Marley.

"Everything's been good?" She lit the cigarette, blew a cloud of smoke at the wall, away from him.

He nodded.

"Medications?" the social worker asked.

He shook his head. "Haven't needed them."

"No judicial intervention?" She raised an eyebrow, held her cigarette limp-wrist, smoke spiraling into a rat's nest of salt-and-pepper hair.

He put up his hands and shook his head. "Been clean."

"Good, good." She pushed herself away from her desk. She wore an African dashiki to hide her immense weight. Her skin was pale and pocked with purplish freckles. "You want to sit in or are you just passing through?"

"Sit in," he said meekly.

She nodded, studying him. "Group doesn't start for

another fifteen minutes, so bring me up-to-date. What have you been doing since we last saw you?" She crossed a hairy leg.

A year ago the therapy had been mandatory. He had been arrested for assault in McKeesport, outside of Pittsburgh. The judge who ordered counseling wasn't exactly playing games.

He didn't like talking about himself, but group was better than time in county lockup and the arrest had scared the hell out of him. It had been one close call when you considered what could have happened next. When you considered they might have charged him with a felony and taken blood for DNA.

He hadn't intended to hurt her, but then, she was a hooker and hookers were used to that kind of thing. He certainly hadn't expected her to call the police. Though this one was admittedly crying when he left and there were those marks around her neck. The judge hadn't liked those marks at all.

The police picked him up at a tollbooth on the Pennsylvania Turnpike. The girl had called in a description of his car.

His court-appointed attorney wanted to see if the prostitute would actually show up when the prosecutor was ready to present his case. He, on the other hand, wanted no part of mounting a defense and quickly pled guilty to a fourth-degree misdemeanor. Preparing a defense might have meant giving exemplars—bite marks or, worse, saliva. If they ever scanned his DNA into the system, his life was as good as over.

So the misdemeanor was a no-brainer, as was staying out of the courts in Allegheny County, Pennsylvania. The judge wouldn't forget him if his name reappeared. That judge said he thought that from what he'd seen in those pictures, he might be the kind of guy who had done that kind of thing before. Did he have a wife or girlfriend, someone he was abusing at home?

He assured the court he had neither and that this was his first time in trouble with the law. He was glad the girl didn't mention the mask. Perhaps that was even too embarrassing a story for her to recount. That mask would have sent the judge over the top, though, and God knew he was looking for a reason to deny him the misdemeanor. The cops had started showing his picture around town. His attorney told him they were trying to find other prostitutes he might have assaulted. But this was his first time in McKeesport; there was no one around who knew him that well, thank God. It was a lesson he'd learned long ago. The judge had no choice but to let him plead to the lesser charge.

"Your urges, would you say they occur as frequently?"

"I listen to the tapes. They help relax me."

"You still have our tapes." The woman smiled, pleased. "Well, good, good. We're supposed to ask you to pee in the bottle, but we haven't seen you in a while"—she patted his knee affectionately—"all that heavy stuff can wait until next week. That is, if you decide to rejoin us. Right now let's get you into group. That's what you're here for, right?"

He nodded.

She clapped her hands together and smiled with coffee-stained teeth, reached for a handwritten list of names thumbtacked to a corkboard. Her Brillo gray hair bounced off the shoulders of her yellow dashiki.

She mashed out her cigarette and leaned toward him.

"We all have lapses," she said. "What matters is that we keep finding our way back." She printed his name on the bottom of the list, handed it to him, and stood. "Give this to Jennie when you go in."

He rose and turned for the door.

"We have some new faces here since you've been gone. I think you'll like the group. One of them lost his mother about the same age as you, but we'll talk about that afterwards. Over coffee and cake."

She looked at her watch. "Well, you run along now. We're using the room to the left, the yellow room. I'll be along in just a minute."

The meeting ended at nine. He couldn't remember anything that was said, but then, he couldn't remember much of anything about the day.

The meetings never curbed his appetites. They only showed him there were people out there even more fucked up than he was. People who thought the world didn't understand them because they were misprogrammed by their parents, suffered the emotional maladies of their age group, had bad genes and chemical imbalances in the brain. There were three generations of emotional cripples out there. That was what the meetings had taught him.

The counselors at Phoenix liked to say that meetings were like lighthouses and clients like boats on the sea of life. The boats could go in any direction on the compass and always see the lighthouse, always find their way back home. It didn't matter what kind of trouble they had gotten into along the way, it didn't matter how high or turbulent the seas, you could always make it home, and lighthouses were constant and forgiving.

The counselors were right about the sea of life. One day you would be sailing along smoothly; the next you were capsized and fighting for your life.

He'd come here because he didn't know what else to do, where else to go. It was a place and a moment to think. The meeting certainly wasn't going to save him. There were things in life that were bigger than forgiveness, things that could never be solved over coffee and cake.

This morning had started normally enough. He was having his usual breakfast at the diner. He'd just pushed a dollar bill through the plastic top of a Lions Club tin and was reaching for a chocolate bar when he saw the headlines of the *Pittsburgh Tribune Review*.

His knees actually buckled. He stepped back into a customer who was waiting in line behind him. He said something to excuse himself, then bent over to grab the paper and flip it facedown by the register.

"Sorry," he'd told the waitress, fumbling in his pockets for a dollar bill, mumbling apologies to the customer behind him. "This too." He shoved the bill across the counter, turned away, head down, toward the door.

"Pirates lost," the waitress had called after him.

He nodded, expression appropriately glum, and pushed the door open to fresh air.

"Fuck," he whispered with his head down as he hurried through the parking lot, mashing the headlines against his side so no bystanders could see. He wished he could buy all the papers in the world and burn them. Burn them from the face of the earth.

It had finally come.

BODIES FOUND IN CUMBERLAND STORAGE CONTAINER.

DOES CRIME SCENE HOLD CLUE TO THE PAST?

His heart was pounding.

There were things that you knew you couldn't run from. Things you knew would overtake you one day. You might not know the time or the place, you might even lapse into hours of restful respite, but deep inside you knew it was coming. There was never an end once you started down certain roads.

It wasn't Cumberland that was catching up with him. Cumberland was but a milepost, a stop along the timeline that was his life.

There were, in fact, several lives and several iterations of himself. He was constantly changing, morphing if you will. It seemed crazy how a person could perform at so many different levels and manifest so many different personalities. Thinking this, doing that, saying something else, you were on cue twenty-four hours a day. It was exhausting at times.

Cumberland had been a major shift, geographically and in maturity as well. He wasn't the man he was in Missouri, who wasn't quite the man he had been in Utah and Kansas. He certainly wasn't the young twelve-year-old boy in Connecticut with the crazy mother he both loved and hated, was both proud of and embarrassed by. He was old enough now to see her for what she really was, emotionally deficient but cursed with the beauty and the power to affect those in orbit about her.

She used to be on his mind constantly. Now he had his days of respite. Not many, but some. He hadn't been thinking about her this morning when he rose. This morning he had been like everyone else, hungry and anticipating the day. He had actually been on his way to meet a friend about a second job at White Water Will's, where one of the girls had suddenly quit to go back home and they were looking for someone to take her place.

He worked only three days a week now, so he had time on his hands. It wouldn't hurt to put extra cash away for winter. When the weather got bad in the mountains, businesses didn't do well and owners had a proclivity to board up and head for warmer climates. You could never count on anything in the winter but that your heating bills wouldn't go down.

He hadn't shown up to talk about the job, of course, not after he read the newspaper.

He almost had to laugh at the idea. Yesterday eighty bucks a week had seemed important. Now it was the last thing on his mind.

He needed company. He wanted a woman to talk to.

There was that one in Cumberland he liked and killed; she was a redhead. Her hair was short and fashionably spiked. She had a tattoo on her lower back, some charcoal swirls that looked like eagle's wings.

He couldn't remember her face—it was hard to remember faces—but she had talked so softly to him. For hours and days she talked about her family and she'd asked about his.

Why could he never remember their faces? It was always like this with him. After a few weeks, the images got muddled, disjointed, like the memory of an old movie, the remnant of a dream.

Details, once so important, eluded him. He knew

only that he had acted out his fantasies; he had played the part that was him in his life.

Cumberland was different in more ways than one. It was certainly the largest geographical leap he had made in two decades. But it was also the longest amount of time he had ever spent with one of his victims.

He was sorry it had to end. Being able to return each day to his victims was advantageous, posed less risk than all the hours spent in unfamiliar places, never knowing if someone would show up unexpectedly. Never knowing if he had missed a panic-button alarm, or a gun in a nightstand drawer, or a phone set to speed-dial 911. Never knowing if cops had come upon his car and were surrounding the neighborhood, perhaps the very house he was in.

The cops themselves gave him the opportunity to leave Cumberland. When they chased and killed those teenage boys from Ellicott City, they had already made up their minds about their guilt. They wouldn't be looking for him anytime soon.

Meanwhile he was able to move and establish another version of himself. You didn't need to move very far to do that. Five miles could work if you crossed a geographical boundary, and a state line was a major bonus. Tourist and college towns were always good, because so many people came and went. Sure, the cops had sophisticated computer interfacing these days, but it was street talk that got you into trouble to begin with. That's where the cops first got wind of you. When people began to get curious about you, even in a good way, they compared what you said to what other people knew about you. Holes in your past might begin to occupy their minds. The more people knew you, the more likely you were to get mentioned, even casually, if the cops got curious about something. One thing was certain. If they ever questioned him about the missing women, he couldn't stand up to interrogation. He had no alibis.

If he had made any mistake in Cumberland, it would be DNA. He was very careful not to be seen or filmed when he abducted the women from their offices and parking lots. He thought he had been careful as far as DNA went too, he didn't think he'd left any, but you could never be sure when it came to things so sensitive. DNA wouldn't be an entirely fatal error. Like a fingerprint, you had to have a body to compare it to. But a DNA match to crime scenes in the Midwest would tell police the killer was now in the East, and the FBI would begin to give the local cold cases in the area a more serious look.

He didn't want that kind of attention.

The last thing you wanted was people thinking about you. Be vanilla, he would always tell himself. That was the key. Never show an interest in anyone that might reflect back on you. Never draw attention to yourself.

As it was, he didn't think the people of Cumberland

would easily remember him. Cumberland was a fairly transient area. It was a freight hub with dozens of machine shops and metalwork plants. Allegheny College was there. Cumberland was the seat of Maryland's mountain tourism. He'd made no friends or enemies, paid cash for an occasional beer in local bars, went about his six or seven menial jobs, doing neither too well nor too poorly. He paid his rent on time, made no noise, and left no mess, and he was sure he was as forgotten by everyone as if he had never come to the place.

The job at Haucht's meat-processing plant wasn't really a job. He had been doing a guy a favor while he was on summer vacation, running over to the plant each evening to make sure that power was running to the buildings and to see that none of the emergency generators had kicked on. Two weeks later, he returned the keys—two of them now copied—and two months later he was out of town.

If they didn't know he was in Cumberland, Maryland, in 2005, they didn't know he'd been living in Pennsylvania the two years since, which meant he fell off their radar in Missouri three years ago. That was what he hoped, anyhow.

He'd begun to like it here in Waterdrum, in the Laurel Highlands of Pennsylvania. He liked all the nature around him. He liked the rivers and the trails that were once railroad tracks, cut through formidable mountains.

It reminded him of his childhood in some ways. The West had its own kind of beauty, but he'd missed the changing colors of the hardwood trees. And it was time. He'd outstayed his welcome in the West and he needed fresh images. He needed to kill again and more often.

It was a shooting star scenario, according to an FBI report based on the confessions of serial killers. The reenactment cycle of fantasizing and killing would accelerate until the killer was blundering about in a bloody frenzy. While he couldn't resist killing, the report found that he often lost any high he once got from it. Even though there was nothing he could add to the act that could help him reclaim the euphoria, he couldn't stop trying. Once that began, he would alter his routine and then he'd make mistakes.

He would have agreed that something was changing inside him. He knew he had trouble remembering. Images that had once lasted a year now lasted only weeks. He noticed a marked loss in his sexual desire; he had developed beyond the puerile, always fantasizing, but not about their bodies. It was their eyes he'd grown to adore.

He remembered the earliest images, how it began those first years in the Midwest—the rental house on Grant Street in Hutchinson, Kansas; the hardships of a new school, new neighborhood; first holidays without his mother and friends.

His father attempted to start a new life, first

taking work as a laborer, then a housepainter for a local contractor, then a gardener at a nursery where he watered plants, but the essence of John Dentin was gone and soon he was back to sitting in his chair with a bottle. What little communication there had been between him and his father ended completely after his mother died. They each moved through the house, living in stark silence, smiling politely, his father offering an occasional pat on the head, a hand on a shoulder. They didn't talk about his new school. They didn't talk about his father's new jobs. They didn't talk about their past or the present or the future. Life became subsistence; it had the dull quality of a play in which you are an unwilling participant, an actor going through the motions without feeling. Just the way his mother had all her life.

He never got used to his new environment, the Midwestern people, his classmates and teachers. He hated trying to explain himself to others. There was no hiding that. Counselors called him into their offices. They knew his mother had committed suicide. The other children could be cruel. He wasn't just unpopular; he was failing in all his classes. The administrators tried to isolate him from harm. They acknowledged that he couldn't focus in class; he must certainly have disorders. Who would wonder that he wasn't doing well or that he went straight home after school and was never interested in making friends?

Then he met Barbara Hunt—everyone called her Barbara the Hun—who was every bit as strange. They often found themselves sitting together in hallways, waiting to see the same counselors. They actually had to smile at each other in acknowledgment of their situation; it was kind of a "hey, you must be at least as fucked up as I am" look.

Most of the kids in their school were into trick cars and the street corner gang mentality. Barbara was Goth and the only one he'd ever seen. She wore black clothes and black fingernail polish and pierced her body all over. They went to the park after one of their many sessions, smoked cigarettes and marijuana and talked about life.

She'd heard his mother committed suicide; she was sorry about that. She said her own parents pretended she didn't exist. They gave her money, a car, anything she asked for. They didn't care if she came home all fucked up on something or was failing in school. They just didn't want to make waves. They wanted to pretend that everything was always okay.

She said she could get any kind of drugs he could imagine, she had an in with one of the older men in town. He had a brother in Brownsville, Texas, who smuggled stuff in from Mexico, he'd said. She paid top dollar, but then she could.

She said the safest place to hide drugs in the whole wide world was in her room. Her parents would not dare enter her room. They believed in treating her like an adult and that adults had rights to privacy. Not to mention they would have been scared to shit to know what she was doing in there. She'd giggled in a rare moment of levity.

The house was enormous, old and Victorian and very purple. It looked out of place in this suburb of the Midwest. Her room was large, with a gabled roof and dormer windows on two sides. She had an intake fan in one window and an exhaust fan in the other. She told her parents it was better for your lungs than air conditioning. If they didn't believe that, they never said so.

He was a virgin the first time they did it, though neither could have recalled the experience, they'd consumed so much Ecstasy and wine before tearing off each other's clothes. The next time he was straddling her, he put his hands around her throat and she liked it. She said it was scary-cool, the feeling of losing control.

She bought wrist cuffs and choke collars for him to use. They tried scarves and belts and nylons as ropes. They progressed to latex masks. He cut a hole where a straw was inserted into her mouth, and he crimped it off until he felt her body go slack under him.

Then one afternoon something went wrong.

There were drugs all over the room. The police spent as much time collecting them as they had looking at her naked body. Her parents freaked out, like he had never seen anyone freak out before. They screamed at him at the police station, but his own father just looked on blankly.

When it was all said and done, he was a juvenile. The sex was obviously consensual. They found photographs of them both; sometimes he was tied up, sometimes it was she. The room was full of sex toys and pornographic magazines. There were near-fatal levels of Ecstasy and amphetamines in her system. The coroner ruled it accidental, with contributing factors. He wouldn't be charged with a crime, but he had been ordered to see a therapist.

His name was Mr. Treece.

Treece was a young man and new to the judicial system. He had new diplomas on his walls and family pictures on his desk and credenza. He had a nice house, a nice dog, smiling children, and a pretty wife. There was a picture of her carrying a candlelit birthday cake through a door.

He liked to write things on his pad of yellow paper; he liked to tap the clicking end of his pen against his knee.

"You found her, your mother, when you came home from school? Do you want to talk about that?"

"Not really."

"Try."

"I don't know what you want me to say."

"I want you to say what you feel. What you felt then." Treece clicked the pen on his knee.

"Bad."

Treece wrote on his paper.

"Did you love your mother?"

"Yes."

"Very much?"

He nodded.

"You miss her?"

"Yeah, sure."

"But you still have your father. You love your father too, right?"

"I like him."

"But you don't love him?"

"I don't really know him that well."

"Meaning?"

"I don't think much about him and he doesn't think much about me."

Treece wrote again, then clicked the pen against the side of his knee. He looked at the ceiling, then at the pictures on his desk.

"Does it bother you that you feel that way? To feel that your father doesn't think much about you?"

"I never really cared one way or another, what he thought. He's my father."

"Which means he's different to you from your mother?"

"You're confusing me."

"You don't consider a father's feelings as important as a mother's?"

"I don't know what my mother felt."

"When?"

"Do you mean in general? I'm really not feeling well."

"Because we are talking about your mother?"

"I just don't know what she was feeling or thinking."

"You seem very tense right now."

Silence.

"All right, we'll leave that alone for the time being. Would you say your childhood was normal, I mean, uh, up until, uh, your mother, what happened to your mother? You didn't consider your parents a threat in any way?"

"No."

He began to fashion nooses of rags, soft enough not to cut into the skin of his neck, quick enough to pinch off the flow of the carotid artery to his brain. He'd started out slowly, putting one over his head and twisting it tight until he could not breathe. Then he tried tying a noose to a doorknob in his room. By the end of the school year, he was adept at hanging himself from an iron pipe in the basement.

It was unrestrained ecstasy, the synchronized orgasm of the body and an oxygen-deprived brain. It was a state of hallucinogenic euphoria, an antidote for life's pain. But it was also highly addictive; he could barely let the hours pass before he tried it again, every experience drawing him closer and closer to what his mother must have felt in the end.

That's when he first began to fantasize. He saw her with the mask over her face, her eyes behind the glass windows staring wildly at him. She could not speak, she could not plead, but oh those eyes and how they changed when she rose up on her toe to relieve the pressure on the noose, you could see the ebb and flow of her very spirit behind those eyes.

He had tried to understand it himself, to put a name to the hunger. What would his mother have called it?

In the library he'd gone to the Internet and found dozens of Web sites devoted to strangulation sex. There were places to read about autoerotica, asphyxophilia, hypoxphilia, or breath play. There were Internet groups and chat rooms devoted to the subject. One site was where teenagers wrote about their fantasies; you could invite members off to the side to correspond with them privately.

But the Internet experience left him wanting. It wasn't in telling that he found pleasure. It was in the power of the moment. For that time he was inextricably bound to someone else, making it impossible for her to think of anything but him, every rise of her breasts, every exhalation reflected in the light in her eyes.

Day after day the fantasy began to evolve. He imagined it in greater detail. From the first few words on a street corner to get her into his car to the last hopeful look in her eyes.

That was something he couldn't explain to Treece. How did you put that into words?

Treece would make much ado about his thing for women in green dresses. Most of the women in his fantasies were brunettes like his mother; Treece would surely make something out of that too. He just happened to prefer brunettes wearing green dresses, like some guys had nylon fetishes or liked to see garter belts or women in high heels.

It was just his own little twist on things, the mind play before you reached the object of your desire, all perfectly normal, all perfectly safe.

He wondered what his mother's triggers had been. He wondered what she first thought about when she put that noose around her neck. In fact, it had become one of his fantasies, watching her lay out the dress on the bed, selecting nylons and underwear, putting on her makeup in the mirror. Over and over he could imagine her doing it. He could see her looking at herself in the mirror, touching her painted lips with her tongue like she did, blotting away at the corners of her mouth with a tissue where it smeared. He could see her eyes looking back at herself, looking down at her pale freckled body.

Treece had asked him to talk about his life, about what he felt he had left behind and what he felt was in store for him. Treece had wanted to know how he perceived the future.

What could he say about himself all these years later? What could he add to the story of his life after his parents?

He was twenty-one when his father died. They had been living in Kansas for seven years. His father had just gotten off work from the tire department at Sears and was driving home when he pulled to the side of the road with chest pains. That's where a state trooper found him two hours later. Foot on the brake. He had managed to put the transmission in park, twelve miles from home, when he died.

There was no funeral. No article in a paper. No one came to the house to say they were sorry.

He couldn't say he missed his father. There wasn't all that much left of him to miss. In truth, his father had died with his mother in Connecticut. He'd just kept walking around like he didn't know it.

The boxes his father brought from New England were still in the basement intact. He carried each of them up to the living room and stacked them around him in a circle. He sat among them and began to slice them open with a box cutter.

He didn't eat that week, he didn't bathe, he didn't open the front door to pick up the mail. He just sat there and cried among those boxes, taking a journey through the remains of his parents' lives.

The boxes pretty much told the story.

If one word could describe his father, it would be *smitten.* He was utterly, inescapably, smitten by his wife, Mary. There were old photographs, love letters, stacks of cards tied with kite string. There were silk scarves, valentines, movie stubs, and notes that had once attended lavish gifts; tubes of lipstick, hairpins, his mother's rings and bracelets, and a half-dozen inexpensive wristwatches.

He found newspaper clippings, police reports, and letters from insurance companies. His father had even kept some of her personal things—nylon stockings and underwear that she'd never opened.

It was a love story and a tragedy all rolled into one and the ending had been written before it ever started, written in the genes of some forgotten ancestor, a code that prompted a syndrome or strain or fatalistic malfunction of her brain.

A physician's report in the boxes indicated that his mother suffered from borderline personality disorder. He didn't know she was supposed to be taking medicine for it; doubted, knowing his mother, that she could follow a regimen of any kind, even if it was necessary to save her life. He would later research the symptoms and begin to consider her in a new and different light. She was never conclusively happy, that much went without saying. She was never immobilized by her depression, not that he was aware, but she was certainly prone to the long bouts of dysphoria, mood swings, impulsiveness, and compulsiveness, and in retrospect, she probably suffered from recurrent suicidal thoughts. He knew she was obsessive. She would brush her teeth every few minutes, then bawl over a torn nylon, a dropped egg, a cloudy day. But that wasn't the whole story; there was always something else about his mother, and it was difficult to put your finger on it. She had this thing about contradicting herself throughout the day.

She tried to be spontaneous, but she was never able to pull it off. You could see that in every move, every word—all forced as if she were living in an alien body and she wasn't yet adept at controlling it. In all likelihood, she had difficulty convincing herself that it was her own; she seemed that uncomfortable being human.

BPD. Borderline personality disorder. The fantasy reenactment cycle of repeated stress, urge, act, and cooling off, wasn't that just like her too? Wasn't that just like him? Wasn't that exactly what he had been doing since he was thirteen years old?

BPD mothers had been known to kill their children. He'd read that in one of the medical magazines. He wondered if his mother ever thought about killing him, decided that she had. BPD mothers knew something the rest of the world did not. They knew that their children were going to turn out just like them.

She knew.

She gave birth to him, for Christ's sake. She raised

him while his father worked three jobs to keep her. She must have looked into his eyes as she fed him, stroked his hair, and patted his rosy cheeks and thought about snapping his neck, every day of her life.

They laughed at her, the policemen who came into the house. They didn't know he was there, on the floor behind the sofa. They took turns walking upstairs to look at her on the bed, some of them many times, until the detectives arrived. He had wiped away most of the makeup she wore, cleaning her face, but she was always beautiful to look at. That's what they said.

He wondered if any of them touched her.

Among the boxes were his father's army surplus supplies he used to buy at discount stores where he worked and peddle on metal tables at the Sunday sidewalk bazaar around town. There were unopened first-aid kits, latex gloves, his father's white uniform smock that looked like a doctor's jacket with a red medical insignia over the breast pocket. He slashed the kits open one by one, scattered them around the living room floor. There were cotton swabs, boxes of gauze, burn pads, ankle wraps, now strewn across the heaps of camouflage shirts, canteens, GI hats, propane field stoves, and gas masks.

He looked at the gas masks staring up at him from the box, so familiar now. He had kept the one his mother used, hid it under his bed all these years. That smooth triangular head like a fly's, round eyes and rubber hose for a snout. His heart pounded as he lifted one from the box and held it in his hands. He put it over his head. He sat there like that and cried.

The day he put the boxes away, he emerged from the house a new man. He had stepped into yet another life, his third. There was life with his mother, life after his mother, and now life after his father.

As it turned out his father had a life insurance policy, no doubt to preserve his mother's lifestyle should anything happen to him. He hadn't paid into it for years, but it was still worth a lot of money. Seventy thousand dollars was proof that his father was indeed worth more dead than alive.

He paid his rent through Christmas, not working the remainder of that year.

He first put on his father's white medical smock in July and drove north toward the Nebraska border. He drove down country back roads, knocking on the doors of isolated homes, pretending to be selling first-aid kits, until he found a woman who was alone.

His first was middle-aged and she lived in a single-wide trailer. He asked her if she or her husband had a proper first-aid kit in the house. She'd laughed. "I might have use for a first-aid kit," she'd said, "but not for any husband for sure." She motioned for him to come in.

Her hair was dirty blond, not that it mattered. He wouldn't see her hair once she put on the mask. He wouldn't see anything but those green-gray eyes behind the fogged glass.

She didn't fight him, she didn't scream. He wondered if, like his mother, she thought her end inevitable. He had tied her hands behind her back and put the mask over her head. Then he made a noose out of clothesline. There was no place in the trailer that would support her weight, so he stuffed the end of the respirator intake hose with wet paper towels and suffocated her on the bed.

He didn't know how long a person could go without oxygen before he or she was dead; his only experience had been with Barbara the Goth girl in high school and they had been so highly influenced by drugs.

He heard her muffled cries beneath the mask. Saw the light in her eyes, the heat of her face, her hot breath steaming the eye windows.

When the light left her eyes that last time, he knew she was dead.

There were two women in Kansas, each a year apart. Three in Utah, over a period of sixteen months, and one in the Ozarks of Missouri six months later. He knew it was getting dangerous. The cops were setting up checkpoints and searching suspicious vehicles.

He had to move far away. He decided to head back east.

Driving across I-68 through Maryland, he stopped for gas in the city of Cumberland. There was no reason in particular he chose to stay.

He worked a variety of places throughout the year, delivering furniture, selling Christmas trees, installing storm doors, loading trucks at a lumberyard. And of course there were the two weeks he bailed an aquaintance out, checking the power to a defunct meat-processing plant.

When he wasn't working, he drove to the outlets in Hagerstown and walked the stores and strip malls, drove up and down I-70, getting familiar with the on and off ramps around the office parks.

The traffic was busy on I-70. On weekends and holidays, the headlights formed a hundred-mile chain between Washington, D.C., and Cumberland. You couldn't help but look at all those cars and trucks and vans and wonder who was inside them. Where were they all going? What kinds of lives did they lead?

The first building he decided to try was a medical park, a dozen or so one-story suites for pediatricians, gynecologists, dentists, and optometrists.

Some of the office lights were on. A cleaning company van was parked by one side door. He saw people through the windows vacuuming the carpets.

He chose one where there was a single car in the lot, a red Honda. He parked his own old green station wagon behind shrubs in the lot of a prosthetics store next door, far from doors and loading docks where cameras might be scanning.

The front door was unlocked, no camera. The light he had seen from the outside was just down the hall.

Like that first time in Kansas, he was prepared to ask directions and leave if he ran into a man or felt uncomfortable in any way.

She was right there when he looked in, sitting on a stool behind a counter. There were envelopes in front of her, eyeglass lenses lying on a felt pad, frames tagged with names and numbers.

It was so easy he couldn't believe it. First-aid kits, of all things.

He told her he shouldn't be doing this but his company had changed wholesalers last week and they were no longer stocking their old supplier. He had two dozen new commercial first-aid kits he had to get rid of. Sixty-seven dollars retail! Years and years worth of bandages, creams, tapes, and compresses. Would the nice lady like to take one for free?

It was dark and rush hour was over. "Heck, yeah." She smiled, and her accent was deep southern. "We all try to keep each other in samples. I get toothbrushes from Dr. Vizzini"—she pointed at her teeth—"and Jim gives me my bleach too."

He explained he was just in the lot next door, just on the other side of the hedges. He said he'd been around the corner, updating supplies, but was on his way to the car now if she'd like to follow.

Whether it was his face or the white smock with that red medical patch stitched over the breast pocket that put them at ease—or perhaps it was human nature to want something for free—it was easy. She came like a lamb to the slaughter, and a syringeful of Darkene was all it took to put her in the back of his station wagon.

He couldn't believe he had done it. Couldn't believe how little effort it had taken.

He took her back up I-70 to Cumberland and up the lane to the old meat-processing plant where he had done the caretaking a month earlier.

He knew the buildings on the grounds, he had toured them extensively. He found the refrigeration container and noted that the walls were heavily insulated, next to soundproof.

The contractor who had asked him to look in on it for two weeks had explained that the job was simply to unlock the gates at the entrance, drive the short distance to the plant, check on three electrical panels to see that each had a power light burning. If you saw green, you kept driving; if you saw amber, the emergency generators had kicked on and you needed to find the breaker that had tripped and reset it. If you couldn't do that, a tree had most likely taken a wire down and you needed to call the main office.

No one went inside the buildings. Even if they did, he had purchased his own padlock for the interior container. No one was going to bother breaking into an empty room. They would probably think it was the owner who put it there.

Time alone with his victims was different from anything he had ever experienced. Once you were behind the locked gates to the complex, you could be sure that no one, including the police, was going to sneak up on you. He could keep her there as long as he wanted, put the mask on her every day, and he did.

She was terrified at first, but in time she didn't react when he got ready to pull it over her head. He would take the respirator hose in his hand and watch her eyes as he covered it with his hand, watching the rubber face piece begin to collapse as she consumed the little air trapped inside. When the glass eye windows began to fog, she would fight the noose around her neck as he raised and lowered her over the table.

"What are you thinking about?"

"I don't want to die."

"But what are you thinking about?"

"It hurts."

"What else?"

"I don't know what you want!"

"Are you thinking about your family?"

"I don't want to die."

"What are you thinking about!" he screamed.

"You?" she answered hesitantly.

Silence.

"I was thinking about you?" Attempting to smile was all but impossible, yet she strained to raise the corners of her mouth.

"I'm thinking about you," she said more assertively. "You're all I think about."

He pulled the rope, lifting her off the table, left her dangling there, eyes looking down at him. He held it until she was dead.

He told himself to slow down. He repeated to himself that it was too early. He didn't need to hurry, but he did. Only weeks went by before he needed another.

She was a woman working alone in a surveyor's office. She wanted a free first-aid kit too.

Two weeks after that, a woman was carrying a tray of desserts by his van.

"Looks good," he said.

"You should have seen the shrimp."

"That your van?"

"Katy Caterer." She made a funny face. She was happy. Business must be good.

She had parked next to him, well away from the building's surveillance cameras.

He was pretending to be organizing things in the back of his station wagon when she returned.

"Couldn't interest you in a free first-aid kit, could I?"

When the women were in the refrigeration container in Cumberland, he moved his station wagon off property and parked along the forest on the side of a rural road. His footprints, if any were left behind, would wash away in the rains. There could be no suspicious cars, no tire tracks, no cause to prompt a deputy to get suspicious and suddenly decide to check out the buildings.

One time he had waited outside the door of the container, standing by the door in the warehouse until the woman on the table began to scream and kick at the stainless steel table. The sound was so faint he might not have heard it had he been twenty steps across the floor. No one would hear her, not unless they were standing right here, and even then the slightest noise would overpower her.

It was almost too perfect. No one was coming to save them. No one would come here looking for them.

Then those two teenagers from Ellicott City kidnapped a woman in Frederick off I-270. She was still in the van when they drove off the side of an overpass near Frederick and killed themselves.

It was like a sign from God. The police were blaming the teens for his kidnappings. The whole thing just seemed to go away.

Only now they must know that they had the wrong suspects.

Why else would they have brought a psychic to the scene in Cumberland? And if there was anything at all to this psychic woman, they might even know what he looked like.

He knew that if he was ever identified as a suspect, they would get a warrant to test his DNA, and when they typed it against their evidence, there wouldn't be a juror in the world who was going to have a reasonable doubt.

He thought about the psychic Sherry Moore again and he thought about the women in Cumberland.

Sherry Moore was blind, the papers said. That was eerie. She'd been in the news last summer when those women's bodies were being excavated in New Jersey. You had to wonder if someone could really do those things. If they could read people's memories after they were dead. He wondered what she would have seen in those women's memories in Cumberland. Would she have seen his face when he met them at the office buildings?

And what if she did? She was blind. Yes, the cops could do wonders with computers these days. Imagery programs like Identi-Kit were so sophisticated they could produce digital likenesses with the guidance of one strong witness. He'd watched them do it on the Discovery Channel. A woman raped in Ontario worked with a technician at a keyboard. She selected the right face shape, then she told the technician to change the hair color, the form of a chin, erase half an eyebrow, thin the lips, and in minutes a real-life image emerged on screen until she had it tweaked to look exactly like the person she remembered.

In that particular case, the information was fed into a face recognition scanner that spit out a sex offender who lived in her town of ten thousand. But face recognition technology was still too new to worry about.

Sherry Moore wouldn't be able to tell a technician they were interpreting her description correctly, but if they were even close, you had to be concerned about your neighbors' asking themselves the question. How much do I know about this person? Where were they before they moved here?

He knew about manhunts. He'd been reading about himself for years in the Midwest. Ninety-nine percent of all suspect sketches and images are shown only to a handful of witnesses. Other police agencies receive them, but there are no media to get them in front of the public. Not unless you are inclined to study post office walls.

Which was why cops vied so competitively for precious airtime on shows like *America's Most Wanted.*

It would hardly be an issue in his case. Anyone who could produce a likeness of the Cumberland killer would get all the airtime they needed.

They would offer a big reward, and a few days later they might get a phone call from someone who thought this guy in Waterdrum looked a little like that guy on *America's Most Wanted.* He could imagine the little river rats from nearby Coal Town scurrying to get their cheese.

It would happen quickly after that. There would be a knock at the door, a set of handcuffs, they'd arraign him, draw blood, and the door would close forever behind him. No judge in the world would ever give him bond or bail, which meant that the day they put the cuffs on him would be the last free day of his life.

Then what?

Prison for a man like him would be an ending worse than death. Call it purgatory or call it hell, he would be subjected to the kinds of things he had done to his victims. He couldn't think of a worse fate.

How much time did he have? he wondered. Was anything in his favor?

The newspapers said the bodies were somewhat preserved, which meant that the compressor had kept running all this time. The papers didn't mention crime scene evidence, but it was difficult not to leave something behind. The cops wouldn't make mistakes collecting it either. There would be no frantic rush for amateurs to get into that room. No rookie cops or medics to trample the evidence while performing CPR. If the FBI was involved, they would carefully preserve anything that might contain his DNA. And if they found it, they might not know his name, but they could certainly test it against the DNA from an unaccounted-for hair root specimen they bragged about in *The Salt Lake Tribune.*

He simply had to keep them from identifying his face or fingerprints. He was a fanatic when it came to wearing the latex gloves.

Few people had witnessed him entering the dark office parks and medical centers outside Hagerstown, which probably accounted for why no one got stuck on recollections of a guy in a green station wagon. Even if they had, two years had gone by. Witnesses forgot things, changed jobs, moved away. Some may even have died. A lot of things happen in two years, and that alone was a setback for whoever was reopening the cases.

He'd been living in the village of Waterdrum all that time. Only ninety miles from Cumberland, it was a tourist-dependent environment, a mountainous community in Pennsylvania known for white-water kayaking. Work was plentiful, employees were transient, students came and went between semesters, tradespeople followed new home construction and renovation projects, then moved on to other states and were soon replaced by others.

It was the ideal town for someone like him. The key was to remain normal enough, friendly, but never too interesting, never too mysterious.

He wondered if he could keep pulling it off or if it was time to move once again.

He stopped the car in Monroeville at a liquor store, then took a ramp onto the Pennsylvania Turnpike heading south. It was cold again, frigid.

The group session left him tense and he wondered if he had made a mistake by going there. It wasn't part of his routine. Like the way he had acted this morning in the diner; it was different. He couldn't start to act out of character or someone might suddenly take notice.

He thought it best not to return to Waterdrum. Not tonight, not until he got himself together. Still, he didn't want to be alone, didn't want to close his eyes on his thoughts.

He knew a girl across the state line in West Virginia.

Salty white buses and slush-caked tractor-trailers hissed along I-76; backseats of passenger cars were filled with children's featureless faces. The sky was dark lavender and spitting snow. He leaned forward to use a rag to clean the foggy windshield.

The radio, its antenna broken, drifted in and out of the droll condemnations of a farm-town preacher, fading to country music before it lost the signal.

A man at a tollbooth in New Stanton gave him change with chafed red hands, his fingernails the size of quarters. He filled his tank at a gas station and used the ice-cold men's room with a gaping hole in the single porcelain urinal.

Route 119 twisted south through small towns and wind-stunted forests, the mountains covered with a crust of dirty snow that refused to melt. At the crown of a hill the station wagon cleared the summit and the road began to descend into forest once more; he saw the double yellow lines falling away in his rearview mirror and thought he was entering yet another phase in his life.

He drank from the bottle, finding it impossible to keep his hands from shaking. This was all supposed to happen, he thought. There was a reason for everything, his mother used to say. The unfinished business of Cumberland was there to awaken it, but what was it he was supposed to see? Rum dribbled down his chin; he blotted it with a sleeve and took another drink from the bottle.

The shooting star syndrome, the serial killer's burnout, came to mind; he knew his cravings weren't the same. The killings had continued, the women along the Appalachian Trail, the one he'd hung in a dilapidated barn, which he then set on fire. He tried to arouse the feelings, but they just weren't there. He was becoming impotent, meaningless. He wondered what this all had been leading to.

The leaky radiators in Room 9 spewed a stale mist upon the unmade bed. The room's meager furnishings, molting lime-green shag soiled to a rusty orange at the corners, heavily brocaded drapes of a former period of elegance, blocked out the streetlights. Pipes in the walls expanded and contracted, uttering a rattle throughout the old house.

She could hear him urinating on the other side of the wall; she reached for a book of matches from the nightstand and lit her cigarette, blowing a line of smoke at the water stains on the ceiling. Goose bumps rose on her legs and belly and breasts.

The toilet flushed and the man reappeared; he came alongside her and stood.

She thought he wanted her mouth, but he took her

cigarette instead, walked to the window, and looked out.

She knew he lived in Pennsylvania. One of the girls saw his car last year, copied down the tags in case anything ever happened to one of them. The money might be good, but he was very, very weird.

Suddenly the old pipes in the house stopped rattling, succeeded by a long, low moan. Then, as if they had only taken a breath, they began to chatter themselves back to life.

She reached for the ashtray, fumbling past the Vaseline and condoms. He was mashing the cigarette out, picking up the mask. She knew there would be marks from the rope he used. He'd wanted to hang her from the light fixture, but she forbade it. That's where she drew the line. She would let him choke her in the bed, but she wasn't standing on any fucking tables and pretending to hang herself. Not for anyone. Not for any price.

She'd taken to wearing a choker to hide the marks, but it was worth it. Three hundred dollars an hour was a week's work in Wheeling, West Virginia.

"Arms." He was breathing rapidly; she could feel him against her thigh.

She rolled on her stomach and put her wrists behind her back. He used her handcuffs, rolled her on her back, and stretched the gas mask over her face. Then he straddled her, looking down at her eyes beneath the glass, put the respirator hose over her breast, cutting off her air, and watched her eyes as the hose began to suck frantically at her own skin. He could see the look of terror in her eyes, the glass steaming, her body overheating; he pulled the hose off, heard her take a gasp of air, then put it back again.

The light ebbed and flowed in her eyes.

4

Baltimore, Maryland

They sat in a conference room in the Garmatz Courthouse on West Lombard Street in Baltimore—Glenn Schiff, attorney general for the state of Maryland, along with senior agent Alice Springer, out of the FBI's St. Louis field office.

"You have to imagine this in the context of what was happening at the time." Sherry Moore's voice came across the speakerphone that was situated between them in the middle of the conference table.

"There is a vast difference between what people are thinking when they know they are dying slowly as opposed to those who are taken quickly. The more time, the more knowledge the person has that death is imminent, the more erratic their thinking, the harder to interpret what I see.

"The victims had all been in the refrigeration container for weeks," Sherry Moore was saying. "Their thoughts must have wandered to most everything that ever happened in their lives. There were times when they might have thought of nothing but food and times they thought about nothing but their loved ones or friends. They might have prayed. They might have exchanged stories. Certainly they thought about the man who assaulted them, but that was only a small part of what they had on their minds. They were cold, frightened, and injured. They were starving at times, and in the end they probably weren't lucid."

Sherry took a breath.

"There are one thousand four hundred forty minutes in a day, more than eighty thousand seconds. They had all lived at least two weeks in confinement. It would have been a moon shot to have caught any of them thinking about their killer in the last eighteen seconds of their lives."

Schiff leaned back, staring at the ceiling.

"Once more"—the agent sounded annoyed—"what's this eighteen seconds?"

"Average human RAM memory," Schiff said.

"Right," Sherry said. "It's the capacity of our short-term memory."

"And this vision you talk about," the agent said. "You said one of the girls was seeing something through windows, something in the fog. I didn't get that."

"The image was blurred," Sherry said patiently. "I felt as though her vision was restricted; she was seeing something or remembering something, it might well have been a hallucination. Maybe it represented a memory from her childhood, a comic book scene, or something from a movie, or an interpretation of something she once read in a book. People who are stressed often relive the nightmares of their lives. That's the best I can tell you."

"So?" Schiff looked at Agent Springer. "Any questions?"

Agent Springer stared at him, unblinking.

"All right, Sherry, I'll call you tonight, after we've talked. Thanks again."

"My pleasure," she said tiredly.

Schiff leaned forward to disconnect the call. "I knew it was a long shot." He walked to a watercooler, pulled a paper cup, and pushed a button.

"We're curious why you chose to do it."

"Mostly because of you." He drained the cup and pitched it in the trash.

"Me?" Springer's eyes rolled upward.

"You rushed into Cumberland like gangbusters."

She stared at him.

"You took over the scene and started seizing evidence from the state police. Since when does the FBI do that?"

"The FBI was involved in 2005. Kidnapping's still a federal offense."

He made a face. "Please."

"I thought we were talking about why you would bring a psychic to a crime scene."

He stared at her a moment longer, wondering what she knew. Wondering why the FBI was so interested in a two-year-old crime scene all of a sudden. It wasn't as if they'd rallied around him when he wanted local law enforcement to keep looking for a suspect after the Ellicott City teens were killed.

"He's not in your DNA file, he's not in CODIS, is he?"

"We don't even know if there is a he," the agent said. "The DNA we found in Cumberland could have belonged to a past employee of the meat company or, for all we know, the Ellicott City teenagers could have been the match. We have yet to attempt their DNA."

Schiff snorted. "You don't believe that any more than I do."

She shrugged. "Mr. Schiff, believe what you want, I came here to hear about Sherry Moore. About why you brought her to the crime scene."

He turned and walked to the window. "I never believed we got him. It's that simple, Agent Springer. And I knew he was smart enough not to leave a trail. I wanted to know what he looked like. I wanted Sherry Moore to see his face before Blackman began to manufacture clues to link her pimply-faced teens to Cumberland."

"That's quite an accusation."

"Who is he, Agent Springer? Do you know?"

"I don't know any more than your psychic, apparently."

"I worked with her in Philadelphia. I saw what she can do, and I learned at a reasonably young age, there are things in this world that simply can't be explained. If there are people out there who take issue with that, well then, that's their problem. How did you come to catch this case anyhow, Agent Springer? You're not from around here, are you?"

Springer looked the attorney general over; her face remained expressionless. She was new to the East Coast. Schiff had called a friend in Washington, learned she was originally from Texas but working on a long-term assignment out of the St. Louis field office. You had to wonder why a St. Louis agent would catch a Maryland case.

"The Pittsburgh regional office is shorthanded right now and they wanted a team they could devote to this full-time. My work was wrapping up in the Midwest, so it happened to be me."

The first time you laid eyes on Alice Springer was nothing less than alarming. She had a coldness about her, a look that was impossible to read.

Schiff's friends in the FBI knew little more about Springer than he did. The FBI wasn't always an open book, not even to its own agents. There were confidential activities within the agency and Springer was rumored to have been working on one until Cumberland broke. Then they pulled her crew from St. Louis and reassigned them. The agent Schiff talked to said she had a reputation for making trouble, for being a cutthroat. Schiff had been around the government long enough to know how they worked. Difficult employees got transferred from station to station to keep them from doing any permanent harm. That would fit the reason she'd been assigned to a task force in the Midwest and was now bouncing between Cumberland and Pittsburgh. She wasn't a team player.

Hearing someone attempting to describe Agent Springer was amusing. Meeting Springer in person was not. She was dark-complexioned, nearly ebony, and her hair was the color of ice, short on top, shaved on the sides like a marine's. She was six foot four and had eyes like black olives swimming in pools of gooey egg white. She had an aura about her that settled over a room like radioactive waste.

"Anyhow, this guy was into breath play. He's probably in jail right now. They don't test nonviolent offenders for DNA," she said. "Even if we had managed to find his DNA, there's a two in ten chance we couldn't match it to him."

"Breath play?"

"Erotic asphyxiation." Springer crossed her legs.

He shook his head.

"When the brain is deprived of oxygen, it induces a

lucid, semi-hallucinogenic state called hypoxia. Combined with orgasm, the rush is said to be no less powerful than cocaine, and highly addictive, both in the giving and taking."

Schiff folded his hands. "You're saying this was rough sex turned murder?"

Springer nodded. "That's what the press calls it. We usually find paraphernalia on the scene, plastic bags, latex hoods, duct tape, snorkels, drinking straws. The practitioners are in the tens of thousands, mostly the young. The chokers are called scarfers; their partners are called bottoms or choke chicks, air walkers or gaspers."

"But the bodies were clean, I heard. No signs of intercourse, no semen. Doesn't that contradict?"

Springer shrugged. It was a fact that had been bothering her as well. "The excitement is sometimes in the watching. Maybe he didn't need the sex any-more. Or maybe he masturbated in a condom. No matter what he did, it's always about sex."

"Masturbated into a condom?"

"Wouldn't be the first."

"You ever hear of one of these people hanging their partner before?"

Springer shrugged again. "It happens, but rarely." She looked at her watch. "Mr. Schiff, you must excuse me, but I have a plane to catch. If you're interested in my opinion, I think you should try to use Miss Moore to your advantage."

"Advantage, Agent Springer?"

"As long as the cat's out of the bag about her being on the scene, I think we should make an appeal for him to turn himself in. Through her, I mean."

Schiff shrugged. "He'd need a real reason to come in."

"So we give him one. We leak that Sherry Moore saw the women's killer. Then we put her on the air."

Schiff watched the odd agent, trying to catch any hint of emotion. "I can't do that."

"You say he's still out there, that they never had the right suspect, and you want to catch him, don't you?"

"I'd have the press to contend with sooner or later."

She sighed. "All right, at least tell her not to say that she didn't see him."

"I'll have to ask her how she feels about that."

Springer sighed, annoyed. "Talk to her then." She looked at the AG, pursed her lips, and recrossed her legs. "We'll throw him a parachute, a phone number for safe conduct, life without parole. Tell her we need her to keep him off balance. If he doesn't know for sure she hasn't seen him, he may take the bait. He won't if he thinks there's nothing to lose."

Schiff nodded. "Let me talk to her."

"Of course." The deep voice soothed. "But don't take too long."

Schiff couldn't see the harm, but there was something about Springer that wasn't altogether right. Something about her that told him he didn't have the whole story.

The morning's headlines were printed on the strength of an anonymous source: PSYCHIC SEES CUMBERLAND STRANGLER.

The article went on to say that Sherry Moore had allegedly confided to a high-ranking police official in Cumberland that she had seen the killer's face.

Schiff, who had yet to talk to Sherry about his conversation with Agent Springer, couldn't prove it, but he was suspicious that Springer herself had been the leak. He'd heard she was cutthroat and ambitious, but this was a bald-faced lie.

As it turned out, the issue became a nonissue the very next day. Sherry Moore was served with a superior court injunction barring her from disclosing information about the Cumberland victims. A lawsuit filed by attorneys representing one of the victim's families charged that Moore's presence at the crime scene violated the deceased person's rights to privacy. It was a groundbreaking assertion that deceased persons had rights and virgin territory for the lawyers representing the plaintiffs and the defense.

The superior court injunction read in part, "It is hereby requested that the defendant be barred from communicating, either in public or in private, either orally or in writing, any portrayal of any vision or description of sounds, thoughts, or images, be they considered sensory or extrasensory, which the defendant claims to characterize as thoughts, memory, or experiences of the deceased. Further that the defendant is barred from communicating, orally or in writing, any personal extrapolation of events based on such visions, voices, sounds, or other means of communications, intended for the benefit of any other person, public or private, or any interests, including promotional and commercial, which we deem to be inherent."

Even if Sherry had seen something in Cumberland, neither she nor the government could say. And since Sherry Moore was unable to say what was going on, the press would go after the attorney general and the state police commissioner.

"Isn't it true, Mr. Schiff, that you used your position as the attorney general to further a personal agenda? Why, if you thought you were doing the right thing, were you hiding Sherry Moore's visit under a cloak of secrecy? What did you hope to learn from a psychic that your own police officials could not tell you? Isn't it true, Mr. Schiff, that you disagreed with the state police position on the kidnappings two years ago? Isn't it true there has been bad blood between you and the state police commissioner ever since? Isn't it true you have political aspirations in 2008?"

There was no limit to the insensitivity of the questions they came up with, including speculation that

Schiff was having a secret relationship with Miss Moore. You always had to throw that one in if you were a reporter, didn't you?

Schiff frustrated the media with refusals to comment on Sherry Moore, and the governor's office was beginning to hear rumblings from Republican legislators about a vote of no confidence.

Not surprisingly, the question most often asked on talk radio and in television polls, on computer plogs and blogs around the country had nothing to do with Maryland's attorney general at all. They wanted to know what the psychic saw inside that refrigeration container in Cumberland.

That, of course, was a question not soon to be answered.

5

Philadelphia, Pennsylvania

Her nightmares continued after Cumberland, but now Sherry Moore was seeing a face shrouded in fog. She was sleeping constantly, forgetting things, drinking too much, taking too many pills. Days and nights became interchangeable; mornings and midnights she felt the same dull aching pain. She couldn't go on like this, she knew that. Something was going to break. Something was eventually going to have to give.

Before the holidays she had felt only the ponderous weight of depression. Since she had begun to mix the prescriptions, she would be laughing one moment and crying the next, and all those moments in between were filled with endless, emotionally exhausting replays of her life and the memories she'd shared with John Payne.

She knew it couldn't go on.

She had heard of people going crazy before, but never understood what that must feel like. It wasn't that she didn't know what was wrong with her—she did. She was conscious that she was self-medicating and losing the battle for control of her mind, which had begun reeling out memory after memory, assailing her with guilt. She couldn't move forward, couldn't think about the future, and she couldn't, under any circumstances, forget about the past.

It was hard to believe that the mind could affect you so adversely. That it could use your hopes and dreams and all that it knew about you against you.

She moved between the bed and the couch and back again, stopping to make a drink and take more pills. She slept fitfully, had nightmares, then long lapses of silence when she lay on her side, knees tucked into her chest, going over the nightmares again and again until one afternoon an elephant seemed to have climbed on her chest.

The spatial world began to alter. She felt as if it were closing in on her. She imagined harm, the air being bad, things gathering around her. She remembered hearing Brigham's persistent knocks on the door, but then that too went away and she lay catatonic, unable to bring herself to move.

When she finally did, she knocked over a vial of pills, swiped some into her hand, and poured them into her mouth, while others rolled to the floor. What pills, which pills did not matter. They were all there to make her feel better or make her sleep or at least to kill the pain, and any of those conditions was preferable to this hell.

She said Brigham's name and remembered he was teaching; he would be gone for several hours. He must have stopped by her house on his way out the door.

Whom could she call if she needed someone? Not her doctors; they would only call an ambulance for her. They would want her in a hospital and in a hospital they would take one look at her and put her in a ward with crazy people.

Crazy. That's what it came down to. This wasn't sadness anymore. This pain was excruciating, an ache from deep within. You couldn't fix this kind of thing. This must be what happens to people right before the end. This is what they must feel, right before they take that step into thin air.

At some point she thought about getting the phone

and dialing 911. She didn't want anyone to see her like this, but then she didn't want to die either. Or maybe with one or two more pills, she could manage to get herself together. Then she would call for a cab and . . . she would tell . . .

She reached for the vial of pills and poured more into her hand, popped them into her mouth. Was that twice or three times today? She just could not remember.

Something warm burned her eye. Something was stabbing the back of her head. She could smell the blood and sour puke when she reached out; her hand came away sticky.

She was on the floor. She could feel the edge of the braided rug under her right elbow. Her legs were off to one side. She reached out and found the coffee table leg. Her arm was soaked with vomit; it made her gag. Something was happening behind her, some noise at the door.

She tried to remember what happened, what last thoughts she could recall. Whoever was at the door was banging on it now, rattling the door against its locks.

She heard glass break, then a bolt turn, running footsteps; someone was looking down at her.

"Three River Road, get an ambulance here," Brigham's voice barked, and he tossed the phone aside.

Sherry passed out again.

Voices faded in and out; there were bright lights and motion all around her. She had no feeling, though, was aware of it only from a distance, somewhere, she imagined, between life and death.

Vivid scenes came to the forefront of her mind, vivid sounds like the slamming of car doors and the weight of the wet tarp across her body. She could remember the smallest details, the draft of fresh air that was near her forehead, the sound of the wind and the rain.

She had not wanted to remember any of it, but this was where she ended up. This was what was at the bottom of her bottles of pills.

She had tried to fight back; she had even consciously attempted to move her body, to sit up, but nothing worked, not her arms, not her legs. She had tried to will herself back down into the mind's great depository of nightmares, hoping she might select another and reenter life in a safer place.

No one could see this but her. No one probably even knew she was alive.

The scene kept on unfolding and at last there was a knock at the door: *Don't-open-that-door!* her mind screamed, but of course she did—she always did—and he was there waiting.

She remembered catapulting backward, backward and away, plunging into the abyss of her memories, layer after layer, until she fell into the netherworld of her mind. Here was the zoo where she caged other people's monsters.

Here was that place where the monsters rattled their cages.

It was dark at first, but then she grew accustomed to the light. Something moved in the shadows. There were others down here. A man walked quickly by; he was carrying a white box. She saw a car by some bushes, dull green paint, the tailgate of a station wagon open.

She saw a hook on a ceiling.

She saw a man at the end of a long hallway, wearing a white jacket; he was walking toward her. She saw something out in the fog, a face, a man—or was it a beast?

She began to understand. These visions, these scenes, all belonged to someone else. She was no longer in the mind of Sherry Moore, she was now represented by many. This place she had fallen into, this nether region of her mind, was not safe. She had crossed a partition separating them, securing her from the repositories of the dead.

She could feel their eyes on her, watching her from the shadows.

She remembered thinking she had to move. She had to get out of there quick. She must cry out for help!

And when she did, they began to run toward her, putting their hands all over her body.

She screamed; she could hear them coming, the footfalls slapping, as more and more hands pinned her down, hands on her thighs and around her ankles, her shoulders, and her wrists.

Something was clamped over her mouth; she fought for air, but they kept pressing it down. It was rubber, she thought. A mask!

"Sherry?" a voice yelled. "Sherry, I'm a nurse. You're in a hospital. Breathe!"

And that was when she came to. *"Sherry, do you understand? I need you to breathe!"*

It was only then that she realized it was an oxygen mask on her face, that friendly hands were pinning her to a bed. She remembered that first cold voluntary breath of air, how it felt like crashing up through the surface of a lake. She remembered how the energy in all those tense hands holding her down relaxed, in relief.

They told her she had been in a twenty-four-hour coma. No one knew for sure if she was coming out of it. Staff neurologists, neurosurgeons, they all came to see the famous medium. They were all there, whispering over the encephalograms, having thoughts of neither hope nor despair. Sherry Moore's medical history was simply too complicated to comment on.

She knew something they did not. Nor would they ever believe or understand. Something she felt in the seconds before she came to. When an adult suddenly dies without explanation, they call it Long QT or

SADS. It really wouldn't matter what they called it if her heart were suddenly to stop. She would be dead and they would never know. Never know that one of the monsters in her zoo had killed her. She was vulnerable to her memories of the dead.

Her admission to Nazareth was hardly a secret. She'd been brought in by public ambulance, then a crime beat reporter saw her on a gurney and every reporter between Maine and Miami knew her face.

Switchboards lit up at the *Philadelphia Inquirer.* The psychic Sherry Moore had overdosed on pills. Better yet, she must have tried to kill herself.

In truth, no one could have hoped to keep Sherry's admission a secret. Not in a hospital the size of Nazareth. Half of Philadelphia knew Sherry Moore on sight. She was a hometown personality even before the Cumberland incident made national news. Countless articles had been written about her in newspapers and popular magazines, and the news was still breaking about her lawsuit.

There had been rumors she wasn't doing well after her experience in Wildwood last summer, rumors of an illicit affair with the married cop John Payne, who was killed. Now the Cumberland debacle with the attorney general, Glenn Schiff, and to top it all off, she was being sued on a privacy issue that could preclude her from ever working with the dead again. What she claimed to be simply memory readings or retrievals might in fact be protected by the Constitution. No one had ever considered the human body a depository of its own privileged information before.

No wonder, the press suggested, she had caved in under all the stress. They patrolled the hospital corridors looking for a photo opportunity or anyone on staff who would talk to them.

Sherry's personal physician was contacted. When Sherry was out of danger, he managed to pull strings and have her moved to a private room. Nurses saw that she was hooked up to monitors and there she remained for two more days.

The halls of Nazareth were dark after ten, the last visitors straggling toward the elevators. Sherry's new room was in a wing in a hall connecting the old and new buildings of the hospital, situated between two dark stairwells and the elevators.

Getting into the staff lounge was easy. No one was going to challenge a man with a white smock and medical patches in the halls of a city hospital.

A security guard was buying a candy bar at a vending machine. He closed the door behind him and dragged a metal chair toward a scarred Formica table. He sat there and pretended to flip through an open newspaper.

The guard looked over her shoulder at him, then back at the machine and what she was doing.

"Nice night." He jabbed a thumb toward the door.

The guard grabbed her candy bar and change and

sat on a chair, trying not to be visible from the glass in the door. She began to unwrap the chocolate.

"Warm," he said. "Not hot."

She was in her late thirties, no wedding ring. A roll of stomach had begun to overtake the wide Sam Brown belt. He could see a Chinese symbol tattooed under the nylon stocking on one ankle, a dragonfly on the back of her wrist. If ever she'd turned heads, that day was over, but she still wore some makeup and her hair was kept long. She looked like a drinker, a pack of cigarettes pressed beneath a buttoned pocket on her uniform shirt.

"I thought they would have promoted you by now." He flipped a page.

She stopped mid-bite and squinted at him. Wondering where she knew him from.

"No, I mean, you've been here awhile, right? Two, three years?" He glanced at the service pin on her lapel.

She nodded. "Three."

He shook his head in dismay. "I know. I've been seeing you around that long. How come you never made sergeant?"

She cocked her head and shrugged, took a bite of candy.

"See, I always thought you were sharper than the others. You can tell that about someone even from afar. I mean it's one of life's things. It's either there or it isn't. You know what I mean?"

She sat a little straighter and pulled in her gut. Nodded.

"Most people in the world like to talk. I keep to myself, like you"—he pointed—"but the others in my business, they're always going around talking all the time. Always on the phone, always talking to the nurses or the doctors, networking they call it, you know what I mean. And do you know what? They're the ones that get promoted. It's a crazy back-ass world." He shook his head.

He was tanned as if he spent a lot of time outdoors. He wore a goatee that was black like his hair. His hands were clean and his nails were trimmed. She liked that he wore trail boots instead of dirty sneakers. All the men she met were slobs. Dirty socks, bad teeth, couldn't keep a steady job if they tried.

"You with Emeritus?" she asked.

He nodded vaguely, sensing she was referring to a private ambulance company.

"That's cool," she said. "Long time?"

"Oh, yeah." He nodded, wanting to change the subject. "You always been a cop?"

She thought about that for a moment. Nobody ever called security guards cops. "Yeah," she said, liking the term. "I was going to be one of them NAs, nurse's assistants, but then I had a kid." She made a confusing gesture with her hand. "Sometimes you just gotta do what you gotta do, you know what I mean?"

"Yeah, I know," he sympathized.

He leaned back and twined his fingers behind his neck, yawned. "Whatever happened to that blind woman we brought in the other day? She die yet?"

The guard looked at his hands; no tan lines where there would be a wedding ring. She wrapped the candy bar as though she was saving it for later.

"You know the one," he said. "That psychic, she tried to off herself."

The guard nodded. "You brought her in, huh?"

He rolled his eyes. "I worked a double that day." He made a face. "Today too, that's why I can't wait to get out of this place."

"They had her in critical care last I heard, but you don't want to go up there."

"How come?"

"Nurses have an attitude up there, all of them think their shit don't stink. I don't even like doing the desk for them at night."

He looked bored, turning another page of the paper. "Cops guarding her or did they stick it with you guys?"

"Cops don't do shit here 'less we let them."

He nodded. "You know, it used to bother me when we got called out to suicides, especially people that have money. I figure everyone's got their problems. I mean, I got problems, you got problems; we don't go around making other people clean up our mess." He jabbed a thumb toward the ceiling. "But some people just don't have the kind of character we do. Maybe

I'm getting sappy, but I been going back to them all lately. You know, when I bring one in and they make it, I go back the next day and tell them I'm glad they're alive. I think it matters. I don't know why I should care, they don't know me from Adam, but I like to tell them so. You know, just tell them that there's someone out here that cares."

The guard looked at him suspiciously, then shrugged and nodded. "Yeah, I guess that's cool."

"Hey, maybe I'll stop back here before I check off duty. You going to be around a while longer?"

The guard put the rest of the candy bar in her pocket and tugged a stray hair away from her face.

"Midnight."

"You ever go around the corner for a beer? That place . . . uh . . ."

"Murphy's?"

"Yeah, Murphy's," he said.

"Sometimes," she said.

"Going tonight?"

She made an attempt at coy.

"I can meet you here or over at the bar." He looked at his watch. "I just want to run up and see that psychic woman . . . say, could you do me a favor, save me a trip. Can you get me in without all the fuss; tell the guys I'm coming up or something?"

She wet her lips, walked to the wall phone and dialed zero, smiled back at him while she waited. A moment later she hung up.

"No need to bother, they moved her to a private room. She's up in 1212. Hey, look for me down here first. If I'm not here, I'll be over at Murphy's."

"Cool." He reached out as if to touch the sleeve of her shirt. But didn't.

"Cool," she said, wondering where she could get a tube of lip gloss this time of night.

He wore the bill of his baseball cap pulled low across his face, careful to keep his head down and away from the security cameras. Talking to the guard was a necessary risk, but he wasn't concerned. By the time he left the building, no one would recognize him.

He checked the hospital directory next to the main elevators, took one to eleven, where he got off and walked a staircase to twelve. The halls were deserted and quiet. There was a nurses' station at the far end of the corridor. He could see only part of it, which meant there was a parallel corridor on the opposite wall of the wing. He walked toward it, hugging the wall, reading numbers, first to the right, then to the left—bed one, bed two, move on to another room.

He checked the convex mirror as he approached the end. No one was standing at the elevators. The nurses were seated behind a glass partition. No one had posted security on the twelfth floor.

He rounded the corner, turning his head away from the nurses, glancing up to catch the next convex mirror, and one of the nurses, a young blond woman, was watching his retreat.

He never hesitated, knowing she could have seen only the back of him, and bent the corner.

An old man in a bathrobe was shuffling along the handrail. He came up behind him, pretending to walk alongside, checking numbers as they went: 1209, 1210, 1211, 1212. And there she was.

He kept walking, leaving the bewildered old man at the handrail, pushed through the exit doors at the stairwell, and put his back to the wall. He stood there taking deep breaths. He had not imagined making it this far, actually being able to do this. And yet here he was and no one was guarding her. It was going to be so much easier than he thought.

He looked at his watch. It was twenty till eleven. He snapped on latex gloves, then removed a syringe from a breast pocket on his white medical smock and held it up to the light. Then he replaced it.

He stepped into the hallway just as a young black man rounded the corner by the nurses' station.

Got to keep going, no turning back now.

The man was in green scrubs, carrying a red plastic trash bag and pushing a wheeled bucket with the toe of his sneaker. He wore an elastic plastic cap and there were headphones in his ears. His lips were moving, he was nodding in time to a beat; he pushed the bucket through the door of a room down the hall and disappeared behind it.

Room 1212 again.

Sherry Moore was lying on her back. Her head was facing him. She appeared to be asleep. There were strips of white adhesive securing a clear IV tube that climbed her arm across her shoulder toward a sagging bag of fluid on a chrome-plated stand.

He wouldn't have to wake her. He could empty the syringe directly into the IV tube.

Her dark brown hair was piled around her head. On the shoulder farthest from him a spray of multicolored wires disappeared under her gown.

She was lovely, he thought. He nudged the door closed behind him with the toe of his boot, crossed the room, and looked down at her from the foot of the bed. He pulled her chart, took the front page of the clipboard, and saw it had a nondriver ID clipped to it. Someone must have given it to the ER and they put it there and no one bothered to return it yet. There was an admission slip as well as a phone number written on the front page, next to the home address. He couldn't say why he wanted them, but took both and stuck them in his pocket.

There was a hollow place at the base of her throat, a lump of carotid artery rising over a protrusion of collarbone. He wanted to reach down and lift away the gown. He wanted to touch it. He wanted to press it, to stop the blood on its way to the brain and watch her face.

Seconds ran off the clock. He had a feeling of disorientation; his hands reached uncertainly for the bed rail, tracing it as he walked around the bed and took a seat on the opposite side of her.

The IV tube was right there, just inches from his hands, and yet it didn't seem right. There was more he wanted to know.

"How are you feeling?"

She turned toward him groggily.

"All right," she said hoarsely.

"Do you feel like talking?"

"Who are you?"

"Just one of the counselors."

She nodded. People had been coming into her room for four days, asking her questions, inane questions, making sure she wasn't about to do something else stupid. They couldn't be sure whether she had accidentally overdosed or was really trying to kill herself. They couldn't be sure she wouldn't walk out the door and do a better job of it in front of a bus.

"You have an unusual history."

She moved her head, barely perceptible.

"You've seen the end, the real end of life. I've always wondered what that looked like."

The room was quiet but for the heater fan, and she wondered if the door was closed; she couldn't hear the constant heart monitor from the room across the hall. That was different.

"I see people die in here all the time, but you always wonder what they were thinking at the end."

She started to move her lips, but no words came out.

"Most people are fascinated by death. I think those last seconds must be like entering a dark tunnel, exhilarating, everything unknown."

Silence.

"They must think about their loved ones, though, right? Everyone thinks about their loved ones when they're afraid. That would only make sense."

His voice had climbed a decibel.

"I would want to know—"

The door swung open.

"'No you can't fear what you don't hear, check yo piece at the door, check yo roof, check yo ho, cause the man he use a traitah when he puts you on the paper. . . .'"

He looked up to see the young man in headphones and scrubs, guiding his bucket toward the bathroom. The man went into the bathroom, tossing towels on the floor, then brought out a trash can, emptying it into his red bag.

"'Pooty say I'm hyper, but I pays that goddamn piper. . . .'" The man's head bobbed as he spoke. He stepped over the towels and looked toward the bed, his eyes on the red bag lining the can on the floor.

He looked down, away from the janitor, feet planted flat and ready to bolt. Something tasted bad in his mouth. He slipped the syringe from his breast pocket.

This was wrong. Something was wrong. He thumbed off the cap. He needed to get out of this room.

He stood and started around the bed, eyes low, covering the floor between Sherry's bed and the door, always conscious of where the janitor was. *Were they earphones or a cop's radio?* He saw something flash out of the corner of his eye, looked up to see the call light blinking on and off over the door. He looked back. Sherry Moore's thumb was mashing the red panic button on the remote. She was facing him again. She looked exhausted, but her eyes were open, looking directly at him, looking at him as if she could actually see. As if she knew who he was.

It was all instinct after that. The janitor bent over for the trash can. He stabbed him in the back of the neck, emptying the plunger of the syringe with his thumb. Then he ran for the door and down the hall, hitting the stairwell exit with his elbow in time to see the brown-haired nurse bending the corner at the opposite end of the hall.

Back in Sherry's room the black man's eyes went wide, and he doubled over, swiping at the needle sticking in the back of his neck.

Don't look back. Don't look back. You can't look back! He took the steps two at a time: eleventh floor, ten, nine; he exited to a dark waiting room and a sign that read Outpatient Surgery. There wouldn't be anyone here until morning.

He found a restroom where he scrubbed his face

with soap. He removed a disposable razor from his zippered pocket and shaved off his goatee. Then he washed the cheap dye from his hair, until it was sandy blond.

He peeled off the white smock and rolled it into a ball. Then he combed his hair, removed his latex gloves, and stuffed them into a rear pocket of his pants.

He wove through dark corridors until he reached the new side of the building, waited for an elevator, and squeezed between two laundry bins and an orderly wearing scrubs and paper shoe covers. He slipped the balled-up smock into one of the open bins as the doors closed. The orderly turned and smiled, asked him what floor, and pushed a button for the parking level.

A guard was running past when he exited the elevator. He walked past a female cashier in a booth at the exit barrier and stepped onto the sidewalk as more cop cars came careening into the block.

He walked without turning, wondering if he had overreacted.

Maybe the janitor was only a janitor. Maybe the headphones were only headphones. Maybe the janitor wasn't an undercover cop after all.

His hands were still shaking. He could still remember Sherry Moore's face. She had opened her eyes and looked at him. She looked like she could see him, but of course that was ridiculous.

He stopped at a Don't Walk sign, waiting for the orange man to turn white.

Take your time, he thought. Nothing can go wrong now. A moment later the pedestrian sign changed and he mixed into a handful of people crossing to the opposite curb.

He should have felt worse than he did. He'd missed the opportunity, but now that he had seen her, he knew it would have been all wrong. Reading about her was one thing, but seeing her as a person was indescribable. She was like his mother, a presence.

"Hey, watch where you're going." A man's hands were pushing him out of the way. He looked up at the stranger, a dark urge to strike him passing over.

"Sorry." He stepped out of the way.

He was blocks from Nazareth now; the sidewalk crowds were thinning out. He was in a commercial district. People were getting onto a bus and he got in line behind them. He didn't know where the bus was going and didn't care. The police would be swarming the downtown parking lots for the next several hours. He'd come back when things calmed down.

Tonight he would be back on the Pennsylvania Turnpike heading west. Five hours later he'd be home in Waterdrum, on the opposite end of the state.

He couldn't stop thinking of how the gown lay

across her neck, the piles of chestnut-colored hair around her head.

He had to see her again. Whatever else he might do, this shooting star had a destination.

He knew now how his life was going to end.

6

PHILADELPHIA, PENNSYLVANIA

"Sherry? You have a visitor, Sherry. A man is waiting for you in the hall."

She stirred, scrunched her nose, wondering where she was. She heard a low television and dishes rattling on trays. The hospital, yes, there was a man in her room and then . . .

"Sherry?"

The effects of the sedative were still wearing off.

"Can you roll a little toward me, hon? There, can you move?"

She remembered all the commotion now. The man had hurt someone. People were running to resuscitate the victim, guards swarming around her bed, and then they were gone again.

"Is he dead? The man that was in my room."

"He's alive, honey, but they're still working on him.

Can you walk to the bathroom? I need to get you standing for a few minutes, so you might as well use your legs going to the bathroom and brushing your teeth."

Sherry walked slowly to the bathroom, closed the door, and used the toilet, threw cold water in her face and brushed her teeth and hair.

"There, that's much better, isn't it?" the nurse said as she opened the door. "Everything's all spiffy here. I've got you a fresh pitcher of ice water." She punched up the pillow and replaced it, then helped Sherry into the bed and pulled her wet hair from her face.

"I'm not working the next two days, so if I don't see you again, you remember this." She pressed a piece of metal into Sherry's hand. "Say a little prayer to Saint Christopher when things get bad. I've been doing it all my life. I tell you, child, it helps. Shall I tell the gentleman he can come in?"

"Thank you." Sherry smiled. "Did he give you a name?"

"Why, I thought he was your grandfather, child."

"You're looking rather good."

"Edward?" she said, surprised.

"Miss Moore."

"I thought we were past the formalities." Her voice cracked.

"It's been a while," he said.

"It has." Her voice now was barely more than a whisper. "A year. I wasn't expecting you, of all people."

Karpovich removed his jacket and circled her bed, pulled a plastic molded chair from a corner, and sat next to her. The same chair the man had been sitting on.

"No more than I." He folded the jacket over his lap.

"Why you?"

"Because I know you?"

Karpovich thought about the first time he'd met Sherry Moore. He hadn't known what she looked like before that day at Pittsburgh International Airport. He certainly hadn't expected her to be blind or beautiful. Just hours before they parted for the last time, he had watched her hold the hand of a rotting corpse and thought there was nothing to compare with that sight. Not in his thirty-two years of police work.

Looking back, his request to bring her to Pittsburgh had been an act of desperation. Probably that was how most cops got involved with so-called psychics and mediums. He had never in his wildest dreams imagined calling one himself; in fact, he'd probably made some rather strong negative statements about their abilities over the years.

But circumstances had left him nowhere else to turn. The criminal justice machine and the state's bureaucracy had both turned their backs on him. He wanted to find a body, even though it served no purpose. There was no one to prosecute. There were no relatives to present the remains to. So maybe it wasn't desperation as much as principle that drove him to it. In any case, an old friend in the Philadelphia Major Crimes Division told him about a psychic who he vowed could read last memories.

Karpovich used the friend's connections to reach Sherry Moore. He really had no idea what to expect when he met her, but that same day Sherry went to his crime scene, took the hand of a dead man, and told him where she thought the body would be. Before the week was over, a backhoe unearthed the victim's remains.

Colleagues later assured him that the psychic had only made an educated guess. It was not an act of mysticism, but a deduction that anyone might have made knowing the facts of the case. In fact, they said, Karpovich would have figured it out himself, given time. He was just too close to the case to see it clearly.

Karpovich wasn't so sure. His mind agreed, but his heart had always told him something extraordinary had happened that day, something outside the realm of his experience.

"Oh, come on, you're far from home, Edward. Pittsburgh is on the other side of the state."

"I got promoted." He watched her face carefully, wondering if it had been too early for this kind of thing. "I work statewide now."

"To what, Edward? What were you promoted to?"

She wanted to hang on to the niceties, to postpone the inevitable.

She must look pitiful, she thought. She was up to her neck in legal issues and the newspapers were now accusing her of playing footsie with one of Maryland's cabinet-level politicians. She knew that everyone thought she had tried to commit suicide. Then someone got attacked in her room. Strangely, the part of it that bothered Sherry most was that she didn't want Karpovich to think poorly of her.

"Colonel," he told her.

She nodded and gave him a weak smile. "I'm not surprised, Edward."

She put her head back on the pillow. "He's alive, I was told, the man who was in my room."

"He's stable," Karpovich said. "How are you?"

"Oh, you know." She tried to laugh. "I had some rough spots last summer and then I took these pills and went into a coma and then a guy tried to kill someone in my hospital room."

Karpovich smiled.

"What was he doing here, Edward?"

"We don't know yet."

"Guess."

"He could have been stealing drugs, saw you alone, and . . . you know."

"Decided to rape me? In a hospital room?"

"It's happened before."

"Did anyone else see him?"

"A security guard and one of the nurses on the twelfth floor. He was wearing some kind of uniform. They're still collecting the videos from the surveillance cameras."

"You're here officially then?"

"Philadelphia city has jurisdiction. I'm just here to see how you are."

"Embarrassed," she said flatly.

"You've had quite a year. I'm sorry about all that happened in Wildwood. I don't even know what to say about Cumberland. It must have been horrible."

She nodded.

She knew it was close, that she'd nearly killed herself. She knew what her own doctor had to say.

"Any idiot can figure out where you're going. You don't have options, Sherry. Not anymore. You've used them up. You're feeding off reserves. You are unraveling under the stress and your brain may just interpret that as a need to shut down.

"You cannot fuck with pills!"

He'd shaken his head, then softened his tone. "We don't know how you're wired, Sherry. We don't know that you wouldn't lose your memory again and go back to your early childhood. We don't know that you aren't on the verge of cataclysmic breakdown and I mean a 'knees pulled into your chest, sucking your thumb' kind of breakdown."

That had scared her, but not half as much as what had happened in that coma. Sherry had been far closer to death than even the doctors realized. There were places in her mind that were too dangerous even for her to stray.

"I'm going to be okay," she said. "I'll be okay."

"I know it," Karpovich said, soothing her. Of course he didn't know it, he couldn't know it, and he was scared as hell she was right. That someone had come to her room to kill her.

Sherry thought about that day so long ago now in Pittsburgh, how thoughtful Karpovich—then a captain—had been the first time she met him. How easily he had slipped into the role of Seeing-Eye companion. He had a natural instinct for what she wanted to hear. He was intuitive about describing her surroundings. He became her eyes for that day, and few people understood how meaningful that was to someone who couldn't see for herself. She had decided at the time that he must be a caregiver to someone. Perhaps a sick wife?

She tried to make a funny face, which collapsed into a single doleful sob.

"I knew what I was getting into, Edward."

"I know." Karpovich leaned over the bed, putting his hand on her arm.

"I'm all right." She sniffed. "No matter what I did, I'm all right now, Edward. I'm back." The tears ran freely now down her cheeks, onto the neck of her gown. "I'm back." She wiped her eyes, taking comfort in the company of this man.

"I know," he said. "I know."

Sherry Moore was taken home by her neighbor Garland Brigham. On the steps of the hospital her lawyer issued a brief statement.

"I cannot comment on the incident that took place in Nazareth except to say that Miss Moore is well and cooperating with the police. Miss Moore is recovering from adverse reactions to medicines that were legally prescribed to her by a doctor. I would offer a word of caution to those who might speculate otherwise."

Cameras flashed and the attorney removed his glasses.

"You have been reporting that Sherry Moore disclosed information to Maryland state police officers having to do with the murders of the three women found in Cumberland last week. I can neither confirm nor deny that report. You may know that federal courts have limited the privacy claims of family members concerning deceased relatives as far as autopsies are concerned. The government's test in the hallmark case was to demonstrate a matter of common public interest in overriding what has become the assertion that the dead or even relatives of the dead enjoy survivors' rights to privacy. In that case the court ruled that dead people cannot speak for themselves and so the government is compelled in the public's interest to learn how they died through the postmortem process of autopsy. Our argument is identical. Sherry Moore's hand-holding experience is far less intrusive, but still an opportunity for the dead to speak for themselves. On the matter of Cumberland, Maryland, state police officials are beginning to back away from the position they took in 2005, being that two teen suspects killed in a police pursuit in 2005 were responsible for kidnapping the women found in Cumberland. Keeping in mind that Miss Moore cannot comment on what took place in Cumberland, she has asked that the public join police in helping them solve their case. I quote Miss Moore now: 'It is not a time for talking about what should have been done by the police in 2005, but to support them in all they do now. If you have any information about the Cumberland crime scene that will help police bring these cases to conclusion, we implore you to call the number on the screen. If you know of anyone who had access to the grounds where the women were found, you should give this information to the police. If you are responsible for the deaths of the women in Cumberland in 2005, I beseech you to call the number on the screen.'"

He removed his reading glasses. "Miss Moore wants to thank her well-wishers for the cards and letters she has received throughout the winter and for those who have prayed for her these past few days. She is sorry that it has taken so long to get back to you and promises to make up for it. Thank you for coming out to hear us today, and once again, we are sorry that Miss Moore could not be here personally."

7

WATERDRUM, PENNSYLVANIA

The Iroquois called it Ama Ahuli, meaning "water drum," the confluence of the Youghiogheny and Casselman Rivers. On a crisp winter's night you can hear it for miles, the rivers rushing to meet above a great waterfall, the rocks far below, white-water pools churning before they run into gorges that meander through Pennsylvania's Alleghenies and into the Appalachians of western Maryland.

The first settlers were trappers, followed by military scouts. In the eighteenth century it was the setting for the French and Indian War. In the nineteenth century the mountains were pocked with great furnaces making coke for fuel.

By the mid-twentieth century the forests were second growth, the coal fortunes had come and gone—though mines and miners remain throughout southwestern Pennsylvania—and by the 1950s a postindustrial population, seeking rest and relaxation from their labors, began to discover the hidden beauty of Ama Ahuli.

Tourists followed dirt roads that followed railroad tracks that followed rivers. The mountains were too jagged to cross, the hollows too scattered to circumnavigate. Inns became popular, and picnickers came from the booming steel towns of Pittsburgh and Wheeling and Weirton, West Virginia. They saw few of the hard mountain farms or the company coal towns tucked over the next ridge or in the countless hollows.

Then came 1970, and a revolution of consciousness put Waterdrum on the map. Armies of tree-hugging environmentalists loaded their Hondas and Toyotas with cross-country skis and snowshoes and came to the wilderness in search of themselves. And as the environmentalists grew older and wealthier, they bought property in Waterdrum and began to take over the local politics.

River houses were revived into B&Bs and restaurants. The first-ever fine-dining menus appeared on windows in Fayette County.

What was once thought outdated became quaint, and carpenters and plumbers and electricians rushed to the area to give the old summer homes and hunting camps expensive face-lifts.

Entrepreneurs rushed to Waterdrum as well, providing cycle rentals, kayaks and canoes, white-water guides. There were backpacking shops, ice cream stands, "authentic" Indian jewelry purveyors, and places to get barbecue and beer.

Every piece of the river that was not protected by the state was built upon, and every former inn or mill swelled with tourists who could afford to hear the eternal beat of Ama Ahuli in their rooms at night.

George Thorpe, retired from the U.S. Marine Corps after twenty years, took a second mortgage on the Trail's End Inn and refurbished the restaurant. Business flourished. His father had been a coal miner in West Virginia, which was why he tolerated the Coaltown boys at his bar. A sepia-colored photograph of a dozen black-faced coal miners hung over a mantel above the fireplace. George Thorpe Sr. was among them, standing off to one side. He was young and had a daring look about him, with a shock of dark hair hanging over his forehead; his eyes burned right into you as if he knew there would be other generations of young miners staring back at him one day.

There were rules for the locals, of course. Piss off a tourist and you were out for a week. Piss off two and you were out for a month. Lose a customer and "you ain't nevva comin' back!" And retired Master Gunny Sergeant George Thorpe was not shitting them when he told them so.

Thorpe had traveled the world and set foot on almost every continent. He'd seen the clash of cultures on a dozen different soils. The dynamics were always the same. Different perspective, different priorities, but, reduced to a phrase, it was mutual envy.

The Coaltown boys envied those college boys with the long leggy blondes and their European cars, designer clothes, and expensive toys. They never grew up to appreciate the wonders that brought city people to their world. They had to suffer its hardships instead: had to hunt the craggy foothills for food, chop firewood for fuel, endure the harsh winters, take an elevator into the bowels of the earth to survive.

The land wasn't always so beautiful either; behind those state parks and national memorials were hilltops razed by hulking cranes with massive toothed buckets that stripped trees and sod from the earth in search of shallow coal. What they left looked like scabs on the mountains.

The land was hard like the people who lived here, the Welsh and Poles and Irish and Slavs.

The towns they lived in all looked the same, with rotting wooden tipples and rusting coal cars on railroad tracks. The state roads looked as if they'd been carpet-bombed, so poorly were they repaired. Hillsides stripped of timber for infrastructure eroded mud and rocks onto the highways to cause horrible accidents.

At the edges of a town were smoldering bony piles that leached nitrates into streams and drinking wells. Whose father hadn't known a kid who walked across or drove up to the top of one and disappeared into a hot shaft that had burned up from the core? It had happened in nearly every county in Pennsylvania over the last seventy years.

Rivers that ran between the towns were coated with orange slime, rocks discolored from the mineral runoffs of overworked mines. The old-timers called it Yellow Boy, but it was a sulfate and it turned your skin the color of rust. No one thought it curious that fish didn't survive in it—not one of the four generations that had played on the banks and swam in the holes for the better part of two centuries.

The towns themselves were a row of identical houses, tarpapered gray and covered with the coal dust that permeates every pore and every cell of every living thing. The number of people in the houses had fluctuated little since the towns came to be. The residents represented three shifts in a mine, which was all that could be said about them; there really was no other story: no one ever lived there who had done anything else.

Tourists, on the other hand, stayed on the main roads, saw the waterfalls and the old iron railroad bridge, the natural rock water chutes to pools where they launched their thousand-dollar kayaks. They saw the very places where Revolutionary war generals walked. They didn't know what lay over the hills; they didn't know that the earth beneath them was honeycombed with thousands of miles of tunnels, or that towns over the next ridge were built over a 200-foot shaft into a vein of soft bituminous coal that ran northwesterly in the direction of Pittsburgh.

But that was how life was, and George Thorpe understood. Each side saw something the other had that they wanted, usually something false. There was something almost akin to wonder, like two tribes meeting at the edge of their known world, suspicious but curious about each other.

George Thorpe didn't run a loose bar—he wouldn't permit a fight under any circumstances—but boys would be boys and girls would be girls and long after the diners were gone and the tourists were back in their cabins at night, he allowed for things to get interesting. On a good night the Coaltown boys might get to catch one of those leggy girls flashing her tits or dancing on a table. On a very good night, one of the Coaltown boys might get laid, but come Saturday morning it was back to the real world and back to the bowels of the earth.

Kenny and Walter were both working the bar tonight. Kenny spun a coaster in front of Cal Mooney and sat a long-neck Bud on it.

Mooney handed him a five-dollar bill, then raised his bottle in a salute to Crisco at the end of the bar. Crisco looked at him suspiciously, nodded his gray head, and mumbled something unintelligible. Crisco was nicknamed for the dozens of rusty vegetable shortening cans he kept in the back of his El Camino; they contained nuts and bolts and old carburetor parts. Crisco, who drank shots of whiskey to fallen comrades, would be back in 1972, wheels down over Haiphong about now. Crisco had never quite returned from Vietnam.

Mooney looked around the room, happy not to see Eric Milner at the bar. Milner was convinced he had called the police and snitched on him for selling stolen wheels out of his garage.

He had.

By four-thirty, the dining room was full. Two miners, Nicky Czerwinski and Dave Blough—scrubbed more or less clean—took stools on the opposite side of the bar. There were dozens of out-of-state contractors who worked on the houses around Waterdrum. Transients looking for temporary work were forever passing through.

"You hear they've got another hiker missing down in Tyler?" Pete Row, the postmaster, sidled up to the bar. George Thorpe, wearing reading glasses, was going through credit card receipts.

He shook his head.

Walter, standing next to him, stuffed a towel in a glass and polished it dry.

"Troopers came in this morning, said they were picking up those hiker's registration cards from the trailheads. Like a fucking murderer is going to fill out a registration card before he goes up the trail to kill someone. Fucking idiots."

Thorpe put a finger to his lips, pointed at the diners waiting by the door.

"Sorry," Pete whispered.

Nick Czerwinski craned his neck to watch a pair of long-haired blondes in hiking shorts squeeze through the diners waiting for tables. The girls took stools next to Mooney, began organizing their cigarettes, cell phones, and lighters on the bar in front of them.

Czerwinski slapped Blough sitting next to him and nodded at the girls, just before Mickey came through the side door. Mickey was covered with gray glue and whatever he crawled in all day long. He specialized in burying PVC, which in plain English meant running sewer lines.

Carl Mooney didn't like Mickey, not since he challenged him to a fight over some bar change. Mickey, who had been renovating houses around Waterdrum for more than a year, was best known for his abilities to make beer disappear. They called him the liquid plumber; he hadn't drawn a sober breath since he moved here.

"Remember that girl that was raped and strangled in the shelters at Tremont a couple years back. They never found that guy either," Pete went on. "Cops might have another Green River killer on their hands. Fucking Ridgeway guy was killing women for twenty goddamned years before they figured him out."

A well-kept middle-aged woman entered the bar. She looked like money, Czerwinski thought, hoping she would sit next to him, and after looking at her options, she did.

"It'll be a goddamn chain reaction, like when those towers got hit in New York. First they'll close the Appalachian Trail. Then the inns will start to lose business. Bars suffer, rental places suffer, then them kids that run the raft trips. No more bike rentals, no kayaks, no business at the gas stations, and the grocery mart will start closing on Sundays again. People need to feel safe in the woods or they'll go somewhere else. Next thing you know, property values drop."

Thorpe nodded, studying the receipts through his reading glasses.

"It'll hurt us all, George."

"That fucking—"

"Take it easy, Pete," Walter said. A family with young children was waiting for a table to be cleaned next to the bar.

"Yeah, okay." The postmaster looked over his shoulder. George Thorpe didn't much care what you said after the dinner crowd left, but when the kiddies were around, you had to have manners.

"Ma'am." Kenny laid a coaster in front of the pretty brunette. She was in her late forties, tanned and taut and quite a looker. "What'll you have today?"

She let her eyes travel slowly down the front of

Kenny's shirt to his waist and back up. "Gin martini, up, dry, with two olives."

Kenny nodded. "Menu?"

"Maybe later."

She opened a floppy buckskin bag and took out a newspaper. She was dressed down, but chic. Her arms were gym-toned. Czerwinski looked down at her jeans, clinging provocatively to her thighs. She wore a gold teardrop pendant that plunged into the exposed cleavage between breasts that, real or not, were nothing less than stunning. She laid the newspaper on the bar and began to flip through the pages with the jangling of hoop bracelets.

Nicky Czerwinski lifted his bottle to drink and leaned over to look down her linen blouse. You couldn't mistake his intention, but she made no effort to conceal herself.

"Thank God for summer." Blough elbowed Czerwinski and they grinned, clinking bottles.

Kenny poured the martini in front of her.

"You guys look busy tonight." She took a sip of her drink.

"Rivers are up," Kenny said. "Spring was dry, so everyone's out making up for it."

"What do people do here for fun at night?"

"Drink." He laughed. "We have a band on Saturdays." He pointed toward the deck. "And Bucks up the street has karaoke if you're into that."

"You go there?"

Kenny smiled. "Everything's closed when I get off."

"You?" she asked Mooney, sitting across the bar.

He shook his head, uncomfortable at being addressed.

"Shame," she said into her martini. She threw back an inch of the drink and tapped the front page. "Can you believe all this stuff down in Cumberland?"

Mickey the carpenter walked up behind her and leaned over her shoulder, pretending to look down at the paper.

Mooney watched Mickey suspiciously, wondered what he kept in the trunk of his Impala. He always parked near the grassy end of the lot. He'd seen Czerwinski follow him over there and do something behind the open trunk. Drugs, he was sure.

Mickey was weird. Mickey liked to brush up against the women at the bar, hand always in his pocket; he looked like he was rubbing himself when he did it.

"Cong moui!" Crisco slapped an imaginary mosquito on the back of his wrist.

"Jesus, look at that." Blough jabbed Nick Czerwinski. The two blondes on the opposite side of the bar had ordered Blow Jobs and were picking up the shot glasses in their mouths, tilting back their heads.

A moment later they let the shot glasses drop from their mouths to the bar.

"Lick it off," Blough yelled, standing on the rungs of his stool.

Thorpe cast him a cautionary look over the rims of his reading glasses and Blough sat back down. One of the blondes leaned over to lick the whipped cream from her friend's face and Czerwinski moaned audibly.

The woman in the designer jeans looked up and laughed. "Youth." She shook her head before going back to the article. "Can you imagine what those women's bodies must have looked like? I keep trying to picture this container they were in; they said it's like half the size of a railroad car."

"They know who they are?" Mickey was still at her shoulder, bumping up against her lightly.

"Uh-huh," the brunette said without turning to look at him. "Same women from Hagerstown, Maryland, two years ago. They said they were waiting to notify the families. One of them had moved away from the area or something."

Mickey leaned over her again, looking at the picture of Sherry Moore on the front page.

"That one of them?" He pointed.

"Wow, have you been out of the country or what?" She looked over her shoulder.

"Nah," he said. "I stay busy."

"She's a psychic," the brunette said. "They tried to sneak her onto the scene and got caught. Now one of the victim's families is suing her and she swallows a bottle of pills and tries to kill herself and on and on and on." She waved her hand in the air.

She rolled her eyes. "Oh, yeah, and while she's in the hospital some maintenance guy gets attacked by one of her fans. Cute headline, huh?" She held up a *New York Post*. VICTIMS OR PSYCHIC—WHO'S THE REAL STORY?

Mickey looked confused. "So what's she have to do with any of it?"

The woman shrugged. "She was supposed to name the killer, I guess."

"Uh-huh," Mickey said, sounding even more confused.

"I read about her." Nick Czerwinski leaned nearer to take another look down her shirt. "Sherry Moore, right?"

The woman nodded. "She's from Philadelphia. You heard about that swamp thing going on in New Jersey last summer? She touches dead people and reads their memories."

"Yeah, right." Mickey laughed, rocking unsteadily on his heels.

Mooney watched the liquid plumber, thinking he must have made a few stops along the way.

The young blondes across the bar were openly fingering whipped cream out of their shot glasses now and wiping it on each other's faces. Half the men in the dining room were hazarding cross looks from their wives, unable to tear their eyes from the action. The girls looked like they were ready to mud-wrestle.

Nick Czerwinski caught a glance from one of the blondes and winked at her. It was always hard getting laid when there were two girls, he thought. You had to factor in what influence one might have over the other. Maybe he should settle for the old gal next to him. She was certainly pretty enough and built like a brick shithouse. He'd bet she was a handful in bed.

Kenny stepped in front of the blondes, replenished their Coronas, and lit one of their cigarettes. Czerwinski heard them introduce themselves across the bar. Debbie and Dawn.

"Can you believe it? He hung them all too. What a horrible way to go."

"That's crazy," Czerwinski said.

A waitress came up between the brunette and Czerwinski to pick up an order for a table. "What's she saying now?"

"Some press conference on the steps of the hospital. Her attorney is asking the Cumberland killer to turn himself in." The brunette snorted. "Like some public service announcement, huh?"

"Trying to get the focus off her, I would think."

"She must have told the police something," George Thorpe said. He pushed the cash register drawer closed and laid his reading glasses alongside it. "They have to know more than they're saying."

"All a big tease." The waitress pointed at the paper.

"Some local reporter claims a police captain told him she saw the killer's face. And now no one can talk about it? The whole thing sounds crazy to me."

"You believe in psychics?" the pretty brunette asked the bartender Kenny.

"I heard some weird shit from a palm reader once." But it wasn't Kenny who answered. It was Mickey standing behind her; his chest was all over her shoulder now. She could feel his arm at her side and had the impression it was moving around. She glanced back and saw his hand was in his pocket.

She leaned forward, away from him. "I don't think she qualifies as a palm reader." The brunette tapped a picture of Sherry Moore's twenty-room mansion on the Delaware River.

Czerwinski was studying the brunette's western boots, expensive-looking alligators balanced on the brass rail.

"What's your name?" he asked.

"Jean," she said. "Jean Farrell. What's yours?"

"Nicky," he said, wondering what she was wearing under the jeans, guessing Victoria's Secret; she had money all right. Maybe if he played it right, she would pick up his tab too.

"If you could really do that, I mean, if you could really see what other people saw when they were dying, that must really screw up your head."

"Fucked up," Mickey said from behind her. He burped.

Kenny was about to call Mickey on his language when a large man came through the patio doors and pushed his way around Mickey, sliding onto the stool to the left of the brunette.

"Fucked up indeed," the big man agreed, leaning over to kiss the brunette on the cheek. He was wearing a fire-engine-red Ralph Lauren Polo shirt stretched tightly over his massive belly and a heavy gold Rolex on his wrist. Czerwinski figured him for sixty or so.

"It's a cluster fuck over there, from what I hear."

Czerwinski, feeling cheated, noted that Thorpe and his bartenders cared less about the out-of-town customers cursing than locals during the dinner hour.

"Why would anyone want to stop her from saying what she saw?"

"Oh, for God's sake, that's not even the point," the man in the red shirt said. "They had to know what would happen if they got caught doing some silly shit like that. It doesn't make any sense unless they wanted to get caught."

"Oh, you think everything has to be explained; it's either this way or that, black or white, hot or cold. You judges are all alike."

"Come on," the judge said. "She's free press for everybody. That's all that makes sense when it's said and done. No one in their right mind would invite a psychic to a crime scene unless they wanted publicity. Vodka rocks," he yelled toward a bartender.

"She'll write a fucking book. *Jacked Up by Justice*

or some such shit. And that black guy Schiff will get votes for being a minority with creativity."

"Oh, Barry." Jean put a hand on his knee.

Nicky Czerwinski, sitting next to her, rolled his eyes. So much for the easy lay.

The situation across the bar was slipping away as well. The blondes had been joined by a boy wearing a Virginia Military Institute sweatshirt.

"Black Moshannon," one of the blondes shrieked. "No fucking way. My parents have a place on the lake."

"I was born in Philipsburg," the boy said, "been going up there since I was five."

"We're number three lot, the only camper with a red awning."

The VMI boy shrugged.

"You should meet us up there. Last week of May, just the two of us." She jabbed a finger into the other blonde's shoulder. "We go down to State College at night. Ever been to Shadrock's?" she asked.

He nodded.

"So are you home for the summer?"

"Me and my buddy"—he stuck a thumb toward the door—"we're trying to get summer jobs in Waterdrum."

"Cool," the one called Dawn said.

"Who goes up to Moshannon this time of year? Must be cold until the Fourth."

"That's why we like it." Dawn smiled wickedly,

licking whipped cream from the rim of her shot glass. "No one's there but us."

The boy nodded and pointed at their Coronas. "Same thing," he yelled at the bartender. "Make it two." His buddy walked in, wearing a baseball cap and cargo pants hanging halfway off his ass.

Dawn stuck out money for Kenny to pay for the boys' beers and ordered another round of Blow Jobs.

Mooney walked to the jukebox and flipped through the racks of different records that he knew by heart. He knew the recipe for gunpowder and nitroglycerin, he knew that a Sig Sauer 2022 had a clip capacity of fifteen rounds for 9mm ammunition and twelve rounds for 10mm. He knew that cops could triangulate the signal from three cell phone towers to locate a particular signal. And he knew that George Thorpe had added a Howie Day record to the jukebox since last Monday.

He noticed other things around the bar as well. The blond girl named Debbie had come back from a trip to the ladies' room with the top of her thong sticking out of her jeans. It hadn't been visible like that before those boys came into the bar. And she'd put on more eyeliner as well.

He noticed there was a picture missing from the corkboard collage on the wall too. There were hundreds of photos stapled to it, glossy snapshots of girls dancing, girls smiling, boys drinking with their arms around each other's necks, some caught mid-shout, some holding bottles of beer for the photographer, some giving peace signs.

Kenny or George took the pictures when the bar got real busy. George wrote the customers' first names and dates on the back or the border. He liked to post them so people would come back every year to see themselves there. He said it was good for repeat business. George didn't miss an opportunity to make his customers happy.

Mooney knew right where the picture had been. He knew the picture well enough, too; Thorpe had taken two photographs of the same woman, one with her husband and kids and one of just her when she came back later without them. It was the family picture that was missing.

The judge leaned into Jean and tapped a finger on her paper. "I'll tell you what else. If she's suicidal, she's a nutcase and serious people don't connect their names to nutcases." He picked up his vodka and drank half of it.

"But the police were wrong in 2005. They're starting to back off those teenagers already. Can you imagine what the real killer might be thinking?"

The judge guffawed. "What do you think he's thinking? If it was me, I'd figure the government was too stupid to do anything about me since they were consulting fortune-tellers. Who would worry about the cops? I'd be more concerned about telepathic vibrations coming at me." He wiggled his fingers and thumbs over his head, laughing so hard his belly rattled.

"Oh, Barry." She waved him off.

"No, no," he said, banging the bar with a fist. "I've watched AGs do this dance all my life. It's like there isn't enough serious work out there to keep them busy, so they got to go out and find themselves some intrigue. It wouldn't occur to them to start putting some fire under their DAs' asses." He shook his head. "Which is why trial calendars will soon need to take into consideration the life span of a judge before they assign fucking docket numbers."

The big man leaned over and kissed her on the cheek. "I'm going to have one more. I put us on the list for a table." He squeezed her thigh.

"Well, I think that guy Schiff must have really believed in what he was doing and, you know, as far as the psychic, I'll admit it seems all so dramatic, but it's still not funny when someone commits suicide."

"Attempted, my dear, she attempted to take her own life, which is another word for I-want-to-be-noticed."

"They found her, Barry. Read the freaking paper. She would have died if her neighbor hadn't found her."

"Whatever." He reached to cadge a cherry from the fruit tray behind the bar.

Kenny picked up her glass and scooped more ice in it. "Didn't she solve some big case for the police, though? She was just in the news not too long ago."

"More bullshit," the judge muttered.

"She's a freak," the postmaster said. "She's got some biological thing where she jumps over into your brain and can read your memory."

The judge rolled his eyes and opened a menu.

"Only if you're dead." The waitress was back. "It's short-term memory. She's supposed to be able to tap into short-term memory. The brain generates electricity; she transfers the impulses from her hand through a dead person's receptors in the skin cells and uses the wiring of their central nervous system to reach their brain."

"Oh, for Christ's sake," the judge said.

A burst of laughter erupted on the other side of the bar, where the girls had just finished their second round of Blow Jobs and missed each other's hands when they attempted a high five. The boy with the VMI sweatshirt now had his hand on Dawn's bare back and his foot on the rung of her bar stool.

Nick Czerwinski was trying to make them out, but he was seeing four blondes instead of two across the bar.

"What else has she done?" the postmaster asked.

"She does a lot of scientific work," a man said from the end of the bar. He had just left his family at the dinner table to smoke a cigarette and look at the blondes up close. "Like she helps researchers and archaeologists. I read in *Newsweek* she did some work for the government trying to locate POWs in Vietnam."

Crisco looked up from the green and brown bottles and tried to locate the source of the conversation. Then he saw Mooney to his left and thought he was looking more and more Vietnamese by the moment. "Dinky-da," he slurred. "Dinky-da?"

"Yeah, right." The judge pounded down another vodka rocks. "POWs."

"Listen to him, hon." Jean nudged the side of the judge's leg with her knee.

Nick Czerwinski, who was on his last ten dollars until payday, pushed off from the bar, slapped Blough on the shoulder, and staggered toward the door, sneering at the college boy with the blondes. He'd have fucked them up if they'd given him any lip. Goddamned college fairies. Why George Thorpe catered to those assholes was beyond him. George thought them tourists' shit didn't stink. Maybe they'd have a car outside with a VMI decal in the back window. Be a goddamned shame if someone accidentally ran a key down the side of it. Probably think it was that retard Mooney or the liquid plumber.

"I'd be one nervous son of a bitch when that woman starts talking, that's all I'm saying," Jean said.

"And she'll talk," the man with the cigarette said. "It might not be tomorrow, but she'll talk, and when she does there'll be a movie deal. Longer they shut her up, the more money she'll make."

Jean ordered another drink, the judge's hand on her thigh, little finger climbing nearer and nearer to her crotch. She was getting horny, but it wasn't the judge she was thinking about.

She thought when the judge passed out for the night she might put on some lipstick and come back for a nightcap, sans bra.

The noise level had risen dramatically. Ceiling fans were flapping Cinco de Mayo pendants on their strings. A wind chime made of Marine Corps Marathon medallions tinkled behind the cash register.

8

HARRISBURG, PENNSYLVANIA

Evelyn Harp, who was the administrative assistant to Colonel Edward Karpovich, wasn't into "feelings," and she'd let more than one commanding officer know it. There was a job and you did it. Either you were good at it or you stank. What more was there to say?

She felt the same way about high-ranking police officials.

Karpovich, so far, was in her good books.

She picked up the phone and put it back down, then peeked over the rim of her tortoiseshell glasses. "The colonel will see you now." She nodded toward the heavy wooden door behind her.

Palmer was a Karpovich protégé, rescued from a dead-end job of answering phones for the bureau following a car crash that took the lives of both his parents and his fiancée, who had been on their way to Pittsburgh to visit him in school.

The department's psychologist sent him to therapy and prescribed medications. The decision to bench him was his former commander's. Palmer, clearly stunned, was in no condition to protest.

Karpovich hadn't known Palmer personally at the time, but he'd read his evaluations and found that he'd been considered an excellent sergeant before the tragedy. Karpovich didn't like to see cops put on shelves. If something was broke, you fixed it. That was his philosophy. More important, Palmer had been a good cop up until the day he needed them most. Palmer didn't need more time to think. He needed something to do. So in spite of a lieutenant's and captain's concerns, Karpovich returned him to the streets the week he took over the division. And was glad he did. Palmer closed cases.

Karpovich knew there had to be dozens of ways to say it better, but in summing Palmer up it always came down to the same thing. Dan Palmer had an innocence that made him a better investigator. It wasn't naïveté. Not by a long shot. It was more akin to purity of thought, but that didn't quite nail it either. In essence, Palmer could see each new crime as if it were through a child's eyes, without preconception, without the prejudice that comes with years of experience. He didn't miss the little things. He had a way of reversing roles and seeing the crime through the eyes of the perpetrator. The old-timers might have said he had the sixth sense.

Karpovich had told his new secretary, Evelyn, that he thought young Sergeant Palmer was trying to emulate the killer's own feelings.

Evelyn had cocked her head to one side. "Don't you go talking about 'feelings,' now, Colonel. There's enough 'feelings' in this old building to make the walls weep."

Karpovich would never have dared tell Evelyn about Sherry Moore. The fact that he had once worked a case with a psychic would have sent her over the top.

It was dark inside his office, little different than the day his predecessor moved out. There were two photographs on a credenza, both of his wife, and two ferns with sympathy cards still stuck in the soil. The plants had been sitting there for a year now; presumably Evelyn kept them alive.

The desk was large and ornate, but Karpovich never used it. He preferred instead a corner chair between two windows. It was a cracked leather recliner under a gooseneck lamp. Stacks of books and case files were on the floor within reach.

Karpovich wore a long-sleeved white dress shirt, the only color he owned, cuffs rolled midway to the elbow. His tie was navy blue with fine white specks; his pants were charcoal wool. The old man's hair was as white as his shirt and neatly parted across a pink line of scalp.

Some of the troopers called him Gramps, but never to his face. Karpovich was the third most powerful law enforcement officer in the Commonwealth of Pennsylvania and he hadn't gotten there the easy way.

"What do we know, Dan?"

"Flunitrazepam. It's marketed under Rohypnol in the states."

"Date-rape drug?" Karpovich said.

Palmer nodded. "But this isn't the garden-variety pills they're putting in women's drinks. It's an alcohol solution called Darkene, sold in Europe predominantly to treat acute insomnia. It's about ten times as potent."

"So why knock her out? She was already vulnerable if he wanted to rape her."

Palmer shook his head vigorously. "There was more. Pentobarb, an anesthetic—the doctor said it was a very lethal cocktail."

"How'd the maintenance guy pull through?"

"He was sitting on top of an emergency room.

Another five minutes and they wouldn't have gotten it out of his system."

Karpovich sat back in his chair.

"What else?"

"Philadelphia PD has videos of a man in a white jacket, like a medical jacket, with an insignia over the breast pocket. He's wearing a baseball cap, keeps his face looking down and away from the cameras. The security guard said it's the same guy, same uniform."

"Will she be able to recognize his voice?"

Palmer shook his head. "I doubt it, she's not even sure what color his hair is, can't describe his eyes, says he sounds like everyone else she's ever talked to. She's not very cooperative or observant. The only things she remembered with any detail were his goatee and boots. He was wearing hiking boots."

"What about the exits?"

"Nine operating cameras; we have lots of film but no white smock." He handed a still shot developed from one of the videos to the colonel. "This one caught our eye. The camera is angled downward, pointed at the street, away from the garage-level doors. The security chief said the painters may have knocked it out of alignment when they were working down there last winter. Why no one failed to notice it, he couldn't explain, but look"—he pointed—"the legs here in the khaki pants. He's wearing hiking boots. This was twenty-one minutes after the attack. We showed the picture to the guard and she thinks the boots are similar. That's the best we can get from her."

"He probably wasn't wearing the smock when he left."

Palmer shrugged. "There are no other camera angles on these doors. The detectives are looking through all the hospital trash before it leaves the building, just in case he ditched it."

"We have any other cases with Darkene or pentobarb?"

"Pentobarb was used in a homicide here in Harrisburg about three years ago. Husband-wife thing, but she's doing time."

"What about security for Sherry's home?"

"I've talked to Philadelphia and they'll increase the neighborhood patrols. Captain Carroll down at K Barracks will do the same. Sherry's got an effective security system, according to Carroll. He says he's been there before over mail threats. That's about as good as we can do."

"Speaking of mail, have you checked it out?"

"She doesn't open even a fraction of it. The number of letters she gets is staggering."

"Might be something there if you have the time."

Palmer nodded.

"Not you," the colonel said, "but pull some kids from the academy. Maybe he's written to her before, maybe we could get something off a letter or envelope."

"I'll check into it. I got to ask, Colonel. You don't think this incident with Sherry Moore has anything to do with Cumberland?"

Karpovich crossed his legs. "I don't know, Dan. Maryland reopened their investigation this morning. Officially this time."

"Really?" Palmer said, surprised.

"They can't put those teens they accused of the kidnappings in that warehouse and they know it."

"State police leading or is Cumberland looking at it?"

Karpovich shook his head. "Neither. The FBI took it and ran."

"What's the bureau doing there?"

"My guess is they would have to know something they're not saying." Karpovich folded his hands.

"They would indeed."

Sherry checked the locks on her front door, took a scalding shower, and put on silk pajamas. She poured a cup of tea and sat on the divan in her dark living room, unconsciously pulling pillows to her sides, wanting to cradle herself in them, wanting to create some semblance of security.

The newspapers had been hard on her after the hospital visit.

CELEB PSYCHO RUSHED TO ER.

MOORE ATTEMPTS SUICIDE.

One article suggested she pulled a Marilyn—found

naked with pills all around her. The newspapers hadn't forgotten Cumberland either, and now that Moore was considered unstable, they were pressing the attorney general as to his wisdom in bringing her there.

Cumberland became the subject of bitter controversy between the state police commissioner and the office of the attorney general. Former judges and trial lawyers on cable news and Court TV suggested to viewers it could be months before the legal entanglements began to unravel. Months before anyone learned what the so-called psychic saw in Cumberland, if indeed she saw anything at all.

The legal ramifications were exciting, one enthusiastic defense attorney told CNN. The argument that deceased people or their survivors had privacy rights could lead to custody battles never before considered between relatives and law enforcement officers trying to extract critical evidence. It was mind-boggling. The attorney practically beamed.

Sherry thought about calling Garland Brigham next door, then dismissed the idea as quickly. She needed to stand on her own now. She needed to put the past and the crutches, the pills and the alcohol, behind her.

She got to her feet and made her way to the kitchen, rinsed and put away her cup, returned to the divan, and pulled an afghan around her. It was late, but then there was nowhere to go tomorrow, nowhere to be.

She'd been thinking about the man in the hospital; there was something about his voice, something off-key. And then there was the face in Cumberland, the blur behind the glass, the fog.

The wind howled and she let out a slow breath. She was still jittery, but then who wouldn't be? The visitor in the hospital wasn't just some offbeat fan. He had come prepared to kill her.

But for what? Because he was the Cumberland killer and thought she saw his face, or was he only some deranged stalker, as the newspapers reported?

She remembered her cat and wondered where he was. "Truffles?" she called. He was always at her feet.

She hated the feeling of being nervous in her own home. Hated giving in to the police patrols, but Karpovich had insisted on them for a week. It really wasn't necessary, she'd argued. She had a security system and could take care of herself.

She thought about the pistol in the drawer of the secretary, crossed the room to retrieve it, felt the weight of the ten rounds in the clip, the telltale protrusion of a small tab on the right side of the frame that told her a bullet had been chambered. She checked the safety and walked quietly through the house.

If anyone thought it odd for a blind woman to own a handgun, they would have been prudent not to wager against comparative skill. Police officers are routinely taught to shoot with a handicap; they learn to shoot with their weak hand, assuming that their strong hand had been hit. They learn to shoot in darkness, loading their weapons by touch, relying on down-range sounds or simulated muzzle flashes of return fire to regain targets. Sherry Moore's extra senses—refined through echo-location and martial arts training—were far more developed than those of any police officer accustomed to a lifetime of sight. Sherry Moore could blow the center out of anything that moved. Anything that breathed. Anything she could hear.

She checked the lock on the front door, then the French doors off the library. There was a chill in the wide halls as she passed a bathroom, laundry room, and pantry toward the solarium.

"Here, kitty, kitty." She made a clicking noise with her tongue. "Kitty, kitty, kitty."

She put a shoulder against a wall and strained to hear.

"Truffles?" she said.

She heard a meow.

"Truffles?"

The next time she heard it, she placed it behind the doors to the solarium. She crossed a long Oriental runner, unconsciously counting the steps to its end, landed on marble, and struck the glass panel door unexpectedly with her forehead.

The door to the solarium was closed.

The house was like that. It was an old home with many

stairwells and chimneys; the changing air pressure was always closing doors. That was why she left windows cracked open in the pantry and laundry room. "Kitty, kitty." She opened the door and the cat squeezed through the opening, yowling and weaving between her feet.

Sherry pushed the door open until it caught on its hinges, then scooped the cat up as the phone rang. She moved quickly back to the living room, put the pistol away, and snatched the phone off the desk.

"Hello."

"It's me, Sherry."

She recognized the voice immediately. It was the man who had been in her room at the hospital.

"I'm sorry about what happened in the hospital. I thought the kid might have been a cop."

Sherry backed up toward the desk, feeling for the button that would record the call on her answering machine.

"You came to kill me." She finally found it and pushed the button, hoping the noise wouldn't come across on the phone.

"I did, I won't lie to you. I thought you'd be different than you were. I read a lot about you, but it's not always the same as meeting someone."

"Do I know you?"

"Oh, I don't think so. Not unless you've seen me in someone else's head."

Silence.

"They say you tried to kill yourself," he went on.

"I've been there myself once or twice, I know how that feels. I thought you were rather clever, though, considering your condition, pushing that call button and all."

"I sensed you needed help."

"Help." He laughed. "I told you I'd been reading about you, Sherry. About what you do. I asked you in the hospital what people were thinking about when they died. Isn't there always one thing? Always one particular person on their mind? Maybe people think about their parents or their children. I'm looking into her eyes now and I see she cannot stay awake much longer. What is she thinking, Sherry? She's knows it's the end, so what is she thinking?"

Sherry's heart skipped a beat. She needed to get the police. She needed them to trace this call.

"Can you tell me where you are? Maybe I could come to you."

"No." He laughed tiredly. "I can't do that."

"Can I talk to her?"

He seemed to stall. "What would you say to her?"

"I'd say anything you wanted. I'd ask her what you wanted me to."

"I can't do that, Sherry."

"Maybe she would talk to me. You know, maybe she'd feel more comfortable talking to me."

"I don't think so," he said. "But you already know what she's thinking. Isn't that true? You've looked into people's heads. You see this stuff all the time.

Don't you suppose she is looking at me and thinking that I'm all that is important right now?"

"I could tell you what she's thinking about if you'd just give the phone to her and let us talk."

Sherry rummaged through a desk drawer, felt around the top of the desk, went into the kitchen, and patted the tabletop.

"I'm sure she wants to say what she's thinking, but she just doesn't know how," Sherry said, walking to the front door and patting the pockets of her jackets on the coat rack. She found a cell phone and flipped it open. It was dead. She pitched it angrily at the couch.

"I want you to go to the police after she's gone, Sherry. I want you to tell them you have to see her body. Tell them I'm going to call you back and ask you what she was thinking."

The phone disconnected.

Sherry dialed 911. She told them about the voice, the man in the hospital, and the conversation she'd just had on the phone. It took twenty minutes to get someone with the Philadelphia PD to listen to her. Finally they traced the call to a cell phone. Sherry had already called the number back several times, and so had the police, but no one answered. Since the number was unpublished and since the subscriber hadn't called with an emergency, there was no legal way to obtain the caller's address without a subpoena.

The police couldn't help her.

9

LATE APRIL
SEWICKLEY, PENNSYLVANIA
(NORTH OF PITTSBURGH)

Laurel Drive was awash in blue moonlight the night that Karen Nestor was hung from the rail of her garage door opener. The neighbors said the dogs had been howling all the way from Fulton Avenue to the Lincoln Highway. No one had ever heard them do that before. Not in the exclusive Pennwood development in Sewickley.

Pennwood was a gated country club community of young professionals, mostly two-income families with tandem baby joggers and Volvo station wagons in the driveways. There were tennis courts and swimming pools, playgrounds and a paved jogging path that snaked through the trees behind all the houses. It was the kind of place you could take your eye off your kids for a minute or forget to lock your doors at night.

It *was.*

It was the twenty-eighth of April and a late-spring frost glazed the fairways along Country Club Road. Newly planted marigolds forming the word PENNWOOD around a clubhouse were singed a muddy brown; landscapers were still replacing them as the last emergency vehicles extricated themselves from the block.

Sergeant Palmer had been waiting for nightfall. He had wanted to see what the scene looked like after dark. To see what the killer had seen.

There were lights on up and down the block. Neighbors numbed by the news had spent the day at their windows and doors, pondering how something like this could have happened here. If you couldn't be safe in a gated community, just where could you be safe?

Palmer studied 20 Laurel Drive from behind the wheel of his Taurus. The house was a massive stone affair with towering peaks and angles that cast jagged shadows across a lawn of Kentucky bluegrass. The orange coal of a cigarette hovered near the top of the driveway, a moment later arcing upward like a missile. A uniformed trooper appeared out of the darkness.

A strip of yellow crime scene tape fluttered from a gas lamp on one side of the entrance to the driveway. A marked state police car idled next to it, its exhaust snaking across the trunk and disappearing under the opposite side of the car.

Headlights appeared down the street, and a white SUV cruised through an intersection, its gold security emblem reflecting off its door. Pennwood's private security force was well equipped and well paid, according to a local state police troop commander. Palmer had spent time earlier in the day with one of their captains, a sharp-looking man in an immaculate uniform who explained the various tiers of security around Pennwood. There was nothing ambiguous about the man or the process. You couldn't even walk into Pennwood by accident, the captain had told him. Not without registering at the front gate and only then with the written or recorded approval of a resident.

All of the residents' vehicles were registered as well, so if you were entering in a car without a current sticker, you had to be on an approved twenty-four-hour list. Either that or the guards had to call whomever you were visiting to confirm.

No one was on the guest list for 20 Laurel Drive this last weekend in April.

The trooper saluted when he saw the sergeant, and Palmer returned a casual wave.

He would be here all night, Palmer knew. Until the house was finally turned back over to the family, the house with its bloodstained floors and its missing sheets and pillowcases. He had known people who could never walk back into their own homes again. He wasn't sure, under the circumstances, that he could have.

There were three other homes visible from the Nestors' driveway. How the killer chose this one was a mystery. Why had it been Karen rather than her neighbors Debbie or Gloria or Josephine in the houses next door? What made this house different?

It was possible, of course, that Karen Nestor was a random victim, her name pulled from fate's hatful of names, as if she'd won a prize.

Or was Karen Nestor his target all along?

The next-door neighbors, Alan and Debbie Collins, had a pair of yellow Orvis kayaks stacked by their garage. That was where the footprint had been found in the soft peat of a flower bed. The kayaks were out in the open, you really couldn't miss them, but the oars lying next to them were in shadow, and whoever stepped in the flower bed must have tripped over them as he neared the side door to their garage. That's what Debbie Collins had told the police when she saw them gathering around the Nestors' front door this morning.

Crime lab techs later made a cast of the print but were skeptical that it belonged to the man who killed Karen Nestor. No other prints were found to match it—certainly there were none at the crime scene—so it didn't make sense that someone would be so careful at the crime scene and make the mistake of stumbling into a flower bed at the house next door. Not to mention that footprints, especially those found in flower beds next to doors, can belong to just about anyone: the mail lady bringing an oversize package, landscapers, delivery people, meter readers, almost anyone who provided a service to the residents of the estates.

But Debbie Collins was convincing. She told Sergeant Palmer that she had just wheeled their garbage cans to the curb last evening and stopped on her way back to the garage to pluck a few dead flowers from the bed she had planted only a week before. She said she was thinking about the unexpected frost that was forecast, and how much she hated losing the mums she bought only a week ago. That's when she decided to replant them in pots and put them in the garage. And when she was done, she hand-smoothed the flower bed with a glove. She was adamant there had been no track in the dirt as she was doing this.

The more time Palmer spent with Debbie Collins, the more he was convinced she was credible. Which, as crazy at it sounded, meant the killer had been standing at her door before he went to the Nestors' and broke in.

So why didn't he go in there?

Palmer had walked the crime scene a dozen times this afternoon. There wasn't anything about the Collinses' home that was any different from the Nestors'. No dogs, no infrared alarms, no outdoor cameras that might have scared him away. Yet he apparently came here and then left here, crossing the lawn to the Nestors', and now Debbie was alive and Karen was not.

Palmer had been thinking about this crime scene all day long, and nothing about it seemed random. There was a mood about the place that disturbed him.

For one thing, even though the killer spent a lot of time with Karen, he had never entered the master bedroom, even though it was apparent that Karen had been lying in bed and reading just before he arrived.

Had he made her leave the room or had she met him halfway? But why then take her to a guest room? A rapist would have taken her anywhere he pleased. Often it pleased the sociopath to defile the family bed.

Then there was the fact that he ignored the obvious valuables in the house. He had remained focused. A random burglar, even a serial rapist, wouldn't necessarily do that. Palmer had an overwhelming feeling as he stood in the guest room that there was something personal, almost intimate about the killing. The killer had carefully undressed the victim and stacked her clothes on a dresser by the bed as if she would be wearing them again. He—or she—had turned on a radio in the guest room, tuned it to a Pittsburgh light rock FM station.

Was it possible that Karen was expecting the man who killed her? Was it possible that Karen gave directions to where she lived and the killer only mistakenly went next door? That he realized his mistake at the last possible moment and corrected it?

These were the things going through Palmer's head as he considered the killer's approach to 20 Laurel. It was easy to rule out a front street approach to the house. There were lights on in people's homes up and down the block and Palmer knew that it would have been little different the night before. All the neighbors said they were home. Anyone walking the sidewalks could have been noticed by them. Them or the relentless security patrols. You couldn't just walk up the street without attracting attention, and if you had come to kill someone, too many things could go wrong.

The woods behind the houses were a different story, though. He climbed the rear stairs to a deck and looked out over an expanse of grass to the tree line. This was a possibility.

The weakness in Pennwood's security was here, in this wooded area behind Laurel Drive. The entrance to Pennwood off Mercer Road was bordered on both sides by a mile of ornate brick wall. The remainder of the complex, the part you didn't see from a highway, was surrounded by forest and thousands of dollars' worth of commercial-grade security fencing. It wasn't alarmed—the cost would have been prohibitive—nor were residentially zoned areas such as Pennwood permitted to string razor or barbed wire across the tops of fencing to keep people from climbing over it. But fencing and No Trespassing signage was enough to say "Keep out," that you were likely to face consequences if you were found inside. And that worked if you were concerned about consequences.

But anyone determined to scale that fence would have done so, and from Mercer Road it was less than a mile along the jogging path and then you were in the woods behind the unit block of Laurel Drive.

If he had come up along the Collinses' side of the privet separating the two yards and decided at the last moment to come over here, he would have had to cross open lawn. Then he would have had to push his way through a line of privet or maybe the rose trellis nearer the house rather than return to the woods to re-enter from the other side. Wherever that happened it would have been impossible not to transfer something of himself, a snag of thread or a human hair, blood or skin on a thorny branch or pine needle. But you couldn't process a hundred yards of hedge without some small indication of where to start, and nothing looked disturbed. Nothing appeared to have been trampled or broken. He was either very good or very lucky.

An approach from the forest presupposed more than just a stealthy and illegal entry into the complex. If he came here specifically to kill Karen Nestor, and Palmer thought that a real possibility, then he would have had to have known by address, description, or a map or photograph what the unit block of Laurel Drive would look like from the jogging path. It was easy standing back there—Palmer had done it earlier in the day—to make the mistake. The houses looked much the same from the tree line.

Next door there was a coach lantern burning by the Collinses' side entrance to the garage. The Nestors didn't have one. There were small landscaping pagodas dispersed through the flora on the far side of the privet. That was different too. Otherwise the houses had a similar roofline; each had two chimneys. It would have been like flipping a coin to anyone who didn't live there.

He studied the kayaks. There was a full moon last night; the killer would have seen the kayaks from the trees. They were the one truly distinct and distinguishable difference between the two homes and they hadn't scared him away.

If someone had described the house to him they would surely have mentioned the yellow kayaks in the driveway. Or maybe they weren't there when the plan was discussed or the photograph was taken or maybe they just never came up.

The even bigger question was still not answered.

The footprint.

If the footprint was really the killer's and he really had intended to go to the Nestors' house first, what made him believe he had made a mistake?

Palmer felt that if he knew that one thing, he would be halfway to solving the case.

Palmer descended from the deck to the lawn and walked across a honeycombed patio, his leather soles grinding into the mortar. The homes in this subdivision were relatively new. Sand still powdered the edges of the new brick. He wondered how long the Nestors had lived here. Six months? A year? Was that all Karen got?

"Sergeant?"

"Yes." He turned, surprised.

"The husband's in a cruiser and on the way back to Harrisburg for interrogation. Two more hours, Corporal Hastings said. She said to tell you they've split the husband and kids up. One of the troopers is driving his car behind them."

"Thank you," Palmer said.

The trooper nodded and disappeared.

Rick Nestor, the victim's husband, and their two children were away at the time of the murder. Rick Nestor had taken the children on a weekend hiking trip near Milford, Pennsylvania, in the Pocono Mountains, six and a half hours on the other side of the state.

They had spent the day on hiking trails along the National Delaware Water Gap—police were confirming the story now—and had just returned to their motel for dinner when they caught the six o'clock news on a corner television in the motel bar and saw reporters standing on the lawn of their home back in Sewickley.

Nestor, a defense attorney, quickly got his kids away from the television, called 911, and was routed to a call center supervisor, who informed him that police had been looking for him throughout the day.

Something had happened, they told him. He should stay where he was until troopers could arrive to talk to him.

The unusual thing about the hiking trip was that Karen wasn't along with the family. Her mother said that Karen was an avid outdoorsperson and that she looked forward to the family's weekend outings. They did things together. If they weren't going kayaking, they were river rafting, and if they weren't river rafting, they were biking or hiking or horseback riding or skiing. She said her grandchildren thought their parents were fun; you couldn't find another kid who could do the kinds of things they did, not even if you could find a twelve-year-old with a driver's license and that much money. The children looked forward to time with their parents.

Palmer noted that the neighbors liked Rick too. Next-door neighbor Alan Collins said that Rick was surprisingly handy for an attorney, handy with tools and quite the outdoorsman. He was savvy. He was the kind of guy who could figure things out and he didn't mind getting his hands dirty.

Palmer wondered how dirty.

The fact that Karen was murdered while her husband Rick was hundreds of miles away mattered little to Palmer. Pat alibis in homicide investigations tended only to make investigators suspicious. Rick would still be their number one suspect until the day they could eliminate him.

No matter what the evidence or the scene told you, no matter what your experience or what you believed you knew to be true, you started with the odds and worked outward from there. The odds told the police that most murders were family affairs, which meant there was a whole lot more they needed to know about Rick Nestor. Was he financially sound? Were there any infidelities by either party? Why hadn't Karen joined her family on the trip? Were there any unusual phone calls placed to the house before—or just after—the murder that might indicate that someone was checking to see if the job was done?

The brutality of the murder, the time the killer took with his victim, the obsession with strangulation, the force with which she was thrown to the kitchen floor—facedown, hard enough to break the cartilage of her nose and snap off teeth—and the signature of the hanging, all suggested the killer was a sociopath with complicated sexual aberrations. Unless the scene was staged, he was someone who either passionately loved or hated his victim, perhaps someone who was coming apart at the seams.

If the scene was staged, it could be a murder-for-hire disguised to look like a rape-killing. Husbands who contracted people to kill their spouses often wanted the scenes to look horrific. There was a reason for that. Husbands wanted the world to say they were incapable of the act. That what had been done to his wife was too far out of character for the kind of person he was known to be. And it worked. Family members often stood by sons-in-law who butchered their daughters because they simply couldn't conceptualize that someone who sat at their dinner table on Sunday afternoons was capable of what police found.

If they were lucky, they would get a DNA match; there were hair and saliva specimens found on the scene. If DNA matched a known criminal, the guy might spill his guts. If the husband was involved, he might want to cut a deal. Things like that happened every day.

Karen Nestor's mother checked into a Harrisburg hotel room. She would be taking charge of the children when the caravan arrived and Rick Nestor was taken to the bureau of criminal investigation to be interviewed.

Palmer was three hours' drive from Harrisburg. He would meet the entourage there, but first he needed this moment to see it all in darkness, to get a feel for what the killer had been looking at.

He took a last look around and sighed. It was time to go inside.

The side door to the Nestors' garage was found by a deliveryman to be unlocked and ajar. There were no tool marks on the door; no one broke in by force. There were no signs of forced entry at the interior door to the laundry room or on any of the other locks on the four doors to the house. All of the locks were new and functional and the house had a sophisticated and operating interior alarm system. Unarmed.

In a neighborhood like this, it was possible that Karen would forget to alarm the doors, but to leave them unlocked? Palmer thought the lack of forced entry was remarkable, especially because it occurred on the rarest of nights when the victim was at home by herself. Coincidence was another thing that didn't sit well with homicide investigators.

He took the walkway around the house to the front door and entered. All of the lights had been left as they were found this morning. Off the foyer was a living room where a lamp burned softly on an antique desk. There were sconces burning next to a rich oil painting of tall masted ships in a harbor. Cameo portraits of children hung on opposite walls in a corner. He turned into a hallway facing the life-size portrait of the victim. He had studied her portrait this afternoon, thinking she looked so unlike the woman he had seen hanging in the garage. It wasn't one of those stuffy family portraits; she was wearing her light brown hair in a ponytail with bangs; she looked girlish and vibrant and the artist had not missed her spirit. Palmer left her slowly, reluctantly.

To the right was the kitchen, where an ice dispenser on the refrigerator door cast a pale glow across a black stain on the white tiled floor. The intruder wouldn't have had to use a flashlight to creep around the house. There was too much ambient light for that. Hardwood floors in the dining room shimmered under a dimmed chandelier; a teardrop fixture illuminated stairs that curled toward the second-floor bedrooms.

He knew that no fingerprints of the intruder were found, only smudges on the hand railings. The killer was wearing gloves.

A bedroom light was on, second room to the left. He now knew that it was the guest room where Karen had been raped. He turned right instead, toward the master bedroom. There was a *Beautiful by Botox* book on a white comforter on a king-size bed, which had been left open but overturned, and a half-finished Diet Pepsi can on a nightstand.

First blood was spilled in the guest room down the hall. All other specimens, per the direction of the blood splatters, were leading away from that room, down the hall, down the stairs, through the dining room, and into the kitchen.

But that was later. First they spent time in that bedroom.

A lot of time.

A man's dress shirt, one of her husband's—his initials were behind a dry-cleaning tag—was draped neatly over the back of a chair by the bed. On the chair were silk panties; under the chair a pair of Karen's house slippers, laid side by side.

Pairs of Karen's panty hose were knotted around the posts at the four corners of the bed. Her killer had bound her hands and ankles for a time. There was a used tampon in the trash can in the guest room.

Blood, her own, on the bedding, and tampon wrappers found in the trash in the master bathroom indicated she was menstruating.

Blood patterns on the walls alongside the stairs and on the carpet indicated that she was standing, walking under her own power down the stairs and into the kitchen. It was impossible to know her condition mentally or physically by then.

Then something happened in the kitchen. Maybe she darted for a knife in a drawer? Maybe she reached for the phone on the wall? Or maybe he only wanted to hurt her again, for suddenly she was thrown to the hard ceramic floor, where she broke her nose and lost a front tooth.

Palmer crossed the kitchen toward the laundry room, following the telltale bloodstains. The victim had been dragged there by her ankles, leaving a smeary swath painted by her own long hair. From the laundry room, her head had thumped down two steps to the concrete garage. There the killer had tied an outdoor extension cord around her neck, tossed it over the rail of the garage door opener, pulled it tight until she was on her toes, and tied it off around the door latch of a classic Mercedes.

Nothing else in the house had been disturbed; no drawers were rifled, no cabinets left open. Mrs. Nestor's purse, with her wallet containing a brand-new driver's license and seventy-two dollars, was found on a hook behind the closet door. Her cell phone was found on the kitchen counter, the cell phone the killer had used to call Sherry Moore at exactly midnight.

It wasn't until early morning that Sherry had gotten through to Colonel Karpovich and told him about the call and her attempts to have the police check on the address.

Karpovich had his secretary, Evelyn, place a call to the wireless carrier. By the time a state trooper arrived at Laurel Drive to check on the owner's welfare, a UPS driver who was accustomed to leaving packages inside the Nestors' garage door had found Mrs. Nestor's naked body hanging from the garage door opener.

"Sergeant?"

"Yes."

It was the trooper guarding the house; he was standing at the laundry room door.

"Sarge, it's Corporal Hastings. She says it's important."

Palmer stared at the floor. A brittle crust had formed on the blood that had pooled under her body. Hastings was the sex crimes specialist in the bureau of investigations.

"Tell her I'll call her right back." He stood and looked at the blood another long minute, recalled the body hanging there, the orange extension cord around her neck. What had the killer been thinking as he stood here watching her die? How long did it take?

Palmer left the garage and walked through the

kitchen to the hallway, stopping once more at Karen's portrait.

"Ah, Mrs. Nestor," he said sadly to the portrait. "What happened to you here last night? Why didn't you lock your doors? You didn't do something stupid, now, did you?"

The portrait stared back at him.

The phone was flashing as he got back to the Taurus. He picked it up and pushed a button.

"Hey, Mary." He undid the top button of his shirt.

"Sarge," the woman said, "I just got a call from the coroner's office."

"Uh-huh."

"The welts all over her face and neck, the doc says they're hives. He thinks it was an allergic reaction."

"To what?"

"He doesn't know, but he says the sooner we get the toxicology reports, the better."

Palmer was silent, long enough to make Hastings wonder if she'd lost the connection. He saw movement in a second-floor window of the house across from the Nestors'. A woman was closing the blinds. Palmer imagined more blinds had been closed in Pennwood tonight than on all the nights before.

"I'm leaving now."

Palmer cut off the call and dialed another number.

The phone rang in Karpovich's office.

"Secretary to the commander," Evelyn said stiffly.

Evelyn always stayed late if the colonel had company.

"He still in, Evelyn?"

"Just a minute." Evelyn never answered that particular question directly.

A few seconds later Karpovich came on the line.

"Colonel, you know anything about latex allergies?"

10

PHILADELPHIA, PENNSYLVANIA

It was dawn and the sun was rising into the windshield of Sergeant Palmer's cruiser on the Pennsylvania Turnpike. Colonel Karpovich was seated next to him. Neither of the men had gone to bed. Palmer had napped on the receptionist's sofa, the colonel in his office. Rick Nestor had been with his interrogators until almost 3 a.m. The man seemed clearly stunned by his wife's murder. Stunned that someone would break—or, worse, walk—into their house on the only weekend Karen had ever begged off a trip at the last minute. She'd said she had cramps. He knew she was having her period, but things like that had never stopped Karen before. Karen loved the outdoors. She lived for those weekend getaways with the family, they all did, which was why she insisted he take the trip without her.

Nestor was no dummy. Stymied, horrified, struck by disbelief or whatever, Nestor was a defense attorney and used to deception and lies. He did not look convincing when it came to defending his wife's last-minute decision not to go with them. Palmer knew he had been wondering about it himself. Why hadn't the expensive alarm system been activated? Why hadn't any of the locks been tampered with? How in God's name had she let a stranger into the house?

They were driving to Philadelphia to visit Sherry Moore. A Philadelphia police dispatcher had logged the midnight activity about her conversation with Moore regarding an emergency and a cell phone call. She'd said her hands were tied. You couldn't just order cell phone providers to give out people's names and addresses to anyone who said they had an emergency call.

Karpovich was looking out the passenger window at dairy farms and cornfields, a small country cemetery on a hillside. He began daydreaming about his wife's funeral.

"Colonel?"

Karpovich shook his head. "Sorry?"

"I still think there's a chance we have a connection to Cumberland? I know the state forensics guy down there. He said those women had been strangled repeatedly. Just like Karen Nestor had been strangled in the bedroom before he actually killed her."

"I think the FBI is holding back. I talked to Glenn Schiff down there this morning. There an Agent Springer is in charge of the Cumberland case," Karpovich said. "He says she's strange, whatever that means. He thinks she was behind the press leak that Sherry Moore saw the Cumberland killer's face. Anyhow, I want you to get your lab requests to her, all of them. I'll call the deputy director in Pittsburgh and explain our interest. If there are any similarities to Cumberland, I want to know sooner rather than later. Meanwhile, don't rule out copycats. Get Nestor's husband vetted and fast. Put your people all over him. Eliminate him if you can, because if this wasn't him we're going to hear more from this guy again and soon."

Palmer squinted, pulling the visor down over the sunrise.

"What do we do about Ms. Moore?"

"Play it by ear."

"I think it would be dangerous to work with her," Palmer said.

Karpovich was silent.

"I think we should tap her phones, but we can't let her near our victim. She's tainted, and if we start giving in to him, he'll keep on throwing bodies under us right and left."

"He's going to do that anyhow," Karpovich said. "We need to find out what he wants."

"He wants to kill Sherry Moore."

"Then why didn't he?" Karpovich continued to stare out the window in thought.

"He was interrupted."

Karpovich shook his head. "He was sitting there talking to her when the maintenance guy came in. He could have hit her with the needle and been gone. He may want her dead, but there's something more. Something he wants from her first."

"He thinks she saw his face."

"I don't think it's that. He got her address when he got her phone number in the hospital," Karpovich said. "He could have gone to her house instead of Karen Nestor's."

Palmer glanced over at the colonel, then back at the road.

"I just think we'd be asking for trouble if we went along with anything, you know, that she might want to do."

"Like touch Karen Nestor's body? Don't worry, Dan. I won't tell you what to do when the time comes. Not when it comes to using civilians. It's your show and you're the one who has to execute it, but take an old man's advice. If he wants to talk to Sherry Moore, we have an open line to him. He's going to call her whether we like it or not. We can watch this from the sidelines or we can get in the game."

Palmer nodded. "I'm all for eavesdropping, Colonel. I'm just not convinced we should allow anyone to draw a connection between the police and Ms. Moore. She's a hot potato right now. She could hurt us more than help us. I mean, let's say we used her, I mean just hypothetically. She's got a court case brewing that could go all the way to the Supreme Court. Every lawyer in the Commonwealth of Pennsylvania would be beating on Rick Nestor's door trying to represent his dead wife. Everyone would want their name all over this."

"That's the con, but is there a pro?"

This was complicated, Palmer knew. His boss had gone to see Sherry Moore in the hospital. Everyone in the department knew he had worked with her once before.

"It's dangerous, is all I'm trying to say," Palmer persisted. "We can't control the conversation. If we put her on the phone with him, we could be accused of provocation or something."

"Provocation?" The colonel looked at his young sergeant.

"I'm sorry, Colonel. I know you've worked with her before. I guess I'm just suggesting it's not like that this time. That's what I heard, anyhow. There was no one out there killing people when you used her. You didn't have anything to lose."

Karpovich nodded thoughtfully. "No, you're right I didn't."

Karpovich folded his hands and placed them on his knee, looked out the passenger window again. He hadn't gone home last night, yet his tie was beautifully knotted and snug up to the collar, his face cleanly shaven with a razor he kept in the bathroom of his office. He always looked imposing, Palmer thought, and he could not help but marvel at the man. He knew he wasn't a man given to nonsense. He knew Karpovich had fought for his oak leaves on the streets and not in the classroom. He had become the third-highest-ranking law enforcement officer in Pennsylvania because he'd earned the job the hard way.

You wouldn't think it to look at him. Karpovich didn't look like a policeman, not of any rank or stature. He looked . . . well . . . grandfatherly. But Karpovich had been around when there was still a Pittsburgh Mafia, had seen Johnny Larocca pass the reins off to Michael Genovese. He'd worked with the FBI and an Ohio underboss named Lenny Strollo, who ratted out "No Legs" Hankish and Louis Raucci. He'd derailed a dangerous alliance between the Warlocks and the Breed, two motorcycle gangs that laced the mountains of northeast Pennsylvania with methamphetamines. He'd participated in two major hostage standoffs, one involving a judge who was shot and killed in an Erie County courthouse and another a religious sect that stormed an abortion clinic in the suburbs of Bryn Mawr. He had used his weapon twice in thirty-three years of service, killed a man and a gun-wielding woman, lost his spleen and the hearing in one ear.

Palmer had never met a man he respected more than Karpovich, but you couldn't help but wonder if age wasn't taking its toll. Psychics and civilians really didn't belong in police work. What happened in Maryland was proof enough of that.

"It was a murder-suicide," Karpovich said. "A physician killed his wife and shot himself. He left a note behind saying he'd killed a young lady the year he was in residency more than thirty years before. It was an accident, he said, and he buried her in a field on his farm. That was all. Nothing else. He didn't tell us where. We checked and there was a woman by that name missing during the same time frame. The local police had questioned him about her disappearance, but nothing ever came of it. It would have been impossible to find a body thirty years dead in a hundred-acre field. The easier thing would have been to let her lie there. After all, the killer was dead, the victim's family all gone. There was no justice to be done. Then a friend told me about Sherry Moore and I pulled some strings and a few days later she came and told us where to dig and we found the woman's remains. We got to rebury her in a cemetery with a name over her grave. That was all. Now, did I witness something paranormal?"

Karpovich's eyes were very calm. "I thought I did at the time, but time dusts our memories with doubt. Maybe I led Sherry Moore to the answer unconsciously. Maybe she made a simple deduction based on what she learned at the scene. I can only tell you that when I saw her take a dead man's hand, I was sure I was seeing something beyond my understanding. Let's talk about what we have to work with before we talk about what we don't have to work with."

Palmer looked at his boss. "What we don't have to work with?"

"Sherry Moore is quite her own woman. If she's not interested in helping us, it's unlikely we'll change her mind. We already know she's in a tough spot legally. Her whole life is likely to change if the court takes this survivors' privacy issue seriously, and I wouldn't want to call it the way the court's been acting lately. Add to that the fact she was hospitalized. Sherry Moore is hardly on top of her game. So put aside your angst and consider what you're going to do without her rather than with her."

Palmer was listening.

"What are you going to do the next time this guy calls Sherry Moore and he wants answers? Do we manufacture them? We could probably get away with that once. But what if he planted something in Karen Nestor's last seconds he wanted Sherry to see?"

"You're kidding, sir."

"No, and what you mean to say is 'Colonel, you don't really believe this mumbo-jumbo.'"

"Colonel—"

The old man waved him off. "What I believe

doesn't matter, Dan. My advice is simply not to make your mind up so quickly. Be flexible. You don't have anything yet to turn down, so don't walk in with your mind made up. Sherry Moore might not even let you put a line on her phone."

Palmer had to concede that that was true.

"Dan, all I'm trying to say is that I think you should worry about starting out on the right foot with Moore just in case you change your mind about her." The colonel's voice had softened.

Palmer looked at his mentor; Karpovich winked back.

Palmer smiled. "I'll be good, sir. I promise."

"I'll give you a tip, for what it's worth. Don't ever treat her like she's blind."

Sherry sat in a corner armchair in the solarium of her riverfront home. She wore a black halter top and cropped jeans; her feet were bare and warming in a pool of afternoon sun.

Brigham had told her that she looked tired, that she looked pale. Maybe she had a touch of the flu and should postpone the visit. He said she was suffering from stress, she needed a vacation, she should do anything but get involved with more policemen.

He sounded just like Payne at times, she thought.

She probably did look tired; she hadn't slept all night. Not to mention she'd been detoxing from the sedatives for several days.

Sherry touched her cheeks. She knew her face not by what it looked like in a mirror, but by what her hands told her, by what others had described her to be. She'd felt pleased as a young girl when a newspaper reporter once described her as pretty, but that was a while back. That was a lifetime ago.

She flexed her legs, the joints stiff from sitting too long in one position. She heard footsteps in the hall. Brigham was coming.

She had been feeling foolish all week for ending up in the hospital, for the condition in which her friend Brigham found her. There wasn't a moment of the day that she didn't go back to it. The memories were like bruises to the touch. It was also a stinging realization that she wasn't as strong-willed as she'd always imagined. She wouldn't overestimate the power of her mind again.

"They're pulling into the driveway." Brigham stood next to her. "You know what will happen?"

"Nothing will happen, Garland, that hasn't already happened."

"They'll want to use you."

"It's because of me."

"Nothing is because of you. You tried to do the right thing down there in Cumberland and look where it's gotten you. Someone tried to kill you, for goodness' sake, and now he's calling you on the phone. Look what it did for the people you were helping.

Your friend the attorney general in Maryland will be looking for a job and he's left you holding a wolf by the ears."

"It's not over yet, Garland. It was a judgment call. Glenn was only trying to do the right thing."

"Their risk assessment was a judgment call too, Sherry. It wasn't supposed to be dangerous."

"No one can predict these things, Garland."

"He might not have been caught two years ago, but that was the cops' screw-up. At least he wasn't calling you."

"You don't mean that, Garland, and you know it. You're always talking about the things that history hadn't put right. You hate it when things don't get resolved. I've heard you rail for hours about Congress and POW pawns and postwar reconstruction negotiations. Half the people you argued with hadn't been born, but it didn't stop you. Truth is, we don't know what this guy has been doing or how long he's been doing it. We don't know who else he's hurt. I held those women's hands in Cumberland. Do you think they want me to leave well enough alone?"

The doorbell rang and Brigham mumbled something. She motioned for him to come near and took his hand. She turned her face toward him. "I didn't think I could do this anymore, Garland, not after John died. I didn't want to do it anymore."

She stroked his hand, a determined look forming

on her face. "Now I'm back. I can't escape this. No more than I can escape the fact of who I am or how I came to be."

She continued to hold his hand for a long moment.

"I have things I need to deal with. I know that. I lied to you before, when I wasn't well. I didn't mean to, but I did, and I'll never do it again. Not ever. Now I need you to trust me."

The onetime Admiral of the Pacific looked down at her. His face was like stone. His eyes were cold, never wavering. More than any cops she might have to rely on, he trusted Sherry's instincts. Cops were like soldiers. They had their own agenda; they might not consider Sherry's life their highest priority.

Brigham clasped his hand over hers and leaned to kiss her on the forehead. It was the most intimate thing he had done in the ten years he had known her.

"Go easy on them, Garland." She smiled.

"They can be such asses!"

"Can't we all," she said softly.

Karpovich introduced Sergeant Palmer to Sherry.

Palmer leaned toward her and extended a hand. She sensed it and met it with her own, shook it, and smiled at his gesture.

Then they sat and Karpovich placed his hat on a table.

Brigham took his coffee standing by a window in

the corner. He was Sherry's confidant now, not her protector.

"Any similarities to Cumberland?"

Palmer was hesitant. He looked at Karpovich, but the colonel was busy with his hands.

"We're waiting on lab work from the FBI."

Sherry's face turned again toward Brigham, then down at her own hands. This was more than she should do right now, more than she should think about. More than she should add to all that was on her plate. And yet there was nothing else to do. She wasn't a bystander anymore.

"I'm here to tell you that you need to consider your safety, Ms. Moore. I want to put equipment on your phones and I want our people to go over your security system," Palmer said.

"And I want to see your victim," she said.

"Not possible."

"Because?"

"Because we don't do that kind of thing." It was out of Palmer's mouth before he realized it.

"What do I tell him when he calls?"

"Just keep him on the phone, anything that keeps him on the phone."

"Because you think he's going to call from a landline and you'll be able to rush in on him."

"We can locate a cell signal too."

"In time you can, but you have to have an idea where he's calling from first."

Sherry turned to the colonel. "Edward, you've been thinking about it. About letting me see her. I know you have."

"Sherry, this isn't your normal situation. The killer has taken a personal interest in you."

"Which is all the more reason I need to do this. Who should I be helping if I can't help myself?" She looked to Palmer. "Sergeant Palmer, I have this guy's attention. We can use that to our advantage."

"Ms. Moore . . ."

"He's going to kill again, and while he's doing it, he's going to call me. That's what I think. What do you plan to do in that moment? What if there is something Karen Nestor knows and was thinking about that would give you a break? Maybe it would even tell us where she met him. Wouldn't you want to know something like that?"

"We don't think you should develop any intimate conversations with him. We just want to monitor your communications equipment to fix the location he's calling you from."

Sherry smiled tightly, folded her arms across her chest, and tucked her feet under her behind.

"To fix the location?"

Palmer looked at Karpovich, who looked away, putting his hand on a china piece on the table next to him. Was he enjoying this?

"If you want to hear his voice, you will need me unless you get a subpoena for my phone line. If you won't help me, I won't cooperate with you, which means if he finds an alternative way to contact me—personal ads, my cell phone, dead-letter drops, you won't be my first consideration—the victims will."

"Ms. Moore."

"Don't Ms. Moore me, Sergeant. I want to see this woman, Karen Nestor. I want to see her last seconds of life and you can decide what to do with my phone lines after I've told you what I've seen. Isn't that fair?"

"Ms. Moore, we're not really able to do something like that." Palmer hoped he sounded convincing, because as ridiculous as it might sound, he was tempted to give in. There was something compelling about her; she made you want to believe.

"Edward, you have to let me do this." She turned to the colonel.

"Sherry, I'm not the whole police department. You're being sued by relatives in another of your cases. I couldn't get this approved in days, let alone hours. She'd be buried by then."

"You're all afraid because I was in the hospital. Because people think I tried to commit suicide, that I'm not stable."

"Because of that, because of Cumberland, because the law is trying to put you out of business. Yes, Sherry, you're hot."

"No one needs to know. For heaven's sake, this isn't about me. Get me in, get me out. I've done these things before."

"I can't authorize it, Sherry. Besides, this is Sergeant Palmer's case. I wouldn't ask any of my people to do something that has to be done in secret, to take on that kind of risk."

"Then how do I convince you, Sergeant?"

"Are you even listening to us?" he asked.

"I want you to get me in, Sergeant. I want to help you. No one needs to know," she persisted.

Palmer watched the determined face in front of him and sighed, yieldingly. There was a moment of uncertain silence. Then Brigham's footsteps could be heard receding from the room.

Palmer sensed the undercurrent; all that the colonel had said now made sense. Even if the claims were extraordinary, she was not someone to be taken lightly.

"I'll give you my answer at the end of the day. Just give me that, Ms. Moore," Palmer said.

Sherry put her arms down and folded her hands on her lap.

"That's fair, Sergeant Palmer."

Palmer wondered what circumstances had led to the choosing of Karen Nestor as a victim. Had they met? Had he seen her from afar? Or was she a finger thrust into a phone book?

From all appearances, Karen Nestor would not rate as a high-percentage homicide target. The same criteria that eliminated her husband told them that.

Her life, her family life, was purely uncomplicated. There had been no sticky past relationships on either Rick's or Karen's part, no large blocks of unaccounted time that were common to people who lead double lives. The parents went to work, the children went to school. They all stayed in one place and came home afterward when they were supposed to. There were no poker games with the boys on Tuesdays or Friday nights out with the girls. No overnight shopping forays for Karen, no unexplained business trips for Rick, no wild drug parties for the kids.

The family was doing well financially. In fact they were doing very well. There were no obvious struggles between parents and children; the kids were above average in school. The family wasn't particularly religious, but teachers, friends, and family members on both sides agreed the four of them had a chemistry that seemed to work. The kids even seemed eager to abandon their friends and electronic toys for the wilderness every other weekend. The outdoors was their church. They were healthy and physical, all of them. The big picture was happiness. The Nestor family unit seemed stable and contented in every sense. They did not thrust their lives into the seamy side of life.

Karen's only negative comment to close women friends was more commiseration than complaint. "She hated getting old; she wasn't immune to that," a friend said. "She missed our younger days; we used to talk about the times we went off together and met boys at the beach or drove up to the lake. I think those memories were still strong in her. She regretted the getting-old part, but who wouldn't like to relive the sexier years of our lives and leave the rest behind? We all do that, don't we, Sergeant?"

Palmer had finally gotten an answer about the red blisters the coroner found on Karen Nestor's face and neck, and it came from a box checked on hospital registration records. His suspicion had been right. They weren't hives, but contact detmatitis. She was allergic to latex.

The coroner contacted her family physician, whose records indicated Karen had a severe Type I contact reaction to latex as a child; she had been working on an art project in school and the children were supposed to bring in protective gloves from home.

They already knew the killer wore gloves. If it was his gloves alone that caused her reaction, what more could a glove tell them? Were they surgical gloves? Those were common household items these days. You could buy bagfuls at any hardware store. But he had been wearing some kind of a shirt or smock in the hospital when he came to see Sherry. The security guard said there was a medical insignia on it and to her it looked official. She thought he belonged to one of the private ambulance crew companies. Could the killer be an EMT or medical care worker of some kind?

Mary Hastings had posed a different theory to Sergeant Palmer and Jerry Fossil, the department's chief of forensics out of their Harrisburg office. Nestor's trachea had been bruised and her larynx fractured, neither injury being consistent with the hanging. The electrical extension cord used as a ligature left but one mark around her throat, a typical V that was common to hangings. If the trauma to her neck occurred before she was hung, then she had most likely been strangled in the second-floor bedroom. Mary said the scene had all the suggestions of sexual bondage, including the use of latex, although no semen was found on bedsheets, covers, or the victim.

Since the worst of the weeping blisters had been on her face and around her neck, Mary thought he might have put something rubber over Karen Nestor's face. A latex mask was often used on persons playing the role of "bottom" in breath play, and repeated strangulations would explain the injuries Karen received prior to death. Had he used a mask or some latex ligature like a tourniquet to strangle and revive her, whatever length of time they were in that bedroom?

The mystery of the footprint at the neighbors' continued to haunt them too. They knew by now that dirt had been transferred from the Collinses' flower bed next door to a coco mat in the Nestors' garage.

"There's no doubt?" Palmer asked the lab chief.

"None." Jerry Fossil peered over his thick-framed

glasses. "Parent soil is similar, as are fertilizers, and the alkaloids are identical. This was our next-door gardener Mrs. Collins's own special blend. Someone was at both houses in a relatively short period of time."

"The impression of the boot?"

"Tread was almost completely intact from the sole forward. It's unique to a boot by Columbia called an Ice Dragon, leather with mesh waterproofed uppers."

"Market?"

"Here," the scientist said, distributing photographs of a hiking boot. "Cold-climate regions. Sporting goods stores sell them, but so do high-end chains, and you can get them over the Internet internationally."

Palmer had personally checked every boot tread at the Nestor and Collins families' homes, as well as the footwear the Nestors had taken with them to the Poconos. No one in these houses owned such a boot.

"We'll show them around the neighborhood, check the maintenance yard, security offices, and playgrounds near Laurel Drive."

Palmer nodded, but his thoughts were elsewhere. "We have a photograph of a man leaving Nazareth Hospital after the attack in Sherry Moore's room and he's wearing something that looks a lot like these."

"Jesus," Hastings said.

"What about entry to the complex?"

"The forest behind the houses was a waste of time," Fossil said. "There's a windbreak of conifers behind the jogging path; the leaves are packed heavy and they stay that way. I was hoping we'd find a print around the perimeter fencing, but nothing's obvious, and there's six miles of asphalt to jog on. He didn't need to leave tracks. He could have stayed right on the jogging path and jumped off anywhere along the fence line."

Eliminating Rick Nestor still left them with a predicament. How could anyone have known Karen Nestor would be all alone in her high-security neighborhood? How could they have picked the very rare day her husband and children were not expected to return? Why, and this was a very big why, had she opened or left open the door for the killer?

Something was very wrong about the Nestor case, Palmer thought.

He had once worked a case in the upscale suburb of Bryn Mawr outside Philadelphia. A teenager who had a crush on his neighbor's wife raped and killed her while the husband and their three children were at the community swimming pool. No one could figure it out at first. No suspicious people or cars were seen going in or out of the small community. No one tampered with the doors or windows.

The woman told her family she was going to join them after her soap opera was over. What she was about to do—it later came out—was to tell her teenage lover she couldn't see him anymore. He wondered if Karen hadn't invited death to her door.

Mary Hastings had been looking into other cases as well. There were eight cold cases in the southwestern part of the state over the past five years. Half of them were women, three still missing from campsites along the Allegheny Mountain trailheads, one young woman found strangled in her parents' home near Nemacolin Woods, southeast of Pittsburgh. In that case, Andrea Teng was to be a freshman at Dickinson College in Carlisle the week after she was found dead in her parents' home off Route 40. Her mother, just returning from a cruise to Mexico, was bringing groceries into the house when she heard a strange noise in the back rooms. She went to investigate; she found an alarm beeping on her daughter's clock radio. Andrea was hanging from a ceiling fan, a long step away from the bed. Her eyelids had been taped open with adhesive from the family medicine cabinet. There were no indications of a forced entry, no signs of a sexual assault. There were no fingerprints, no saliva, no sperm, no bleeding. In short, no DNA. It appeared to investigators by the numerous ligature marks around her throat that she had made several attempts to step off the bed and hang herself before she finally got up the nerve.

The ligature in that case was a pair of her navy blue tights.

The case was labeled a suicide, although police spent some time looking at one of Andrea's neighbors, a man who worked as a groundskeeper at a local resort. He had a history with police, had once been arrested for statutory rape of a sixteen-year-old, and was on probation for larceny of a lawn mower he'd stolen from a previous employer.

The similarity in Andrea's and Karen Nestor's murders was evident in the number and variety of injuries to the neck. The coroner noted—perhaps erroneously—that Andrea Teng showed evidence that she had strangled herself with the ligature multiple times before she at last succeeded in killing herself. The telltale V discoloration caused by the dead weight of her body against the ligature for a period of time was the last of those injuries.

A trooper stuck her head in the door. "Sergeant Palmer, the FBI's here. Agent Alice Springer."

Palmer nodded.

Agent Springer walked into the office. Palmer rose to meet her and extended a hand.

Springer looked around at the walls, the books, and the pictures for a long moment before she looked at Palmer, then she took off her sunglasses, lowered her head, and glared into his eyes. Palmer was six foot two, but she had him easily by two inches. A corner of Springer's lip actually curled when her hand finally went out to shake his. "Special Agent Springer," she said. Her voice, deep like a man's, emphasized the word *special.*

Palmer turned to the lab chief and the young policewoman seated in front of his desk. "Jerry Fossil from our lab and Corporal Mary Hastings." He introduced them. "Mary's our sex crimes specialist out of Harrisburg."

Springer was wearing frost white lipstick and her nails were done with French tips. She liked to occupy the ends of life's spectrums, a Harrisburg FBI agent had told him. "From clothing to speech to sexuality, she's all woman," the agent said, "and man enough to kick your ass if you don't believe it. Don't ever try to feed her," his friend had warned. "You'll get bit."

Springer swiveled her head and focused on Mary Hastings. "Specialist," Springer repeated. Her eyes moved up and down Hastings's body; her lips, artfully outlined in beige, ejected the word *specialist* like the objectionable pit of some fruit. "Erotica, I suppose you mean. Is that your specialty, Corporal Hastings?" Springer looked like she wanted to devour the young policewoman right then and there.

Palmer leaned forward, about to intervene, but Springer's head swiveled back to him. "Let's just get on with it." She glanced at her watch. "What are you doing with her?"

"Her?"

"Don't play games with me. How do you intend to handle Sherry Moore?"

"That's why I called you, Agent Springer. We're discussing it with her now. We want, of course, to put equipment on her phone lines, but that's Moore's choice ultimately. We're just as concerned about our evidence, however. If there are similarities or matches to Cumberland, we need to know what you know."

Springer laughed. "What I know is that in all likelihood you have a copycat working in Pennsylvania. You know the odds. Your case is as different from Cumberland, Maryland, as it is the same. Cumberland was a crime committed with great patience and stealth. The man who visited Sherry Moore in the hospital panicked when a janitor came near him. The man who killed your woman in Sewickley left footprints next door and there was no forced entry, giving cause to believe she knew her attacker, a next-door neighbor, a lover, one of the security guards or a waiter at the country club. Anyone on the inside could have killed her." She paused. "What your man isn't, is the kidnapper who managed to take three women from busy office parks during the evening rush hour. He isn't the kind of man who would call some celebrity psychic to brag about what he was doing. We haven't heard one word from the Cumberland killer for more than two years. Not a whisper, not a word."

Springer walked around the side of his desk and backed up against the windowsill. "Sergeant Palmer. Every time something like Cumberland happens, something like Sewickley happens too. Mention a woman was found tied to a railroad track in New York and we'll have two in Arizona before nightfall. You don't see these cases on a national scale. Cumberland's architect is probably dead or in jail, but we aren't blind to the fact you've had a hanging. We want to know what your evidence looks like too. What concerns us is Sherry Moore. You've seen the reaction to her presence in Cumberland. She's bad news. She might have seemed like a good idea at the time, but you can bet the attorney general, Mr. Schiff, is regretting his decision now. You don't want some pill-popping civilian, a psychic no less, smeared all over your case when you finally go to trial. The defense will eat you alive, just like they are going to eat Mr. Schiff alive when we learn who killed those women in Cumberland."

Springer hoisted herself onto the windowsill. "She will appear as an act of desperation, which means it will look like the government would go to any lengths to prosecute their case. If they'd bring psychics to scenes, maybe they'd plant evidence. Or maybe they'd just start arresting people based on feelings rather than facts, and let's not forget the legal ramifications. If everything she told you miraculously turned out to be true, you still wouldn't be able to use a word of it in a courtroom," she said. "This survivor privacy issue isn't going to go away. It tells the gullible public that something is wrong about using her, and you know as well as I do that public perception, informed or not, is all that matters in the end. It's not about right and wrong."

"I don't think it's insignificant that Sherry Moore was attacked only days after someone leaked she'd seen the Cumberland killer's face. I don't think it's insignificant that all four women were hanged."

Springer's expression was blank. "Agreed, but it's still not a connection," she countered. "Let's stick with evidence."

"We have a footprint." The lab chief Jerry Fossil spoke up. "We have the knots on the ligatures. Toxicology from the autopsy indicates Karen Nestor was exposed to a latex product, something she had a violent physical reaction to. We want to know if you had indications of latex on your scene, cornstarch powder used in surgical gloves, or perhaps you have reason to believe there was a mask."

"A mask?"

"A rubber mask," Fossil said.

Springer shook her head, took a business card from her jacket pocket, and handed it to Fossil. "Send me your work with my name on it. I'll see they expedite it and run comparisons. Do you have a record of the conversation with Miss Moore?"

"Yes."

"I'll want a copy."

"Because?" Palmer asked.

She swiveled her head at him. "Because I'm interested in everything, Sergeant Palmer. We'll have the tape enhanced and turned over to voice analysis, just as we will compare your evidence to Cumberland. One last time, I want to caution you about using Sherry Moore." Springer came to her feet. "This killer of yours, he's fix-ated on Sherry Moore. He's emulating the Cumberland killer, but only to get her attention. He was just another unbalanced nut waiting for a trigger when Sherry Moore went to Cumberland and now he's found it. I'm sure Miss Moore gets communications all the time from people taking credit for murders she's looked into. I'm sure she gets her share of stalkers as well. Your man is only trying to get her attention, and you may be leading her into his hands. We'll talk again soon, Sergeant. We'll be taking temporary quarters in Pittsburgh until the Cumberland matter is over."

Palmer looked at Hastings, then at Fossil. "Why Pittsburgh?" he asked.

"It's the closest regional office that can accommodate us. Cumberland's just a stone's throw from Pennsylvania."

Outside Elmerton Avenue a car door slammed and a black Crown Victoria lurched from the curb. Agent Springer put her head against the leather headrest and punched the speakerphone.

"Agent Samuels," a man answered.

"Gabe, they know about the mask."

"Anything else, boss?"

"I think they'll use her."

"I would."

Springer was silent.

"We could bring them all into the fold."

"And blow a five-year investigation?"

"Cumberland was a lucky break. We'd still be sitting in St. Louis if it hadn't been for Cumberland."

"It was our break, Gabe. Not theirs."

"He's going to kill again."

"And when he does, he'll call her, and this time we'll be listening."

Palmer watched Springer's car pull away from the curb. "What did you make of that?" he asked Hastings.

"She's nervous about Moore."

"Did you see her face when I mentioned a mask?"

"She blew by it like she didn't even hear it."

Palmer nodded. "There's more to Agent Springer than meets the eye, I believe. I'm calling Sherry, then I'm sending a car to get her."

Hastings smiled. "I knew you were going to say that."

"I'll have the colonel clear it with the doc. Can you get things set up at the morgue?"

"My pleasure." She grabbed her jacket.

It was five miles to the Dauphin County Coroner's Office.

DAUPHIN COUNTY MORGUE

At first she thought she had tripped; that was the way these things started. One minute you'd be sitting in a cold, dry room, the next you were falling face forward on some stranger's kitchen floor.

That's what happened when Sherry took a dead person's hand. She was instantly transported from the present to the past, someone else's past, and she often landed in the strangest of places.

She was naked and cold, a memory of breakfast crumbs rushing up to meet her, a split second later the cartilage of her nose shattered against white ceramic tile, she saw blood splatter and felt the crunch of teeth breaking away.

She saw dust bunnies and a purple crayon under a refrigerator. The toe of a man's hiking boot, he was standing over her.

She was looking up through her tears; there was a face looking down at her but it was wavy and indistinct. She saw a barn with a weather vane pivoting in the wind. She saw the handle of a broom strike the floor just next to her eye; he was moving her. An orange rope, he was reaching for it, tying the tourniquet to one end before he put it over her head.

A three-legged dog limped through a barnyard past black chickens that pecked in the dirt. A man whistled; he was in a rocking chair on a porch and he pointed at the black sky above the corn. She looked up at the weather vane; it was wobbling maniacally in the wind as if it were going to tear away and fly at any moment.

A man, children, a flag that read Cinco, a photograph, a man and a woman; she was turning it over, writing on it. A metal box, a ceiling, a long metal rail;

she was being lifted off her feet, moving toward it; she looked down and the floor was dropping away. . . .

She saw a photograph in a gloved hand. He was holding a Polaroid photo of two women. They were young and they were blond and there was a pair of crossed oars on the wall behind them, a picture of men on the wall, yellowed with age. . . . The gloved hand flipped the photograph of the two women and there was handwriting on the back . . . names, it looked like people's names, but the letters were blurred by her tears, and then he was putting the picture down.

"Ms. Moore?"

Somewhere down the hall a phone was ringing softly.

"Ms. Moore?"

Sherry took an audible breath and laid the woman's hand gently back on the steel table. She held a trembling finger in front of her face. *Wait, it pleaded.*

She could hear the trooper shifting his weight from one foot to the other, the nearly imperceptible squish of one of her bare heels against leather. Heels, she thought absurdly. She's wearing heels and they are bothering one of her feet.

"Restroom?" Sherry whispered hoarsely.

Hastings stepped forward and took her arm, leading her across the room to a door. "I'll be right here," the corporal said softly.

Sherry nodded, closed the door behind her. She sat there in the darkness and cried.

Ten minutes later, face rinsed, hair pulled behind her ears, she emerged. The trooper led her out of the room and down the hall to an office. The antiseptic aroma of a cleaning solution along the way made her nauseated.

"Here," Hastings said, guiding her into a room. She was led to a chair.

"Water?" Palmer asked.

Sherry nodded and Hastings brought her a bottle.

"Can you identify him?"

She shook her head. "I saw a face behind glass, fogged wet glass, I think. His face was indistinguishable. I saw the toe of one of his boots, Dan. It was made of leather and rubber."

Palmer nodded to Hastings, thinking about the Ice Dragon boots.

"What was around my neck, something red or orange?"

"An extension cord," Hastings said. "An outdoor extension cord."

Sherry nodded. She heard the steady tick of a wall clock, a phone ringing in a distant corridor, the squeaky wheels of a gurney passing by their door. She massaged the fingers of one hand. She knew what they were waiting for and she wasn't sure how to say it.

"He showed her a picture . . . a photograph. He held it up in front of her face."

Hastings leaned forward, elbows on her knees. "Tell me about the photograph."

"It was in a room; there were people in the background. The walls were wood, not painted. Two blond women, they had their arms around each other. Both of them were holding glasses in front of them"—she indicated their size with her fingers. "Shot glasses, I think. They were smiling, posing for the camera. There was a flag on a string that read 'Cinco.' Crossed wooden poles on a wall. He turned the photograph over and there was writing on the back." She passed a hand over her face, and her lip started to tremble, then she started to sob. "There were names on it, but my tears blurred them out. I couldn't read the names," she cried. "I'm so sorry."

"Her tears, Sherry, not yours," Palmer said.

"Did I die quickly?" she asked.

"Yes," Palmer lied. "She died quickly."

11

Waterdrum, Pennsylvania

A For Rent sign was nailed to a tree by an entrance off Route 211. You couldn't see it from the road, not even in winter, when the leaves were off the trees. The lane going into it would best be described as two tire ruts. No one would want to turn around there, much less see where it went.

The roof leaked over the kitchen and in two of the three bedrooms. The wooden stairs to the front porch were rotting and the boards beginning to splinter. The walls and paths were overgrown with poison ivy. There was a barn that had collapsed around a yellow ceramic brick silo, and corncribs and chicken coops in similar states of disrepair.

The owner had family in Ohio and wanted to go live with them. The rent would be cheap, he said, only $325 a month.

It couldn't have been more perfect. He had been subletting a trailer in a park a dozen miles south of Waterdrum. He had no lease, no phone to change. He could move his things here quietly and no one in the world would know. And that is what he had done just over a year ago.

He sat at a white paint-chipped kitchen table with a bottle of Maker's Mark bourbon and a water glass with yellow flowers painted on it. There were newspapers spread out in front of him, headlines from Washington, D.C., Baltimore, Pittsburgh, and Wheeling, West Virginia; they read SHERRY MOORE—FACT OR FICTION? PSYCHIC IS NO STRANGER TO POLITICS. POSTMORTEM MEMORY THEORY SHOCKS SCIENTIFIC COMMUNITY. MOORE—ACCIDENT OR SUICIDE?

There were magazines that dated back to 1994, old editions he found in the computer library archives. He'd had them forwarded from Pittsburgh to a local library in Dunbar. Some were scientific explanations of Sherry Moore, some featured cases she'd worked on over the years. He read about her searches for people lost in the wilds of Canada and archaeological finds around the world. She had helped the police find missing bodies, murder weapons, people trapped by disasters, children kidnapped by parents, almost anything, the articles went on, that could be gleaned from the final memory of a dead person.

Sherry Moore was like a "dying breath," one reporter said; "a voice from the grave," wrote another.

She found it difficult to interpret the last seconds of the dead. "So many things come into play in those final moments," she'd said, "it seems a mad rush at times, and at others cool, calculated, introspective."

Sure, the images were interesting, perhaps the most-talked-about aspect of what Sherry Moore did. Everyone wanted to know what she saw or imagined or envisioned, but Sherry said the real job was in deciphering the information. That was the key. You had to decide what was important and what wasn't. Were these images real or imagined? It wasn't always that easy to tell the difference, Sherry said. Most certainly, she explained to one reporter, the things you see before you die are hard to discount. Almost always the things that are happening "real time" are part of those last eighteen seconds of working memory. In other words, it would be difficult for people to hide where they were in their last eighteen seconds of life. It would be hard not to reveal something about their present physical environment. But, Sherry pointed out, there were always exceptions to the rule. She had recollections of memories so deeply immersed in religious verse or so highly concentrated on a loved one that they obliterated what was happening to the people right up until the moment of death. Sometimes the deceased was so intensely involved in some lifesaving activity that nothing but the act itself occupied their final moments.

When people were dying and knew death was upon them, it was likely that they would recall the most important people or events in their lives. She saw these memories as images, she said. Often there were memories of faces changed by years in a matter of seconds. She would see people as they looked as children and then suddenly as adults, or she would see a home changed by time. Memories of childhood were commonplace, memories of loved ones nearly universal. How many times had she seen children come and go in those final seconds of life?

He pored over the material, reading and rereading the articles, studying her face. She had been in Cumberland. She had seen those women and held their hands, just like he had. Had they been thinking about him? Had Sherry seen his face?

For the longest time he was sure it was about sex. He became obsessed with thoughts of women. He fantasized about them throughout his days. He imagined what it would have been like with almost every woman he met, right down to the finest detail.

He knew now how wrong that had been, all those years, all those women. It was never about sex. It was about power.

For a single moment in time, there was nothing more important, more vital to those women, than he was.

There was a cigar box on the table. He pulled it near and took out Polaroid photographs. They had staple marks and thumbtack holes around their borders and he spread them across the table.

Most were taken at the bar in the Trail's End Inn. He remembered Karen Nestor and her family. First they were sitting in the dining room together. It was the husband's birthday, so the waitress took their picture at the table.

Later that night she came back to the bar alone. They'd been kayaking all day, were sunburnt. She said her husband had a headache and went to bed early. That the kids were playing a board game before they turned in. She sat next to him, ordered a vodka tonic and drank it way too fast. She had a look of desperation on her face. She laughed too hard, flirted too quickly. He could see that she wanted someone to talk to. Someone to tell her she was still beautiful. She wanted for a moment in time not to be Mom or some guy's wife. She wanted to be desired.

He wondered if *he* was that easy to read. Did people ever look at him and think there was something deficient about him? That he was lacking something everyone else had?

He remembered Karen Nestor's knee under the bar, touching his knee, moving away, then coming back to stay. He kept the pressure up, leaned into her elbow in animated conversation. She kept watching the door, checking her watch, wetting her lips, and playing with the pendant around her neck.

After a while she got up and used the house phone. The family was staying in one of the guest rooms. She must have found them asleep for the night, for when she came back, she appeared more relaxed. Ordered another drink and later another.

A photograph? Why, sure, she'd told George Thorpe. First one of her alone, smiling and holding up her drink in salute. Then one of the two of them sitting together. Could he keep that one? he asked. Of course, she told him.

He picked the photo up now and looked at it, touched her face, her hair, her lips.

Just before the camera had flashed, she had put her hand on his knee and squeezed. It wasn't a conscious act; she was just caught up in the moment.

After that she was young and silly again, doing something wild and wicked. Her new look was determined.

He turned the photo over. Karen Nestor, 4/14/07. An address written beneath it.

He remembered the look she gave him just before she left to go back to her room. It was a look of excitement and despair all at the same time. He recalled how she took the photo back out of his shirt pocket, picked up a pen from the bar, and scribbled her name, a date, and her address on it. "It's a Saturday," she said. "Don't come until after dark."

He didn't know what to make of it at first.

"Pennwood Estates. You know Sewickley?"

He shook his head.

"Turnpike north of Pittsburgh, you'll see the exit at Mercer Road; it's a gated community right off the ramp, just past the car dealership. If you park anywhere near the entrance off Mercer Road, you can slip over the brick wall and security won't notice." She wrung her hands, eyes darting toward the door. "Everybody knows everybody and my husband is an attorney. You can't come through the gates."

He thought she could just as easily have torn the picture up right then and there, turned and headed for the door, she looked that nervous.

"There's a jogging path on the other side of the wall, go left, a quarter mile, and two houses appear on your right, first house with two chimneys. If there's a black SUV in the driveway, something's happened, my husband's home, but don't worry, it won't be. Use the side garage door. I'll be home alone."

Then she got up from her bar stool, paid her tab, and walked unsteadily toward the door.

He knew at once he would do it. He wanted to see that look in her eyes once more. He knew she went back to her room and lay next to her husband, thinking of him, nervous butterflies in her stomach, wondering what she had done. He knew that the next morning she would have her regrets, but then as the day progressed, that nervous anticipation would come back again. She would be thinking about him constantly. All that week and the next, wondering if she could really go through with it, wondering if he'd even show.

He almost made a critical mistake by trying to get into the neighbor's garage first. There were kayaks in their driveway and the Nestors had been kayaking the day he met her. He'd assumed he'd only gotten the order of houses wrong. It seemed too much a coincidence, the kayaks, but then he saw the large house number painted on the garbage cans at the curb and realized his mistake in time.

It was awkward at first. She met him in the kitchen. She was wearing a man's dress shirt and a pair of panties, gave him an awkward hug, and laughed at the backpack he'd brought.

"Are we going to have a picnic?" she joked.

"Wine," he told her. "You like Merlot?"

She relaxed at that and he nimbly proceeded to open a bottle with his own corkscrew.

"You've done this before." She smiled, eyes darting everywhere but at him.

He knelt with his back to her, worked with his hands in the bag for a moment, and produced a crystal glass. She laughed as he poured her wine. Then he took a bottle of beer from the bag, picked up his pack, and said, "You lead."

She took a fast sip, started toward the back of the house, one hand trying to cover her behind, but by the time she was midway up the stairs she seemed to relax and took the handrail the rest of the way, a little more sway in her walk.

She'd told him that she had to confess she took a Valium earlier, to calm her nerves. She didn't think he'd really show. She wasn't sure she could really go through with it if he did. It was nice to see him again. She had forgotten how tall he was.

She was suggesting they "sit" in the guest bedroom. She led him down the hall and by then she'd taken another sip, and when she turned the corner, he noticed her clumsily bump the door frame.

"Must be the Valium." She smiled back at him, walked unsteadily, and sat on the edge of the bed as he laid his backpack on the floor.

She looked at the pack with a silly grin on her face. "More surprises in store?"

He smiled back, taking a long pull on his beer.

"I have another confession to make," she said, nodding exaggeratingly. "My period started early." She watched his face. "I hope that doesn't bother you. I mean, we don't even have to do anything but talk."

"Drink, drink your wine and relax," he soothed her, unbuttoning the buttons of his shirt.

She nodded, taking a drink, then another, until her eyes became glassy and she started to say something she couldn't finish. He took the glass from her carefully so that it would not spill. He pushed her gently back on the bed, and she lay there staring wide-eyed at the ceiling. Then he went to the bathroom and poured the wine into the toilet, returned, put the glass in his backpack, and pulled on a pair of latex gloves.

He took off her shirt and hung it over the back of a chair. Removed her panties and laid them neatly on the edge of the dresser. Then he rummaged through the guest room's dressers, finding scarves and leotards that he used to tie her to the bedposts.

Then he turned on the radio and drank his beer.

It was 9:30 before her eyes began to move. "You're back, I see."

"What . . . you . . . happened . . . are . . . you . . . doing . . . to me?"

"A mild sedative. I didn't plan on you taking Valium, I'm sorry. You'll just be groggy for a while, but you won't need to do anything. I'll do all the work."

She tugged at the knots around her wrists.

"Please let . . . go."

"In a while," he said. "I did bring more surprises, however."

He bent over and brought up a black hooded mask with glass eyes.

"No!" She tried to resist, but her effort was weak and the radio was loud.

"Have you ever worn one before? Probably not." He reached for her head and slipped it on chin first, then tugged the hood tight behind her. He straightened the front of it, looked at her eyes through the glass windows. "You can hear yourself breathe. Isn't it different, isn't it exciting?"

Her cries were muffled now. He took the respirator hose and put it next to his cheek, felt the hot breath from her lungs.

Her eyes were wide and she was terrified, arms and legs straining against her restraints.

He put a hand over the end of the hose and waited until the rubber collapsed around her face. The glass portals steamed. Her eyes began to tear; she fought harder.

He let his hand off and heard her suck a breath of air. Then he covered it again.

Two hours later he undid her hands and feet. Her face was raw and red and she was aware that she had begun to bleed between her legs. She was weak and panicky, but he made her stand and walk to the stairs. She tried everything she could to get him out of the house. Her husband was coming home early; she was supposed to call a neighbor after the news. In the kitchen she went for the cell phone and he ripped it out of her hand and threw her to the floor. He had already decided where he was going to hang her, where everyone would see her when they pulled into the driveway on Sunday, and pushed the button to open the garage door.

They would see just how thoughtless she could be. They would all know that she wasn't thinking about her family in her final moments. That she had bigger, better things on her mind.

He wondered what Sherry Moore would say when she took Karen Nestor's hand. He wondered if she would see his face. Sherry said the dying saw their loved ones, but Karen could hardly think of family when he was right there in front of her, holding up the picture of his next two victims.

He picked up the photo of two blondes with their arms around each other. One had whipped cream smeared on her cheek and the other was sticking her tongue out, posing and pretending to be licking it off.

They would be at their parents' camper in Black Moshannon all next week, number three, the only trailer with a red canopy. And they were going to be staying there alone. Would Sherry understand?

He poured another drink and lit a Pall Mall, smoke rising into the old domed lamp over the table. There was meat boiling on the stove. First dinner and then he would head for the Trail's End Inn.

It was ladies' night.

12

BLACK MOSHANNON, PENNSYLVANIA (NORTHEAST OF PITTSBURGH)

"That's really creepy."

"What's creepy?"

"There, on the other side of the lake." Debbie pointed with a free hand. "That man with the binoculars."

Dawn backed out of the trailer and squinted into the dying sun. "Where?"

"There, over there." She pointed. "Wait, he's gone." She swung the binoculars across the rocks to the tree line. "He was right there. I could see his binoculars looking back."

"Didn't you promise to make sandwiches if I cleaned the refrigerator?"

"I will, I will." The girl stared across the lake, wondering if someone had really been watching them or if he had been looking at something else on this side of the lake. She turned and saw nothing around her but more trailers and trees.

Dawn looked at her friend and sighed. "Can you at least get the stuff out of the car?"

The girl nodded. She carried the binoculars at her side as she walked toward the car.

"Don't forget the backpacks and my CD case. It's under the seat."

Someone was there all right, Debbie thought. One moment there, gone the next. "You tell Eddie we were coming?" she hollered over her shoulder.

"What do you think?" Dawn yelled back from the camper.

Her friend grabbed the backpacks and CD case and a plastic bag full of marijuana.

"I told Tom," she said, coming back up the path.

"Oh, you bitch!"

"You know you wanted Eddie to know you were here."

"Fuck you."

She laid the backpacks in front of the camper, sat on the picnic table, and rolled a joint. "You want one?"

Dawn stuck her head out, wet sponge in her hand, and shook her head.

"I'll bet they're down at Shadrock's tomorrow night."

"And I'll bet they're not."

"Yeah, why?"

"Because Eddie Fortuno will be in Niagara Falls tomorrow with his parents."

"What?"

"They're going to their cousins', the whole family, so don't expect to be seeing Tom."

"And he didn't invite you," she taunted.

Dawn shrugged. "I told him I was busy." She ducked back inside the trailer.

Her friend looked at her. "Yeah, right." But Dawn had one of those looks going on that meant she was up to something.

"You ever talk to that guy Dave, from VMI?"

"Who?" Dawn called out innocently.

"You know who. The boys we met in Waterdrum."

"Why would I talk to him?" Dawn stuck her head around the corner of the door and grinned.

"No shit," her friend said in awe. Dawn had a way of turning the mundane into the marvelous.

"He's bringing his friend Troy. Tomorrow night."

"You didn't tell me."

"Nothing to tell." Dawn pretended to yawn.

"We didn't do anything that night, Troy and I. When you guys left us in the room."

"But you wanted to."

"How about you? Did you guys do it?"

"Let's say I gave him something to think about."

Her friend laughed. "You slut!"

Dawn stepped out of the camper and reached for the smoldering roach in Debbie's hand, took a hit, and looked around at the empty campers. It was cold at night still. The few families that came were in on Friday nights and out Sunday afternoons. The week-days were going to be dead until June.

Dawn sucked on the joint, handed it back, and

pulled her shirt over her head. She was wearing a white sports bra and boxer shorts. "If Eddie wants to keep hanging out with the boys every weekend, maybe I'll start doing the same."

Her friend laughed. "You'd shit a brick if he blew off his parents and showed up here instead."

Dawn shrugged. "Yeah, well, maybe I would and maybe I wouldn't. Maybe that's what he needs, a little wake-up call."

"You go, girl." Her friend nodded, impressed, offering her the joint. "Maybe you'll find out Eddie isn't the be-all, end-all you think he is."

Dawn took it and inhaled sharply, looked at her friend sideways. "You know something about Eddie?" she asked suspiciously, handing the roach back.

Debbie shook her head, pinched off the top, and let a cloud of smoke out of her lungs.

"I just think you could do better. I've always said that."

Dawn leaned over and rolled her socks down to her running shoes. "I'll be back in thirty minutes," she said.

"Don't go running off to call Eddie," her friend teased.

"Fuck you." Dawn raised her middle finger and jogged down the dirt path to the parking lot and hooked a right toward the lake.

Debbie sighed and went into the camper to get hamburger meat. She cracked open a beer and cradled dinner, utensils, and the beer in her arms as she went back outside to light the grill.

Something snapped like a twig behind the camper. She took a swig from her can and stood on the picnic table to look across the lake. Someone was definitely over there.

A foot struck the gravel behind her and she grinned without turning. Dawn could never smoke weed and finish a run.

"You slut—" She started to turn, but the rest of the words never got past her lips. A strong arm encircled her waist, pulling her off the table, while a hand went over her mouth, stifling a cry for help.

It was a large camper, twenty feet, with a double bed and two berths that folded into table space. The blinds were pulled and the windows closed. The man was kneeling on the carpeted floor between them. He was wearing a gas mask that covered his entire head and face, the hose hanging from the front of it like some giant insect looking for something to attach itself to.

The girls were facing each other, naked and on their knees, hands bound behind their backs with clothesline. Dawn could see her friend's eye, black and green and blood-engorged, bulging, by the shadowy lights against the cellophane. Her mouth and nose were covered with snot and flecks of blood from a split lip. He had hit her twice when she tried to bite him. That was before he wrapped their faces with layer upon layer of plastic wrap until he had exhausted the roll from a box in a kitchen drawer. Fogged hollow holes marked where their mouths sucked for air; only their nostrils were exposed and he pinched them off until they passed out and then revived them again and again.

He was facing Dawn now. Debbie could barely make out her friend's face, pressed flat and sucking at the plastic wrap. His head was large in the gas mask, smooth and black, the rubber intake hose bouncing in front of him as he twisted the rope around Dawn's neck.

He had been working on her too long. Debbie knew by now what she was going through, the first minute without air, when you could feel the effervescent tingling in your head, a lightheaded sensation as if you were lying down and stood up too quickly. At a minute and a half, you tried to find air anywhere you could, sucking hard at your nose, but he held it closed and nothing was coming to relieve you. He watched you carefully through those glass eyes. You could tell he was getting high from it, his eyes wild, intense, always studying. At times he cut off his own air while he was doing it. Dawn's eyes rolled up into her head. Debbie watched her, swaying on her knees. She couldn't believe how long this had been going on. It had been two hours, according to the electric blue numbers over the stove.

Dickie Rohr and Chuck Matthews had just gotten back from the Burger King when a man burst into the township office and rushed to the chief's battered desk. Walter Hilliard owned the Black Moshannon campground. He wasn't quite making sense to Rohr and Mathews, at least not the first time they heard him say it, but that had much to do with assimilation, the mind trying to comprehend the meaning of words that when first put together made no sense.

He told the policemen he was surprised to find a car by Tilton's campsite this morning. He had never known Robert Tilton or any of his friends to fish, and his wife was far too warm-blooded to be out on the mountain before July.

When he noticed that the car had Maryland tags, he recalled the Tiltons had a daughter in school in Maryland. Out-of-state tags usually meant family members were in the park, but you couldn't rule out thieves. There were hordes of fishermen on the lake for the first day of trout season. Sometimes they got nosy and ignored the private property signs on either side of the beach that fronted the campground.

Walter said he could see the camper with the red awning through the trees, but he didn't notice the women until he was halfway up the path. They were both naked, hands bound, and hanging from a tree.

He didn't know the Tiltons' daughter, nor would he have been able to make out the faces if he had. Both women had plastic wrap bound tightly around their heads, flattening out their faces. He thought it curious that in all the years he had known Robert and Bessie Tilton and never met their only daughter, he was destined to meet her dead and naked.

Chuck Matthews had never been on the scene of a homicide before. In fact, the only dead body he had ever seen was on an ambulance gurney at a multiple traffic fatality, and that one had already been covered with a sheet.

Dickie Rohr, the new police chief of Candle Township, was a boatswain's mate third class in the coast guard and worked five years as a volunteer fireman in Tarrytown, so he had seen a floater or two, but he hadn't yet been through the state's municipal police officer's training course and was not quite sure what they should do about a double hanging on the campground next to Moshannon Lake.

"We should call the state police, Dickie."

Rohr shook his head, staring up at the bodies. "We are the police. Get down to the entrance and padlock that gate. Then you take a ride around the park. If anyone's home, get their name and phone number. Tell them there's been a crime and they should be expecting me to drop by. Tell them if anyone gets nosy and comes up here rubbernecking, they'll get to make their statement in the Township Building."

Rohr saw that a clothesline was cut and frayed,

hanging from a retractable reel hooked to a tree. "Take a look and see if their clothes are inside." He walked toward the spool and studied the cut end of the line.

Matthews looked doubtful. "You want me to go inside, Dickie?"

"How else are you going to find out?" Rohr scowled.

Matthews stepped up to the partially open door and pulled his revolver, nudged it open, and blinked several times until his eyes adjusted to the light. Things were knocked over, but not like there had been a heavy struggle inside. There was a beer can on the floor and a pile of cigarette butts ground into the light blue carpet. He could see that the carpet was wet in places and there were drops of blood on others. The girls' clothes—shorts, tops, and underwear—were scattered around the interior. Panties on a bed, bra on the floor, shorts on a table, top on the stove. As if they had undressed, standing there, randomly tossing what they took off in any direction.

"Everything's in here," he yelled.

Rohr accepted it with a grunt, examining the clothesline nooses around the girls' necks.

One girl, whose hair was light blond, lighter than the other's, had blood smeared between the plastic wrap and her mouth. One of her eyes was twice the size of the other, black, as if she'd been hit.

He could find no other serious cuts or bruises under the plastic and moved on down their bodies, put his face close to the skin, and sniffed. Matthews stood watching him from a distance, uncomfortable and wishing they'd call someone for help.

The chief felt the officer's eyes on him and looked over, sighed, and told him to get the hell down to the main road and padlock the gate.

"Shouldn't we cut them down, Chief?"

Rohr shook his head. "We don't touch nothing. Not yet. Just give me some quiet time so I can think. In fact, hurry up and get down to those gates and put that chain back up."

Chuck shook his head and started for the truck.

Rohr went into the trailer, opened and closed drawers, and examined the stains on the carpet that Chuck had seen. He noted the cigarette butts, same brand as Chuck smoked. He thought for a second about Chuck, then snorted. Mandy, Chuck's wife, wouldn't let him out of the house by himself unless he was strapped onto a gurney in an ambulance. Certainly not long enough to kill anyone.

There was underwear on one of the beds. He held it up to the light with his pen and turned it around. Then he looked at a woman's bra on the floor; he considered outlining it with his pen to mark the exact location, then taking it outside to see which one of the girls it fit. In the end, he decided it wasn't relevant information.

The cigarette butts on the carpet could mean only

one thing. The killer had spent time in here. Whatever had happened, it had happened over the course of several hours. Each one was smoked to the filter. They had to be full of DNA. There were tiny drops of blood around as well, most likely from the bleeder, the girl with the lighter hair.

He was concerned that other campers or fishermen working their way around the lake might see the girls' naked bodies hanging over the picnic table. Maybe even the Tiltons themselves. They wouldn't know about their daughter's death, not yet, unless of course the parents were involved, and he knew from watching *Dateline NBC* that that was a possibility you didn't discount. There were always stories about sicko parents out there. And what if she wasn't even their daughter, he wondered, struck by the thought for a second. He hadn't run the Maryland license plates on the car when he got here. He didn't know who he was dealing with or how they ended up in this trailer. He had to make certain he searched the car thoroughly too. There were too many things to do before he was ready to turn over the scene to anyone. Too many questions that needed answers.

Rohr finished searching the camper. There were no purses, no driver's licenses or IDs inside, which meant the girls left their personal belongings in the car. He found the empty plastic wrap box and put it aside for fingerprinting.

There were no small number of tracks around, but

Rohr thought tracks were pretty much useless when you had shit like DNA to rely on. The last ones leading up to the steps of the camper—before his own—were probably Chuck's, anyhow, he thought.

If anyone criticized the way he handled the scene, he would remind them he didn't know what he was walking into when he got here, a lifesaving emergency or a homicide, not to mention that there could have been more victims in other trailers or out in the woods somewhere. Time was of the essence and saving lives always came first. That would shut up the critics.

He made a mental checklist of what he would want to tell them when they got here. Did the killer know the girls were here or had he happened upon them by accident? That meant checking the girls' cell phones for recent calls and messages. He would need to see if there were any maps or letters in the car, maybe business cards or a laptop computer.

In his opinion, the girls were alone, probably out at the table doing drugs and making a ruckus with their boom box. Couple of men came along, probably fishermen, maybe thought they'd come join the fun.

Maybe the girls started the whole thing. Or maybe the killers came with them. Rohr had never heard of anyone being hanged before, but Moshannon was a small-town community and God only knew what went on in the rest of the world. For all he knew, hanging coeds was a college sport these days.

Sherry collected her coat and wallet. Palmer would be coming to get her. He had told her about the two young blond women found in Black Moshannon.

She felt as if she was responsible for the latest murders. She should have been able to tell the police more. She should have been able to read the names on the back of the picture; it was surely them he had killed. He had shown Karen Nestor a picture of his next victims, but not when and where it was taken. He was teasing her with clues and she wasn't getting them in time.

Palmer assured her that she had played little role in what the killer did. He would have taken lives with or without her, and at the rate he was moving, there would be little time to ponder the evidence in between. Sherry knew Palmer was right, but it still didn't make her feel better.

She knew all about the serial killer's grand finale, the frenzied attention to display, that each new killing was meant to illuminate the superiority of the architect. This one had abandoned his standard MO. He was taking chances, venturing into territory that was beyond his control. Otherwise they would have seen his work before. The FBI would have known about him. What was once his filthy secret was now being shared with the world, he was sharing it with Sherry Moore. What did he want her to know? Or was it more? What did he want to know?

It wouldn't go on, it couldn't go on. Sadly, the death rattle of a serial killer was most often expressed in more bodies. More sorrow. That was the downside.

Sherry was sorry for the lives he had taken and would take in the days in front of them, but she would never have wished him back in his lair. For the first time this killer was out of his element.

She heard a car in the driveway, grabbed her bag, and met Palmer at the door. He tossed her bag into the backseat and then opened the car door for her.

"Where are we going?"

"Airport. We'll fly northeast of Pittsburgh; way out in the boonies there's a state park called Black Moshannon."

Sherry nodded, reaching for her shoulder harness. "What do we know?"

Palmer looked at her. *We?*

"The women were in their early twenties; the owner of the campground found them hanging from a tree."

"He's displaying his work," Sherry said. "You said they were found before noon?"

"Some yokel police chief decided to play Dick Tracy, hung bedsheets from tree limbs all around them, and wasted the day interviewing residents in the area. By the time the county got called, the bodies were beginning to bloat."

"How long have the women been dead?"

"Best guess is yesterday evening. He must have put them in the tree after dark."

Palmer turned on Passyunk to pick up I-76. His face was strained. A car was racing up behind them, cameras at the windows. "Paparazzi," he said.

Palmer crossed into its lane and held it in traffic until he reached the airport exit and at the last minute shifted across two lanes to the exit. The photographers weren't quick enough to react and he shot them the finger as they rolled by.

"Regular celebrity, you are."

"It happens." Sherry sighed.

"I want you to wear a vest. This may be exactly what he wants from us, to get you out in the open."

"Okay."

Palmer looked at her; he had expected that she'd be stubborn. Expected an argument.

"You don't have to wear it all the time, just when you're out of the car."

"I'm really not hard to get along with, Sergeant."

"You called me Dan in your house."

"I was trying to butter you up."

They flew in an old Cessna 182, crossing the state in two hours to land at Mid-State Airport in Centre County, just a dozen miles from the campground outside Black Moshannon. The plane ride had been smooth until they reached the Alleghenies, then the wind started whipping them sideways. Sherry didn't mind the turbulence as much as the sudden horizontal pitches. She was glad to hear the tires hit the tarmac, letting go of her knees as the four-passenger plane taxied to the tower.

A state police sergeant was waiting to meet them on the tarmac. Palmer had her slip into the Kevlar vest, then her jacket, as they waited for the props to stop turning and the door to open.

The ride to Valley Rehab, a regional medical center, took only twenty minutes. The sergeant behind the wheel used every minute of it to curse the township police chief. He was one of those things that weren't supposed to happen anymore. Still, every now and then, some little community hired one and he put on the badge, taking himself all too seriously.

Palmer kept watching his surroundings for any signs of trouble. He crowded Sherry once they were out of the car, keeping her against his left side and to the wall, as he escorted her to the front door.

Sherry measured the size of buildings by footsteps and acoustics. From the hospital's parking lot to the front door and then to the reception desk at Valley Rehab took decidedly less time than Nazareth in Philadelphia had, and decidedly less time than it took to reach the prescription counter in her local grocery store. She imagined from the echoes that the ground floor of the hospital was about the size of a basketball court.

"They're in the waiting room down by the elevators." The receptionist pointed. "Just go to the end of the hall and turn right. You'll see them standing there."

"They" turned out to be a state police captain and two state troopers. The captain rode the elevator to the morgue with them and Palmer took Sherry inside, where she removed the Kevlar and used the rest room.

Palmer was talking to the captain when she came out and it was apparent the captain wasn't too pleased about how the day was turning out. First the township held back on a homicide scene for the better part of a day and then headquarters brought a blind woman to "see" the bodies. She knew what they were thinking. There wasn't a cop on the East Coast, maybe in the entire nation, who didn't know who Sherry Moore was or how much chaos she'd left in Cumberland. Karpovich might be a highly respected police official, and colonels ranked right below God, but he was still sticking his neck on the chopping block. Palmer didn't have the kind of rank or authority to bear that kind of responsibility alone.

No, if things went bad for them, if someone got killed, even Sherry Moore herself, it would be the colonel's head that rolled.

"Are you the people here to see the remains?"

He was a nervous little man in a plaid shirt and blue jeans, clearly rattled by all the police officers in the corridors, sorry that he was the only person with a key to open the temporary morgue. It was a room that was used solely to secure the remains of deceased patients until they could be picked up by a funeral home. The bodies lying here today were awaiting a representative from the Centre County Coroner's Office in Bellefonte, which had been closed for the coroner's own wedding.

Palmer and Sherry followed the man's short-gaited stride to a door at the end of the hall. Palmer could smell the bodies, even though they were bagged, when the door closed behind them.

They were on steel gurneys. Sherry wasted no time, asking the attendant to place her between them in a chair from which she could reach their hands.

Sherry preferred to sit when she was doing this, not always certain what would happen to her during the experience. It was extremely rare, but she had fainted in the past and took no chances by standing.

The attendant demurred throughout, expressing concern that the facilities administrator wasn't present or that they hadn't waited to do this at the medical examiner's office, where someone else could approve it. But in the end he unzipped the body bags and Sherry slid her hand inside to find the hands, which she clasped tightly in her own. The horrified attendant backed away. A moment later the door closed behind him.

Blurred, pale face in clear plastic, dark hollow places

where there would be eyes and mouth and the protrusion of a bloodied nose.

A woman, middle-aged and pretty, was looking down at her, reaching, pulling covers up to her chin . . . a man in front of a classroom, a teacher at a blackboard . . . he smiled at her and looked down at her legs beneath her desk.

A dog . . . it was black with large white spots and its ears flopped as it rose to its hind legs.

She saw a car, the passenger door was open, that teacher was inside leaning toward it, waving for her to hurry, to get in.

She was looking out across a body of water, something reflected light, perhaps binoculars?

The blurred face again, only now she could see hair, blond and wet with sweat.

A photograph and in it a dark-haired woman, middle-aged, pretty, something illegible written across the border. The woman was sticking her tongue out at the photographer, arms crossed, wrists in bangles, hands gripping her top at the waist as if she was going to pull it up over her head and flash the photographer.

There was a boy with black letters on a gray sweatshirt, his hair was dark, a flashbulb explosion, beer bottles on a bar, bartender smiling, reaching toward her with whipped-cream-covered shot glasses. . . . The teacher's hand was on her leg, beneath her skirt in his car . . . a picture on a wall, old, yellowed, there was a dark-haired man standing next to it, black shock of hair and piercing black eyes, watching her, watching everyone.

She looked up and saw a pair of oars—not poles—crossed and mounted on a wall.

When Sherry took the second victim's hand, she saw that same building, same room, something in the last seconds of death reminded them both of that place. But then the second woman was thinking of something else too, a hideous black face, eyeholes covered with glass, she could see a long hose for a snout, it was reaching for her. . . .

Sherry was choking when Palmer ran in behind the attendant. "You okay?" He put an arm around her to steady her and she put her forehead on his arm, taking a few deep breaths. She coughed. "I'm okay."

"Sure?"

"I'm sure. Dan, it was a mask, black, made of rubber, the eyes are large glass ovals and it has a triangular shape, like the forehead is wide but the chin is very narrow, and there's this long hose coming from the mouth of it."

"Gas mask?" Palmer said.

"He was watching them. You said they were camped at the edge of a lake?"

"Uh-huh."

"The first girl I touched. She saw someone across the water looking back with field glasses, I believe."

"What else?"

"They were thinking about a room, a restaurant or

maybe a bar, I saw those crossed poles on the wall, remember, when I held Karen Nestor's hand. They aren't poles, though; they're oars. And there were other things, snowshoes, old wooden skis, and fishing rods. They were in the same room, Karen Nestor and these girls."

"Who else was there?"

Sherry shrugged. "Boys, young men. There was a boy in a gray sweatshirt with black letters on it, VMI, a bartender. Someone else took their picture; there was someone, an old man, in the corner, but she focused on a dark-haired man standing near them, watching them."

"Go on."

"I got the impression the one girl was having a relationship with a schoolteacher. She was in his car. I can describe him too. I don't know why she thought it important just then, maybe it had been weighing on her mind, or maybe . . ."

"He's the killer." Palmer finished the thought. "Go back to the room, Sherry. It was crowded?"

She nodded.

"See the people once more, before you forget."

Sherry concentrated. "There was a woman across the bar, dark hair—wait . . . oh, wait, Dan, he showed one of them a photograph, and the woman in it was there in the bar with them, same time. She was sitting across from them, next to a heavyset man in a red shirt."

"His next victim," Palmer said softly. "Do the room again. Where is it, Sherry?"

"Outdoor stuff, animals mounted, a stone fireplace. There were colored ribbons and shiny metal coins hanging behind the bar. I think I saw the front end of a canoe, a small rowing boat, suspended from the ceiling."

"A kayak?" Palmer said.

Sherry caught the tone. "What's wrong?" she asked.

"Probably nothing," Palmer said.

"It didn't sound like nothing."

"There were kayaks in the neighbor's driveway, next to the house Karen Nestor was killed in."

"What are you thinking?"

"Remember I told you the boots were important?"

"The ones Karen Nestor saw."

"Uh-huh. The guy that killed Karen Nestor stepped into a flower bed next to her neighbor's garage door. That's where we found the boot print. A hiking boot, like you saw. He'd gone there before he killed Karen Nestor and we could never figure out why. I thought it had been a mistake at the time, but now it might make sense. I mean, what if he saw those kayaks in the neighbor's driveway next to Karen Nestor's and just assumed it was her home because of them? What if that's how he knew her, if that's how they met? With the kind of place you are describing he might have met her on the water or rented her a kayak."

Palmer helped Sherry into her vest, arranged for the state police sergeant to return them to the airport, and called Mary Hastings along the way.

"Mary, get ahold of Rick Nestor and find out if the family went kayaking or canoeing or river rafting in the months before she was killed. I want to know where they were, and if you can't reach him, get her mother or the neighbors or anyone you can find and ask them the question."

The flight home was little better than the flight there, but Sherry's mind was on the faces now. It was a gas mask, she was sure. They were beginning to see him, the face in the fog. Was he the dark-haired man at the end of the bar, the boy from VMI, the bartender, or the unknown person who took the photograph of them? Or was it a schoolteacher who lived nearby or the heavyset man in the red shirt or any of the other faceless people in the background? If only she could see the eyes, she might know him, might know those eyes that she had seen beneath the mask.

She mourned his victims and she feared for the dark-haired woman she had seen in the photo, the woman with the heavyset man in the red shirt. Who was she? How could they stop him in time?

She thought about the room, the crossed oars on the wall, the canoe, kayak, whatever. It was someplace real, someplace all of the victims had been. They needed to find that room and they needed to find it fast. Through all the sadness, the thought that they were actually doing it, getting a little bit closer, was encouraging. They were coming at him.

He parked his car in the lot at the William Backus Hospital in Norwich, walked up Lafayette Street to the entrance of Yantic Cemetery, and followed the curvy lanes toward the southwest corner of the cemetery to a tombstone visible from the nearby railroad tracks. It was there, two rows in and seven rows deep, the man had told him over the phone.

His father's insurance would have enabled him to afford a plot for his father here too, right next to his wife, but his father had expressed no wish of any kind regarding life or death, and so he didn't think his mother would mind if he left his father in Hutchinson, Kansas. He hadn't been to his mother's grave since he was thirteen. Her grandpa was just to her left. There were other relatives he never knew.

He looked around, first at the river, then at the railroad tracks and distant trees, thinking that nothing looked familiar about the place. He remembered little about the funeral, only a preacher who was upset that he'd stepped in a pile of dog shit, a dull coppery casket suspended over a wrinkled grass rug. It had felt like a bad way to leave the world. Depressing.

He knelt and put his hand on the earth. She was down there, just below him, just six feet from his hand. He wondered if her eyes were open or closed. He wondered if her face was black and leathery or if she still looked the same. Wondered if the embalming fluids preserved you into eternity.

Sherry Moore knew about these things. Sherry, he'd read, had taken the hands of people long dead and managed to read their last thoughts. She had described the experience to a reporter from *New Scientist* magazine, likening the hand-holding, especially those involving dated corpses, to the English game of Lucky Dip, where a child puts his hand into a grab bag of potential treasures.

"Sometimes you don't know what you've got, even after you've looked at it," she'd said. "The true gems of memory are only discernible when you are able to put them into context with the life of their master, their history."

"What would anyone see if they looked into your memory?" he asked the grave. "Would I be there? That's what it really comes down to in the end, isn't it, Mother? Hasn't that always been the question?"

He leaned back against the stone and looked out across the fields.

If the situation were reversed, there could never be a doubt. He thought about his mother almost every waking hour of his life. He had carried that last impression of her, her eyes wide open, her face a blur of lipstick and snot. That was her legacy, her gift to commemorate all his later birthdays. The dead often thought last about what mattered to them most in life. That one thing they could never escape, that thing that made them who they were.

Had he made his mother's list? Was he that all-important accomplishment or reality in her life?

Jean Farrell stepped off the stair climber and pulled a face towel from the rail. She mopped her forehead and looked around the gym. It was full of kids, or what might as well be called kids if you're closing in on fifty. She got hit on now and then and sometimes took the plunge. There was little doubt she was still in great shape, but you knew when you were pushing the envelope, and there was always a sacrifice of self-respect when you began to stroke an aging ego.

She thought about Barry. You wouldn't catch the judge in a gym. Not unless they were serving martinis in the whirlpool, and then he'd be too lazy to get out to take a piss.

How she ended up with the men she did, she couldn't say. She kept promising herself she'd do better, that she'd put limits on what her tolerance would be. She promised she would now require some semblance of framework in a guy before she climbed into his bed.

Dating seemed so complicated when you got older. You didn't want the breakneck pace or the emotional spikes you went through in your teens through thirties. You didn't want to relive the desperate forties, but you still wanted to feel something besides charitable when you were sitting across from someone at dinner. Where was the romance, the excitement? Did it only come in a cocktail glass after you turned thirty-nine?

Barry wasn't happy with her. In fact he'd been yelling at her all afternoon. He'd wanted to drag her out to the country club to a retirement party so she could wear a short skirt and he could grab her ass in front of his geriatric friends. Those pastel green pants and gold bracelets on pasty white wrists were like *Night of the Living Dead.* She wanted to jump off a high board. She wanted to do loops in the sky. Life wasn't supposed to be this dull, this weak, this empty after all you went through to get here.

She lied to him. She told him she was going to her sister's for a week. Next week, when she got back, she was going to end this relationship or whatever you wanted to call it. Let Barry hire an escort to drive around in his Mercedes. For that matter, he should hire one he could drop off at the escort's place on the way home, because Lord knew he couldn't get it up after five of his vodkas anyhow.

She was heading southeast. A week back in Waterdrum would clear her head. She missed the sounds of nature and the distinct lack of civilized noise.

When she returned to Pittsburgh next, she would be a brand-new woman, she promised herself.

HARRISBURG, PENNSYLVANIA
ELMERTON AVENUE
STATE POLICE HEADQUARTERS

Mary Hastings looked over her shoulder as Palmer came through the door.

"There was a call from *The Philadelphia Inquirer* asking if the Pennsylvania state police were consulting Sherry Moore about anything."

"They tried to follow us to the airport."

"They're going to ask the right person sooner or later."

"I know," Palmer said. "Let's just hope it's later rather than sooner."

"You're a believer, I take it."

"Weren't you when you watched her with Karen Nestor?"

"She's more than interesting," Hastings admitted.

"That's an understatement. Unless she's out-and-out lying, these women were in the same room. You have any luck with Rick Nestor?"

"Karen's mother said he pulled the kids from school and took them to his brother's for a week. The brother lives in Indiana. She said Rick didn't want them going to school while the story was still in the headlines."

"Can you reach him?"

"No answer on his cell phone. I left a message at his brother's, but he's got a plane. They all may be traveling. Karen's mother said Rick's not the kind of guy who can sit still."

"Did she know anything about their recent trips?"

"She remembered they went kayaking somewhere, early or mid-April. She didn't think it was all that far from home."

"No shit." He slapped his hands together. "Kayaks. It really was those kayaks all along. That could fit timewise too. Can she do better?"

"She thought she'd written something on a calendar, but she can't find it now. She said there were several trips, though, somewere in Pennsylvania; one she thought they went to Maryland or maybe it was West Virginia."

"Can she name towns, rivers, anything?"

Mary shook her head. "I reached Mrs. Collins, their next-door neighbor. She said the Nestors had borrowed their kayaks on occasion. She knew they went to Deep Creek, Maryland, and some rivers in southwestern Pennsylvania, but their own daughter was home with her kids all through April and they didn't have opportunities to exchange stories with their neighbors like they usually do."

Palmer nodded.

"And Dan, I was looking into a case in Nemacolin in 2006. A college kid was found hanging in her parents' home outside Pittsburgh. It looked like a probable suicide to the cops, but the coroner's report mentioned multiple ligature marks. He thought they were hesitation marks, as if she'd tried to do it several times in the same day, before she finally got up the nerve to push the bed out from under her feet.

"I called central records and the supervisor told me I was the second request for that case in a week. The FBI wanted a copy of it the day after the Cumberland news broke."

Palmer was silent a moment. So the colonel had been right about Springer. She knew more about this hanging MO than she was saying. Springer was only telling the truth, he was sure, when she told him she had a better view of the national picture than he did. Maybe the FBI had been following a serial killer's trail all along.

"You remember when you first heard about Cumberland? Didn't anything seem odd to you at the time?" he asked.

"What do you mean, Sarge?"

"The fact that the FBI jumped on it so quickly. I mean, I was with the colonel when he met their attorney general, Glenn Schiff. He said they hit the crime scene running, took over the forensics in twenty-four hours. He said they had a camera crew filming the scene when Sherry Moore arrived. They had to wait until they were done to sneak her through the door. That doesn't just happen," Palmer said. "The FBI doesn't run toward anything. They hold meetings just to decide where they're going to eat."

"Why would they keep it a secret? I mean, if you're right, we're all working on the same thing. And why would Agent Springer leak to the press that Sherry Moore saw the killer but now wants nothing to do with her?"

Palmer shook his head. "I think she saw Moore as an opportunity. There was no escaping the fact that she'd been on the crime scene. She just decided to use her to shake this guy out of the bushes. Now she's afraid Moore will hurt her case."

"So what do we do?"

"We have our own leads to concern us." Palmer got up and walked to the window. "We have the common denominator now, kayaks. Sherry Moore is describing a place where there are people, a bar, a restaurant, something with an outdoor theme. If the girl in Nemacolin wasn't a suicide, maybe she had been to the same kind of place. We need to find that town, that room. That's where our killer is. Find that and we have him, Mary."

"I'll call Teng's mother." She picked up a pencil and flipped through the file.

"Keep on Nestor too. We need to know every place they went on those kayaking trips.

"Just make a list and we'll hit them one by one. Get some copies of the victim's pictures you can take along. Someone had to have seen them. Someone should be able to place them with our killer."

Mary Hastings was still in her office when the last of the investigators went home for the day. The Nemacolin girl's mother, Mrs. Teng, now living in New York, remembered a kayaking trip her daughter took the week before she was murdered. She couldn't say specifically where, however, or even what state Andrea had been in.

Hastings found more than a dozen kayak rental places between Kittanning to the north of Pittsburgh and Deep Creek Lake, just south of the Pennsylvania border in Maryland.

She cut them in half, deciding to take seven, starting in Somerset County and working her way southwest across the Laurel Highlands in Fayette. It would take weeks to sift through rental records and credit card receipts, assuming they even existed, but she added that to her long list of things to do. She had also asked Andrea Teng's mother to preserve any computer hard drives or paper records of her daughter's that might have included information about the trip. She learned she was a month too late on that request. The week Mrs. Teng moved to New York, she had finally disposed of her daughter's things.

Hastings sifted through five years' worth of cases involving strangulation assaults in the cities and counties across Pennsylvania. Another interesting find was an "undetermined cause" in Bloomsburg, a woman found in the rubble of a large fire. There was little by way of evidence; the wooden floors had burned away and her bones were found in the core of hot ashes that ended up in a root cellar foundation. But high above the ground where a hayloft had once been, sixteen-by-sixteen-inch ax-hewn beams managed to complete the skeleton of century-old framework. Around one of the beams was an inch-wide band that was pale, as if something had been protecting it as the wood began to soot.

No one knew what to make of it, but a trooper who was on the scene added something to the case file that she thought interesting. It was only one word handwritten in a margin, and it had a question mark after it.

"Noose?"

Hastings was no stranger to researching cases; her position in the sex crimes office took her into the deviant sex scene. She was accustomed to looking for child pornographers, pedophiles, Internet predators, and the like. She didn't have access to library systems or magazine subscriptions, but there were always ways to scan keywords through Internet forums and chat rooms, and she studied sites devoted to S&M, bondage, breath play, and snuff films.

Had anyone chatted about kayaks or hangings, gas masks, or tourniquet ligatures, or had anyone used the names Nestor, Karen, Andrea, or Teng? There were hundreds of sites to sift through, hundreds of hits on keywords—most easily eliminated, but always those few requiring deeper attention.

Site after site, she read the same things. She knew that researchers considered pornography the seed from which many serial killers sprouted. Early sexual fantasies had spawned Ted Bundy, Ed Kemper, and Jeffrey Dahmer. Pornography, the experts wrote, builds on natural desires that exist within us all. The difference is that the serial killer, somewhere in his childhood, overrides "normal" expressions of intimacy and substitutes it with control. Often the modus operandi of a killer—the particular role he likes to play in acting out his fantasies of murder—equates to intimacy. No matter how twisted the act might seem, in his mind he may see what he is doing in a far different light. He may see it as love.

Mary thought that this killer was driven to communicate with his victims, nonverbally. If Andrea Teng were indeed one of his victims, he had taped her eyes open to watch her die. With Debbie and Dawn, he had used clear plastic wrap. With Karen Nestor she was sure he had used a mask but watched her eyes.

He either wanted to watch them or wanted them to watch him or both. He wanted to convey something between them with the eyes. Perhaps it was simply power. Perhaps the murders were the only times in life when he was able to see himself as important or dominant when it came to women.

Hastings was sure he hadn't started out murdering women. There was always some form of progression in these kinds of cases. Serial killers grew on fantasies, performing minor acts as they refined the killing scenario in their mind. By the time they sought their first real victim, they had imagined the act a thousand times, had planned every move. The first time someone died at his hand was the turning point in his life. If the killing matched the thrill of the fantasy and he got away with it, he would be compelled to come back for more. He would no longer be able to live off the fantasy; he would need the physical act from that point on. The next time his work might look a little different, details changed, his fantasies always evolving until he needed only to refresh the memory with different faces.

It was likely, given his fascination with breath play, that he had practiced autoerotica. The hanging might have begun as an early form of his fantasy, first alone, then with a willing partner. Hastings knew that the use of masks and plastic bags and air hoses was common between willing partners, but breath play was rarely performed with a noose. There was more to his fantasy than met the eye, she thought.

There were people around who would remember him, she was sure. Not necessarily the people he knew and worked with, even lived with every day. It would be someone he had tried to be intimate with. Or had he visited the underground scenes around the state? In the red-light bars where S&M was common, he would be known as a bagger, someone who liked to cover his partner's head. Did he like hookers or even men? Had he ever gone too far and someone called the police for a domestic dispute?

Hastings knew he'd subjected Karen Nestor to breath play because Karen was still alive when the killer hung her. They knew that because her heart was still pumping blood while she was hanging. The coroner said she would have gone unconscious in less than a minute in a normal hanging, except that the killer had elevated her just above her toes, just where she could arch her feet and take the pressure off her neck. She would have tired after a while, standing, breathing, falling, suffocating. It could have gone on as long as an hour, the coroner thought. Not to mention the number of times she was suffocated and revived up in the bedroom. The surprise was the absence of intercourse. Surely this had begun as a sex game with him, but what was it evolving into now? And why was he mentally connecting Sherry Moore to his game?

The phone rang.

"Corporal Hastings," she answered.

It was Rick Nestor.

"Yes, yes, transfer him now."

"Mr. Nestor?"

"Do you have something, Officer?"

"Maybe, Mr. Nestor. Karen's mother said you were on several kayaking trips not long before Karen's death."

"Yes," he said cautiously.

"We think it's possible Karen's killer first saw her on one of those trips."

"Why . . . what makes you think that?"

"I'm afraid I can't say quite yet, but it's important that we know where you were. Everything you can remember."

He hesitated. "Jesus, we were everywhere. We went four weekends straight in April. Uh, Kittanning and Perryopolis, Waterdrum and Deep Creek; I don't know where you'd start."

"How about a restaurant or barroom with oars on a wall?"

He laughed. "You're kidding, right?"

"Lots of those, I guess," Mary said, disappointed.

"I still don't understand what you're saying. That someone saw us in some place and just randomly decided to kill Karen? I mean, he would have had to know where we lived and . . ." Nestor cleared his throat. "You aren't implying Karen met someone on that trip?"

"I'm not implying anything, Mr. Nestor. I just need to know if you got gas anywhere, ate at a restaurant, bought something with a credit card, maybe a check. It was someone who was able to get your address."

"Christ," Nestor whispered. "We did all of that, gas stations, hotels, kayak rentals, not to mention half the stores along the way. We had to fill out all kinds of waivers and liability forms at the kayak places. I paid for them with a credit card too; they certainly had our address. We bought gas in Kittanning, Ligonier, Waterdrum. I always used the same American Express for gas. Why would anyone want to kill Karen? I mean, I wouldn't have expected a random burglar in the kind of place we live, but it makes more sense than to believe she was targeted."

"Mr. Nestor, I'm no closer to explaining this than you are. But the investigation is telling us it's a possibility. We have to check it out. Do you think you could supply me with a list of places? Let's just start with towns you stayed in, as many as you can remember right now. That's where you'd have had the most exposure, then the kayak rentals. The forms you mentioned, you said they had a lot of detail about you."

"Yes, yes, of course," he said distantly, "you kind of caught me off guard. Can I call you back in thirty minutes? I just need some time to sit down with a pen and think."

Thirty minutes later he was on the phone. Mary was ready to write.

Rick Nestor read them off. Mary was on her fourth sheet of notebook paper when he started on the last trip the Nestor family had taken. "We ate in a restaurant on Glades Pike. We were driving Route 31, just between Somerset and Donegal. Uh, we rented kayaks outside Confluence one morning on the Yough Dam, Jack's or something. It's a one-word place, you'll find it, just ask around. We stayed at the Trail's End Inn in Waterdrum, that's higher on the Youghiogheny River. We got our kayaks at White Water Willi's there, but we stopped at tons of places in between, tourist places, maple syrup and honey, hand-carved rockers, antique stores, those kinds of things."

"You didn't have any problems on the trip that you can recall? Someone upset over a bill, someone that seemed irrational? A fender-bender, lost wallet, purse, unexpected conversation, or any unusual interest paid to any of you?"

"Nothing," Nestor said, "really, nothing like that at all. The trips were unremarkable. We spent the days on the river alone. The kids didn't even make friends."

"I'll do the last trip first, the inns and kayak rentals starting in Somerset and moving west. If you think of anything else, I want to give you my cell phone number."

"What are you going to ask them?"

Hastings imagined telling him she was looking for a room with oars and kayaks as seen through the eyes of a psychic. How ridiculous that story would have sounded even to her.

"I'm taking Karen's pictures with me. I just want to find out if anyone remembers her, to find out if anything happened that might have drawn attention to her."

"You'll let me know what's going on?"

"I promise."

"All right," he said, "I appreciate it. We'll be back in town Sunday. I'll call you if something comes to mind before."

Hastings hung up the phone and stood to reach for her jacket. Somerset was a two-hour drive. By nightfall she'd be on the Youghiogheny near Waterdrum. Wherever she ended up at dark, she'd get a room. If she found someone who recognized Karen Nestor, she'd stay there and get Palmer to come help her in the morning.

She scribbled a note and put it on Palmer's desk, grabbed keys to a motor-pool Taurus, checked her wallet to find thirty-three dollars, and credit and ATM cards. She took her overnight bag from a locker and turned off her desk lamp.

Three hours west, the lights were on in a second-floor office on East Carson Street. Special Agent Alice Springer and Gabe Samuels paced a boardroom in Pittsburgh's FBI field office.

"Where did it come from?" Springer took a seat.

"They're running it now, but it looks like a commercial line in Fayette County. Just a few more minutes, they said."

"Good, good." She rubbed her hands together. "I want to do this right, Gabe. Everything right."

Samuels nodded. He didn't like all the secrecy. He especially didn't like withholding information from the state police when he knew there were likely to be more victims.

But Springer was the supervisor in charge and even Samuels had to admit that things, at least for the moment, seemed to be going her way.

The call had been transferred to the Pittsburgh field office from a toll-free tip line in Washington, D.C. It was brief. Someone claimed to have seen the two women who were found hanging in a campground near Black Moshannon State Park in a bar together just a week or so before they were killed. He wanted to know if there was a reward for information, but when the operator asked him his name, he hung up.

There was a knock at the door; a woman opened it, handing Samuels a piece of paper. He unfolded it, looked at Springer. "The town is called Waterdrum. The call came from a pay phone at the Trail's End Inn."

Springer put her hands palms down on the table. Her eyes were drifting around the room. "Gabe, get me some history on the place. I'll call the cable companies."

She located a broadband company, Penn Cable. Fifteen minutes later she had a supervisor on the line.

She got a user name for a high-speed modem assigned to the account billed to the Trail's End Inn in Waterdrum; it was TET@Penncable. High-speed computers in Washington, D.C., interfaced with the system, scanning passwords associated with the account at the rate of 2,000,000 combinations per second. Twenty minutes later it logged on to one using MARINE1. She was into the Trail's End computer system, browsing through its history until she located Expedia hits in Internet Explorer. She opened each one until she found driving directions to Black Moshannon State Park.

Someone who had access to the inn's computer was their killer.

Next Springer got into the business's data management systems, located employee records, copied names and Social Security numbers, and downloaded a guest history file. The owner had used it as a mailing list for promotional purposes.

In the payroll records on Excel software, she was able to determine the hours and days employees were at work, which days they were off, how they corresponded to the homicide cases.

Subpoenas would later produce financial records, credit card slips, and incoming and outgoing phone records for the inn's office, restaurant, and guest rooms.

There were seventeen employees listed on the payroll at the Trail's End Inn; nine were active and each had received paychecks within the past six months. Three of the nine employees were women and were therefore put on the bottom of the list. Agents would still want to know who their husbands or boyfriends were; anyone with the password could get into the system, and employees had been known to let friends and families onto systems where they work.

The remaining six males included the owner, George Thorpe, a housekeeper, three bartenders, and a maintenance man.

She ran all of their names through the FBI's National Crime Information Center and started to compile a list of documents she would need.

There would be room registration logs, restaurant/bar credit card receipts, and dinner reservation journals that might tell if any of the victims had been at the establishment and when. That list would then be compared to employees who were working and present. All of it would aid prosecutors when they brought their suspect to trial.

While she was waiting on criminal histories, she took the time to research Waterdrum on the Internet and discovered that it was a resort village noted for kayaking, white-water river rafting, and hiking and biking trails.

There were at a minimum a dozen competing restaurants and inns in the town, not to mention clothing and sporting goods stores, tours, rentals, and a gas station. All would need to be checked and cross-checked to see if they could put any of the victims in town. This, Springer thought, should bear fruit and quickly.

What she had no intention of doing was to show

her hand. The investigation would not be a success if it served only to scare him away. They needed to be absolutely certain before they asked a judge for a probable cause warrant to search his house and draw his blood.

Five long years she had waited for this, from East Carbon, Utah, to Mankato and Sabetha near the Kansas-Nebraska border, to Willow Springs and Dexter, Missouri, to Cumberland, Maryland, and now the town of Waterdrum, Pennsylvania.

The gas mask killer had first appeared on their radar in Utah in early 2002. For the longest time, they thought he might be one of two men killing prostitutes and topless dancers between Colorado Springs and Las Vegas. But the woman he killed wasn't a prostitute—that had worried them some—and then there was the unusual result of a highly sensitive spectroscope examination during autopsy. The woman's face bore traces of dithiocarbamates, used in the processes of vulcanizing rubber. The killer had put a rubber hood or mask over her head. She had been strangled repeatedly, had a fractured larynx and hyoid, which assumed a violent attack.

They had to wait almost two years to find out that they had a whole new identity out there. Another strangulation homicide; a remote country home where the victim had lived alone. She was found hanging. Saliva and mucus smeared across her face seemed to indicate that her head had been covered as well.

Serial killers all have a cooling-off period; those who kill multiple people in a short period of time are called spree killers and their life span is considerably shorter. By the time this one reached Sabetha, Kansas, his cooling-off period was just under a year. When he started killing in Missouri, he was finding a new victim every six months. On the first of them, he actually left her hanging with the gas mask on her face.

The gas mask murders were unique. The period of time he spent with his victims seemed long and busy. What made the gas mask killer so unlike his serial killer counterparts around the country was the ever-widening divergence taking place between technique and sex. This man was going through all of the motions, including ligatures and masks. He was prolonging death, while constantly strangling and releasing his victims, but the scenes steadily progressed to suggest he was losing his interest in sex. In fact there was doubt that he was sexually assaulting the victims at all.

Then he disappeared. No one could understand why. The best guesses were that he'd gone to prison for something else, died, or moved to another part of the country. But even if he had moved, they should be seeing his handiwork by now.

And they weren't.

Across the country in Maryland, there was a spate of kidnappings taking place. All of them were from office buildings and over a single summer, all along an interstate between Hagerstown and Frederick.

The cases caught the attention of the gas mask strangler task force in St. Louis, but in the end, Maryland state police closed their case on two teenagers killed in a high-speed pursuit. The kidnappers had a fourth victim in their van at the time. The FBI as quickly dismissed the cases and went back to looking in Missouri.

When news of the hangings broke in Cumberland, it all came together. The FBI could see it on their wall-size maps. The killer had moved directly from Missouri to Maryland. His attacks by then came only weeks apart, no longer months. He was stepping up the pace. Then he was suddenly reprieved by fate when the two would-be teenaged copycats from Ellicott City ended up getting killed and taking the blame for his kidnappings.

The FBI began to focus on Cumberland and the surrounding mountains of West Virginia and Pennsylvania. There were women missing from campsites along the Appalachian Trail; some were said to be the work of a crazed mountain man, but without bodies to tell the story, who was to say the women weren't strangled to death and thrown into some crevice for the animals to feed on and scatter the bones? Then they found the suspicious suicide by hanging of a young girl in Nemacolin, Pennsylvania. Had he simply moved across the Pennsylvania state line?

Waterdrum, where the tip-line phone call about the blond victims had come from, was less than twenty miles from Nemacolin, an hour and a half from Karen Nestor's home north of Pittsburgh in Sewickley, and two hours from Black Moshannon, where the blond girls were found hanging from a tree.

Springer could sense the end was in sight. All she needed was to keep a lid on Waterdrum until she could put her people in place. She knew Agent Samuels was at least half right. It was necessary to pay attention to Sherry Moore, to keep the cops from doing anything stupid with her and scaring the killer away. Springer had Samuels put a tap on Moore's phone.

She watched the record scrolling across her computer screen, National Crime Information Center histories of employees at the Trail's End Inn. When she was done, she picked up the phone, called a court clerk in Allegheny County, and gave her a case number, sat by her fax, and waited for the response to arrive.

When it came, it was more than she had hoped for. There wouldn't be any lengthy files and records to sift through, no legwork to be done, no interviewing cops or lawyers or teachers or doctors. It was right there in black and white.

Kenneth George Dentin, white male, thirty-three years of age, arrested 12/11/2005 for assault in

Allegheny County, Pennsylvania, just four months after Cumberland.

The government's case—he pleaded to a fourth-degree misdemeanor—would have included testimony that the defendant used a ligature to strangle the complainant. As the defendant had no adult criminal history and the complainant had a lengthy record for prostitution, it was easy to assume that prosecutors had been reluctant to put a prostitute on the witness stand. Either that or Dentin pleaded quickly to avoid the felony. The court would have had no choice but to let Dentin off with a slap on the wrist. A fourth-degree misdemeanor was little worse than a speeding ticket.

He had been ordered to attend group counseling through the Allegheny County Department of Human Services for a period of not less than six months. Since no DNA was brought into evidence, Kenneth George Dentin might have faded into history unnoticed.

Springer picked up the phone, punched a button.

"Samuels."

"Gabe," she said, typing into her keyboard. "I think I have him. I'm sending you a profile on Kenneth George Dentin. Take him apart—where did he come from, relatives, schools, jobs, I want his whole life. Draw a surveillance team from Pittsburgh and find some decent undercover agents. Make sure you're getting the best. I want people around him, but I do not want him spooked."

"What about the state police? They've got narcotics operatives we could borrow."

"Not a chance. I don't care if you have to get someone from California; FBI agents only, no cops."

"Alice?"

"We're taking our time, Gabe. I want total preparation before we move in to surround him. We'll know everything there is to know by then and we'll have search warrants for his car and his residence. We've waited five years for this, Gabe. We can wait a few more days to see that it's done right."

"Where do you want the agents?"

"Here. We'll have briefings and divide the assignments as we learn more about him. He works at an inn, so we'll send in some of the agents as guests. All we need is one cigarette butt, one empty Coke can, a chewed pencil—anything we can definitively say came from him—and before the end of the week CODIS will match his DNA and you and I will have the gas mask killer. And he will never see the light of day again. Now let's get a team together."

13

PHILADELPHIA, PENNSYLVANIA

Sherry awoke from a long and deep sleep feeling more refreshed than she had felt in a very long time. The jitters were all but gone. In her dream, the memories of others laid still in their cages while she and John Payne danced slowly to the sounds of waves crashing. Their bodies were pressed tightly together, each leaning into the other, warm cheeks touching. He whispered something in her ear.

"I can't hear you," she whispered back. "I can't hear you anymore."

He stopped dancing and lifted her chin. "I want you to be happy, Sherry. It wasn't your fault."

Their eyes met and she could see him, although in life she never saw his face.

"I am so sorry," she sobbed. "I didn't know we didn't have time . . . I couldn't see . . . I can't see . . ."

"You see me now, don't you?"

"Yes, John. I see you."

"Keep your eyes on me, sweetheart. Everything's going to be all right."

Sherry knew she was dreaming and willed herself to stay in it longer. Awake now, she lingered in bed, less afraid of her mind's occupants. John was with them.

The phone rang. She had expected to hear from him soon.

"What did you find?"

"Are you asking me what they were thinking about?" Sherry questioned smoothly.

"Yes, what were they thinking about, Sherry?"

"Didn't you ask them yourself?"

"They lie."

"Do women always lie to you?"

Silence.

"I think you're looking for your answers in all the wrong places."

"Cute."

"You think you know how people feel about you, but you don't."

"I know," he said loudly.

"They were thinking about their families, but you know that."

"Uh-huh."

"They were thinking about a night out together. A night they were having fun together. You were there too, weren't you?"

Sherry thought she heard a sound.

"They like you, don't they? The women, I mean. They come on to you sometimes?"

They had been talking nearly a minute. Sherry wondered if the police had a location on him by now.

"How do you decide? Were they special in some way? Did they remind you of someone?"

He laughed. "Oh, don't start."

"You always cover their faces. Sometimes you cover your face. You know why you do that, don't you? You're trying to separate them from what you're doing to them. You don't want them to be people, individuals. You're killing someone else every time you put on the mask, aren't you? You're not even there, you're somewhere else in your mind."

Silence.

Sherry wondered how far she could go with it, wondered how long the police needed.

"Because when you're wearing the mask, they can't see how afraid you are."

"You're lying."

"No, I'm not. You like people to think of you. You want people to remember you. To think you're important."

The phone went dead.

"Shit," Sherry said, putting the receiver down.

The phone rang.

"Sherry, it's Palmer. He was on a cell phone. It belonged to Dawn Webber, one of the Black Moshannon girls."

"Where was he?"

"Still in western Pennsylvania. We have him twenty-five miles from a tower on the Alleghenies. We need another call from that phone."

Sherry sighed.

"How long would it take?"

"An hour, maybe less, we need three towers to triangulate from."

"He'll trash the phone. Maybe I should call him back."

"Wait, just an hour."

"Meanwhile?"

"Mary is running down some leads on where his victims might have met him—"

Call waiting beeped.

"Go on, take it," Palmer hissed.

Sherry pushed the flash button. "Hello," she said. "Hello?"

"I think we'll talk one more time today."

"What do you want to talk about?"

"My next victim."

"You don't have to have a next victim. You could just talk to me."

He laughed. "You and me, we'll just talk. Just like that."

"Why not?"

"Because I won't get what I want from you. You care about what you want but not about me."

"Why are you always so concerned that people care about you? You assume things to be true that you don't really know. You can't expect people to be honest with you, to answer your questions the way you want them to when they know they're going to die.

They don't know what to say to you. They don't know what you want to hear and that's all they can think about, saying the right things to you. I wouldn't know what to say to you."

"I want . . ." He stopped.

She waited. "You want what?" she said gently.

"I want to know . . ." His voice cracked.

He really was coming apart, she thought. He was very, very close, but how to land him? She wasn't quite sure if she should press him or go easy on him.

"I could try to meet you," she said.

"Yeah." He laughed softly. "I know you would like that. I know you would all love to meet me. All of you listening in."

"Okay, I'm sorry; that was wrong. I wouldn't be allowed to meet you alone. The police wouldn't let me. But I could still talk to you if you turned yourself in. I would answer your questions as best I could."

"You wouldn't do it if I didn't make you do it."

"Do what?"

"What I want you to do."

"What is that?" Sherry asked.

"I have to go now."

"Wait," Sherry said. "Let's keep talking. There must be—"

He hung up the phone.

It rang again. "You heard?"

"I want you out of that house, Sherry, just until this is over."

"He's not coming here. He knows I'm being watched. This is the last place he'd show up."

"Maybe, maybe not. But I can't take that chance and I can't afford to put security around your house. You'd be better off in a smaller place, maybe a hotel here in Harrisburg. I can register you under another name."

"I can't leave this phone and you know it. So let's focus on getting him the next time he calls, not on me. Please, Dan. I know what I'm doing."

14

Pittsburgh, Pennsylvania

Agent Springer stood in the conference room, white board on an easel, laptop computer ready to do a PowerPoint presentation.

The subject was Kenneth George Dentin.

Tomorrow morning the first agents, undercover agents, would enter Waterdrum, each taking up points and places until the net was fully functional.

"Gabe." She nodded at the lights.

The room was filled to capacity. There were agents

from evidence control systems, a team dedicated to the preservation and comparison of evidence in more than seven cases now, including Maryland, Pennsylvania, Utah, Kansas, and Missouri.

There were five undercover agents, two couples and a single woman with brown hair. One of the Cumberland women had been a redhead, two of the women in the Midwest had been blondes, but Dentin's mother, who committed suicide—for whatever that was worth—was a brunette and so were the majority of his other victims.

The undercover agents were to play the role of outdoors enthusiasts. They would check into rooms at the inn and in cottages already reserved. They had day trips booked on the river in the morning, but none of them would actually make it to the water. By switching on and off in the restaurant and bar, they hoped to cover all hours that Kenneth George Dentin would be at work.

When he came on duty, the brunette would sit at the bar alone and try to engage him in conversation. Other agents would locate Dentin's car and see that it didn't leave the lot again.

Members of the FBI's Special Weapons and Tactics response team would raid the trailer park where he lived, twelve miles south of Waterdrum. The registered owner of the trailer, a man named Lawrence Whidden, would need to be located and interrogated as well.

"This is our man," Springer said to the group. "Photograph taken for a Utah driver's license; you can see that it's five years old. We'll update photographs with everyone as soon as our UC's in place." She nodded at the two couples and the brunette. "It's a tourist town, so they'll be able to take pictures at will. We also have street and topographical maps for everyone. I want Gabe to go over this with you next. He's studied the maps and aerials, but the good news is, there aren't that many ways to get in and out of this town. There is one main road north and south, one mountain road east and west. It will also be easy to cover the trailer owned by this guy Whidden." She held up another photo, an aerial shot of the trailer park. "Whidden has no history outside the state of Pennsylvania, so we don't believe he's an accomplice, but we rule out nothing."

She nodded toward the SWAT commander. "We don't want any foot chases. That's why we have Larry's experts here. But everybody needs to know the layout of the land if he breaks and runs on us. Dentin has been living in Pennsylvania for two years now; he knows his way around. If he thinks you're a cop, he'll step out the back door and we may never see him again. We are not going to let that happen. We are going to be prepared for every contingency.

"Gabe."

Another aerial photograph of Waterdrum centered

on the Trail's End Inn and a string of fourteen cottages that made an L shape from the inn to the river's edge.

"This is the bar." She touched the screen. "Bring it back just a little, Gabe."

The picture zoomed outward, revealing a parking lot with two exits and entrances and access to a walking bridge suspended across the river.

"This suspension bridge will be closed tonight at midnight. Pennsylvania Parks and Recreation will announce safety concerns and put up signage with a barricade. We'll have an agent on the other end, just in case."

She pointed. "That leaves the north-south road from Waterdrum and this farm road running up the side of a mountain. Our SWAT team has two helicopters at its disposal. Both will remain outside the perimeter until we need them. When we are ready to spring the trap, we'll call them down and, of course, they will be available to assist us should anything go wrong. Questions?"

"Are we going to take him at the bar? He's liable to get a call when we go through the door to his trailer."

Springer nodded. "We're taking him then, so it's all about timing. Whoever is on him undercover in the bar at the time will take the lead. We want to get him out of there with as little fuss as possible. Agent Samuels and I will return with him to Pittsburgh to interrogate. McKullkin and Dell will direct forensic efforts both at the trailer and the inn."

She tapped the screen.

"Everyone starting to get a feel for this? Okay, let's move on to the press releases."

15

Waterdrum, Pennsylvania

Hastings had been to no fewer than a dozen bars and restaurants between Laurel Mountain and Waterdrum throughout the afternoon. The route led from Route 31 across the Laurel Highlands to the resorts of Seven Springs and Hidden Valley, before veering into the village of Waterdrum, where the rivers rushed south toward Maryland.

A few people remembered the women's faces on Mary's clipboard, but only from the newspapers and television reports after the murders. None of them had seen the women in person.

The bars along the mountains were typically rustic, with gravel parking lots occupied predominantly by pickup trucks and motorcycles and a few camouflaged all-terrain vehicles, a few vintage muscle cars. The men wore baseball caps; the women wore T-shirts. Everyone smoked and beer was the beverage of choice. Southwestern Pennsylvania had changed little in a hundred years, and big-city tourists were inclined to accept cigarette smoke and a dose of healthy profanity as local color. They were not about to change this world.

There were guns on walls, and stuffed animals—bears and coyotes and pheasant and deer. There were woodstoves and fireplaces, old snowshoes and wooden skis, antique sleds and ice box saws on the walls.

Every bar seemed to have a clutter of Polaroid photographs tacked to the walls. Pennsylvanians liked to take pictures of one another.

She ate a hamburger and drank a beer with a couple at a bar near Laurel Hill State Park. The kayaking had been good this spring, they had said. They had Class III rapids in Waterdrum and the inns had been filled to capacity in April.

It was late when she started out for Waterdrum. There weren't any hotels since she'd left the ski areas, so she kept going, hoping there would be vacancies there.

The bar at the Trail's End Inn was busy for a Tuesday night. Crisco was staring into his beer with a concentrated look on his face. He was often trying to remember names of his platoon, repeating them out loud: "Captain Mills, Miles, Miller . . ."

Jean Farrell had unpacked her bags, taken a shower, and eaten a salad at the bar next to Crisco. Mooney—she remembered him as the one who was always checking everybody out—was hanging around the jukebox, peeking at her from behind the pine pillar beams.

Nick, the boy with the Polish last name, and his friend, another coal miner, were on the opposite side of the bar, looking her way, but she wasn't looking back. She was here to relax, to think, to do anything but complicate her life, even for another night.

Nick had a habit of flicking ashes while looking around the room; perhaps he thought it looked cool even if he missed the ashtray. She had to admit he was a hunk and there were nights in her life she would have been tempted, but this wasn't one of them. No more boys, she thought. No more trouble. She was here to reinvent herself and she had no intention of bringing home even one more piece of unwanted baggage.

If she wanted a neophyte, it was going to be someone who wanted to learn about life, not sex. Someone who was ready to dump the candlelight river cruises and pick up skis, or scuba gear and mosquito netting to dive the Amazon. How long did you have to live before you became conscious of how you wanted to die? What did you want to look back on in those final hours, minutes, and seconds? She didn't want to leave the world disappointed. How pathetic would that be?

All you had to do was be honest with yourself. Things that felt good seldom stayed around. Things that were good stayed with you forever.

It was late, almost eleven, when Mary Hastings reached Waterdrum. The last twenty miles of mountain road had been as random as a shot of Silly String, twisting S curves and ridges as steep as roller coasters. The road was dark as hell, the trees overgrown to the point that they deprived the land of even moonlight. Occasional lights from cottages twinkled in the woods, then suddenly the sky opened up, and the land cleared and the road widened to cross a moonlit river. Even in darkness you could see the reflections on the white water, churning pools, slapping rocks, rushing to disappear in darkness.

The town was built around a natural waterfall. She thought in darkness it looked like the facade of a western movie town. Outback gear, kayak rentals, white-water river tours, "Old Tyme" restaurants, bicycle rentals, bed-and-breakfast inns, and parks overlooking the falls.

The B&Bs were dark, but the vacancy sign was lit at the Trail's End Inn.

She pulled into the lot under a halogen lamp and parked next to an orange El Camino with a bed full of Crisco cans. She put on her jacket, pulled out her overnight bag—you learned to keep one at the office in her line of work—and locked the doors.

There was a bell sitting on the empty maple counter and soft noise coming from an entrance to a bar. She tapped the bell and studied the dozens of colorful brochures on a carousel rack. A minute later a young man appeared from the bar.

"Help you?"

"You have rooms?"

"Sure do, just you?"

She nodded, fishing for her wallet.

"Ninety-nine dollars, with a ten percent discount on breakfast in the dining room."

"American Express?"

"Sure." He pushed a large bound register toward her. "We still use logs." He smiled. "Owner says it's folksy. Don't worry about the tag number."

She smiled, tiredly, filling in her home address. "Sounds busy." She nodded toward the door to the bar.

"Stays this way till Labor Day. Kitchen's closed, but the bar's open till one-thirty if you want to join us."

She stifled a yawn. "Maybe I will."

He gave her a key. "Go out the way you came in and take the path to your right. It's lit the whole way. We had a cancellation, so I gave you the last cottage overlooking the river. If you leave your windows open, you can hear the falls."

"Thanks." She smiled. "Very nice of you."

She grabbed a handful of brochures, took the bag

to her room, and put it on the bed. Then she washed her face, brushed her teeth, and went to the sliding glass door of the balcony. She needed to call Palmer and leave a message about where she was staying. She picked up the cell phone and pulled open the slider. The moon was three-quarters full and spotlights overlooked the river below her, dark and churning. There were fireflies along the bank in the dark trees. The clerk hadn't been kidding. The river was rushing and loud.

Suddenly she felt alone.

It had been almost four months since she broke up with her boyfriend. The room reminded her of the trips they used to take; she had always liked that he was spontaneous. That was before she found the vial with traces of white powder that had rolled under the floor mat in his car. He said it belonged to a friend, like a kid who got caught by his parents.

She didn't believe him then and she didn't believe him now. There were things she could accept—everyone had some little quirk in their life—but drugs weren't even remotely an option with her.

She didn't leave him immediately; she felt she owed him the benefit of the doubt, but she didn't kid herself either. Once her eyes had been opened, she began to see. She would question rather than accept the high and low moods, the nosebleeds, the odd bouts of nervousness, the difficulties he had concentrating. Things she once thought curious had now begun to take on new meaning. Her boyfriend had a mistress and her name was cocaine.

She laid the phone back down. The call to Palmer could wait until she got back; it would only go to his voice mail anyhow. She began to kick off her shoes, then stopped to look in the mirror over the bureau and pulled her hair behind an ear. Why not? she thought. Why not go to the bar and have a drink? She would be around people and that's why she was here after all, to ask questions.

The bar was crowded, the restaurant dark. There were a few women; one in particular, nicely dressed and sitting near the end of the bar, appeared to be alone. She put a hand on the stool next to her.

"Anyone sitting here?"

The woman smiled, shook her head. "It's all yours."

She slid onto the stool and looked around the bar. There were some very local-looking guys in their twenties, tradesmen, not professionals. Two younger women were talking to them. There was an older couple sipping martinis, a sandy-haired man in his mid- to late thirties, nice looking; the man seated two stools to her right, just on the other side of the brunette, was mumbling into his beer.

A young dark-haired man at the jukebox was watching the room, paying close attention to the two youngest girls. A man with tar-spattered pants came out of the men's room, walked up beside the brunette next to her, and pushed his chest against her shoulder. "I see your friend got here."

The brunette turned to her. "Yes, and we have some catching up to do." She patted Mary's arm and winked. "Give us girls some alone time, okay? We haven't seen each other in a long time."

"Alone," the man repeated, hand in his pocket. He hadn't shaved today and he kept rocking on his heels, brushing up against the brunette's back.

"Yeah," Mary said. "I've been driving all day and I'm tired. Why don't you just give us a break?"

"Break," he said, "you want a break." He nodded drunkenly, backing away, and he pivoted with some difficulty toward the other end of the bar, attempting to walk a straight line to an empty stool.

The brunette laughed. "I kept telling him I was expecting someone. Thank God you came in. I'm buying your first drink."

"Oh, forget it." Mary put a hand up, but the brunette picked up a twenty and waved it in front of her. "Kenny," she called, "my friend over here."

Hastings ordered a Grey Goose and orange juice.

"Cheers," the brunette said, holding up her martini when the drink came.

"Cheers." Hastings raised her glass, starting to take a sip, then froze; the glass never touched her lips.

"Don't worry"—the brunette waved a hand at her—"they're really very clean around here. You can drink out of the glasses."

Hastings forced her eyes to the woman, smiled falsely, nodded, and took a drink. But then her eyes drifted back to the oars on the wall. Just behind the man who was mumbling in his beer.

"You're staying in the cottages?"

Hastings nodded again, head turning, body swiveling on her stool, taking in the rest of the room: the jukebox, the stone fireplace behind the dining room tables, the Cinco de Mayo pendants flapping under the ceiling fan, an old wooden kayak hanging from the high beams on chains.

"And you?" she said in awe.

"Second time this month," the brunette said. "Great place to shake off the cobwebs"—she pointed down the bar—"as long as you can keep the locals from rubbing up against you."

"A universal problem," Hastings said absently; she was studying the green pendants in disbelief.

The brunette nodded. "He was only getting started, though, not that I can't handle myself when I have to. The bartenders are great here too. One sign of trouble and they'll step in." She picked up her glass in salute. "But then you came along and spared us all the pain. Cheers," she said again. "Which suits me well. This is a week of R&R and I refuse to let anyone spoil it."

"You know everyone?" Hastings nodded down the bar; a man was talking on his cell phone, another was adding numbers on a bar napkin with a three-inch pencil. She remembered just then that she had left her own phone on the bed and had yet to leave a message for Palmer.

The brunette shrugged. "Not really. I mean, this is only my second time here this year. I know the bartenders. Kenny's the one who checked you into the cottages." She pointed at their bartender. "That guy down there, good-looking guy in a white polo shirt, that's Walter, another bartender. He's off-duty tonight. Then there's George Thorpe"—she crossed her arms and made fists—"big square-looking guy, ex-Marine. He's the owner of the place. You'll see him around if you're here tomorrow. The locals are carpenters and Nick-something-zinski, over there with the tight T-shirt and the great chest, is a coal miner, if you can believe it. The jerk you chased away that likes to rub up against me says he lays pipe for a living." She put a finger in her mouth and said, "Gag."

She pointed to the end of the bar. "The weirdo over there by the jukebox just likes to watch everybody, and my friend sitting next to me"—she thumbed and lowered her voice—"they call him Crisco. Walter says he's sniffed too much napalm. He thinks we're all in Hanoi."

"Wow, you're good. I mean it. You never got a sense of any trouble here, though? Like nobody really skeeves you out? I mean, besides the pipe layer." Hastings looked concerned. "I can't tell you how many bars I've walked into and out of without finishing my first drink. You know, you get the looks. You get the touching, the really creepy guys."

The brunette shook her head. "It can get crazy late at night, especially on the weekends, but not to the point you'd feel unsafe. Not from the little I've seen. And like I said, the bartenders seem to keep an eye on things. I would imagine there's a line the locals won't cross. Food's great, restaurant has a reputation, tourists are what brings the big bucks here. The owner makes his money on food and rooms. I don't think he'd put up with too much crap for the sake of a little local beer business. Not this guy."

Hastings nodded.

"These miners, though, I think it's amazing. I didn't even know people did that anymore. I mean, you hear about the men trapped and the explosions now and then, but it never seems quite real to you, like you just don't think about people spending their lives in tunnels under the earth."

Hastings was still taking it all in, but now it wasn't the room, it was the people that she was seeing.

She had to admit, she'd been skeptical until now. Sherry Moore was definitely the real thing. There was simply no way she could have known about all the things she identified in this place. She could not have known that Rick Nestor had brought his family here, to a place where two women whom she had never met in her life had seen the identical room.

"You kayak?"

Hastings shook her head. "No, I was in Pittsburgh on business and thought I'd take the scenic route home."

"Where's home?"

"Harrisburg," Hastings said.

The brunette looked at her. "You drove fifty miles out of your way to get here? You must not want to get home very quickly."

"I'm off until next week; there's no one at home waiting. I had some time to kill, so why not here?" Hastings had no reason to lie about being a cop; she just didn't want to draw attention to herself right now. This room, the objects on the walls, it was a lot to accept all at once. She could apologize in the morning, set things straight, but for the moment she preferred to remain anonymous.

"I'm like that sometimes, impulsive." The brunette nodded vigorously. "Jean Farrell." She stuck out a hand. "Are you a one-drink girl or are we having another?"

Hastings looked at the oars on the wall. "Oh, I think we should close the place up." She pursed her lips impishly, took the brunette's hand, and smiled. "Mary Hastings."

"Good deal, Mary Hastings." Jean pushed her glass toward the bartender. "Keep 'em coming, Kenny. The girls are out tonight."

They talked about everything, Hastings snatching tidbits of information about the bar. Walter had joined them for a time, then left. Kenny, losing customers rapidly, had more and more time to spend talking to them.

"I'm going white-water rafting tomorrow," Jean said. "Want to come along?"

"Never done it before," Hastings said.

"That would make two of us then."

Hastings shook her head. "I'm a landlubber at heart. I think I'll just do the shops and restaurants."

"To each her own," Jean said.

It was almost two. Jean Farrell bade her good night, after making vague plans for breakfast with Mary on the deck. She was in Cabin 12, she reminded her; she should call or leave a note at the desk if anything changed.

"Big staff?" Hastings asked the bartender.

The only other person at the bar was the weird dark-haired guy who had been standing by the jukebox earlier. He was drinking a draft and playing peekaboo behind a pillar that stood between them. Was he hanging on for a chance that he would get lucky or was he looking for a woman to suffocate throughout the night? Hastings couldn't read him. He hadn't said a word to anyone in the two hours she'd been here, but he sure seemed interested in everyone.

It was late. She looked at her watch, then at her drink. What more could be learned? she wondered. It wouldn't be easy to get a subpoena for employee records on the strength of a vision, but she could probably learn more from Kenny and the owner, George, than from anyone else in the place. She already knew the Nestors had stayed here and the oars and the Cinco de Mayo pendant were part of both Karen Nestor's memories and the memories of the two blondes from Black Moshannon. She couldn't believe it, and yet she did.

She moved just to her right, where the guy across the bar couldn't see her. Called Kenny over, waving him closer until he was standing between them. "The guy behind you," she whispered. "Do I have to worry he'll follow me out the door?"

Kenny shook his head and whispered, "A little crazy, but harmless. He does odd jobs around town, comes in acting like he's some kind of a private eye or something, seldom talks. I don't think he's got any other place to go."

"What's his name?"

"Billy Duda. He lives down in Confluence."

She nodded, reaching into her purse, and took out pictures of Dawn and Debbie. "Have you ever seen these girls before?"

Kenny took them from her, looked them over under the light. "Absolutely," he said. "They came in a few weeks ago. Cinco de Mayo, I think. Are they friends of yours?"

She shook her head, taking them back, replacing them, exchanging them for a picture of Karen Nestor.

"How about her?"

Kenny looked at her oddly. "You a cop or something?"

"State police." Hastings discreetly produced her badge.

He looked at her a moment, took the picture hesitantly, looked across his shoulder at the man behind him, and put the photo under a gooseneck lamp over the cash register. "Jesus." He looked up at her.

"She was here?" Hastings said.

He shook his head no. "If she was, I didn't see her, but I know who she is."

"Who is she?"

"That woman from Sewickley that was murdered in her garage. I saw her picture all over TV." He stared at Hastings, his eyebrows raised. "She was here too?"

Hastings nodded.

The bartender dropped his towel and leaned toward her. "What happened to them," he asked squeamishly, "the blondes?"

"You don't know?"

"Huh-uh." He shook his head.

"They were found hanging in a state forest north of Pittsburgh." She watched his face for a reaction.

"Jesus," he said, stepping back. "I was gone for two weeks, fishing in Boulder with my father. I'm a Colorado boy." He picked up the photos and looked at them.

"Do you know"—he shrugged—"who did it?"

She shook her head. "That's why I'm here."

"You meet the owner? George Thorpe?"

She shook her head. "I really just got here tonight. I haven't talked to anyone but Jean and you."

Kenny nodded and wiped his hands on a bar towel.

"Why don't you come in in the morning? I'm doing brunch, which starts at ten. The older crowd orders Bloody Marys and Mimosas, so I'm stuck at the bar, but George will be here. George is the best. He'll tell you anything you want to know. Walter, the other bartender you met tonight, he took my shifts when I went home to Colorado. He'll be in by three. If that lady that got murdered was here, he'll remember her."

"The other two, the blondes you saw, you remember who they were talking to that night? Did anything seem odd about them?"

"They were making quite a spectacle of themselves. Flirty stuff. You know your friend that was with you tonight?" He turned. "She was sitting right back here. Came in with a guy that same night, you should ask her."

Hastings nodded. "Good memory."

"I try to remember drinks and names, it's good for tips."

Mary thought about Jean Farrell in cabin 12. She'd be keeping that breakfast date after all. This was getting better.

"The regular locals were in that night, and both those guys with the blondes, I never saw them before. College types. I don't know if they hooked up here or if they knew each other from before."

He looked at her and leaned on the bar, coming nearer. "Duda was here."

She looked over his shoulder. "You said he was harmless."

Kenny looked blank. "I'm a bartender, not a cop."

Hastings half smiled. She put Nestor's picture away and nodded.

"Tell you what," he said. "I'll give him last call and you'll have time to check out his car. Stop me if I'm sounding stupid. I don't know. Is that the kind of thing you do or not? Get tag numbers and stuff?"

"What's he drive?" She smiled, thinking he was cute.

"Blue Firebird, no front bumper." He nodded toward the door. "Just go like you're going to the ladies' room and keep walking, the hall circles the desk by the kitchen and you're right back at the front door. I'll refill your drink, like you're staying for another."

"You don't need to—"

"You want straight up orange juice instead?"

She smiled. "Yeah, sure, that would be great. Thanks," she said sincerely.

The man across the bar looked around the pillar at her and then moved back out of sight. She became conscious of the 40-caliber Glock tucked into her waistband.

She needed to get things in perspective, she thought. What she hadn't expected to find so unexpectedly was the place all three women had been in, just weeks apart from their deaths. It really was likely those women met their murderer here. She looked around the room at all the tables and stools along a bench that ran the length of the wall. It was a big room, a quarter of it devoted to the large bar, three-quarters to the restaurant; it was probably noisy at its busiest. She could imagine someone sitting here, or over there where Duda peeked at her from behind the rough-hewn pillars. She turned toward the jukebox—that now familiar-looking board with glossy Polaroids curling under thumbtacks.

Photos. That's where he was getting them from.

Hastings was from York, Pennsylvania. She'd gone to school in New Jersey, criminal justice with a minor in psychology from Caldwell. The whole picture-taking thing in bars wasn't big where she'd grown up, but in western Pennsylvania it seemed part of the regular decor.

She needed to talk to Palmer in the morning, early in the morning. She could feel it. This was right. This was where they needed to concentrate their efforts. Maybe someone saw something out of the ordinary or heard an inappropriate question. Maybe the dead women all took the same kayaking trip, had the same guide. The police needed to show their pictures around town. They needed to be here at night, to catch the regulars and the other bartender, Walter.

Did any of the locals exchange words with the dead women? Or how about with the men they were with? Could that have been the motive? Was it envy that drove him to kill?

It was time to take a step back. To figure out who was who.

"What's your last name?" she asked.

"Dentin," the bartender told her.

"Mine's Hastings. They do that a lot around here." She pointed at the board covered with pictures. "This is the third place I've seen one today."

"Customers love to see themselves on the wall. Even the ones we only see once a year. George thinks it makes them feel special. He says it's good for repeat business."

"You take them?"

"And Walter and George and sometimes the waitresses when the kitchen quiets down."

She was conscious of the man named Duda; he was still watching her, but trying not to be seen. He seemed to favor that place by the jukebox or the far end of the bar behind the poles.

She was certain this was where the photo of Dawn and Debbie came from. Had the killer taken it himself or had he walked up and snatched it off the wall? Duda could have walked up and taken one of those photographs off the wall.

"The night those girls were here?"

"Uh-huh," Kenny said.

"Did they have their picture taken?"

Kenny looked thoughtful, then shook his head. "The way they were flaunting it, it wouldn't surprise me, but I didn't take any. It would have been George or Walter. I'd ask them tomorrow."

She looked at her watch. It was time to get going, she thought. She did want to look at Duda's car before he left. Duda, who was here so late, so interested in everyone, so mysterious.

"Last call." Kenny turned to Duda, who ordered a beer.

Hastings walked toward the ladies' room, then passed it, along with a hall to the kitchen and a glass oval-paned door, a time clock with employee punch cards on the wall just behind it.

She circled into the lobby, walked out the front door, and picked up her pace into the parking lot. The blue Firebird was easy enough to find. She put her penlight on it, wrote down the tag, watching over her shoulder at the door. It had damage all over it; the tires were threadbare. She saw a naked hula girl dangling from the mirror with half a dozen scented Christmas trees. There was lots of junk in the backseat and on the floor, but nothing particularly interesting.

There were a few other cars in the upper lot outside the restaurant. Tags from Maryland, Delaware, Ohio, New York. She saw several cars with Pennsylvania tags: a Mercedes, an Acura, a Volvo, and a Cadillac convertible. The only other car that didn't look like it belonged to one of the guests at the inn was an old Chrysler. Probably it belonged to Kenny the bartender. She wrote the tag down, circled it, and played the light inside. There were old newspapers on the floor, jackets and ball caps, and an empty Taco Bell cup.

She thought about the employee time cards behind the kitchen door. All the staff's names would be there. All the dates they were working would be stamped on them. Come tomorrow everyone in town would know the cops were here and things like that might begin to disappear. She thought she should have a look at them.

Billy Duda was slowly finishing his last beer and the Dixie Chicks were on the jukebox when she returned. He must have put a quarter in after Kenny gave him last call. She could see his hands; he was playing with his folding money, then his head would come around the corner and as quickly disappear. He was definitely weird, she thought. Definitely worth a run through NCIC.

Fifteen minutes later, Duda stacked a handful of change for a tip, took a final look at Hastings, and stood, weaving just a little on his way toward the door.

Kenny winked, finished polishing a glass, walked to the windows, and pulled the plugs on the neon lights. He locked a patio door. "You mind sitting here just for a moment while I switch one of the kegs in the basement? The township cop comes by every night at two A.M., shines his light in the window, and I flip this light switch here, outside lights over the parking lot. He likes to know everything's all right. It makes him feel good. They really don't have anything else to do around here. But just say no if you want to get going, I understand. I'll wait until he comes and do my work later."

Hastings looked toward the kitchen entrance where the time clock was. "No." She shook her head. "Go on, do what you have to, I'll watch for your policeman."

She felt tired suddenly; the clock on the wall said it was five minutes till 2 A.M. That last drink had hit her a little harder than she'd expected.

She waited until his footsteps receded to silence, then moved quickly toward the kitchen door, tripped over her own feet, and bumped into a dining room chair, cursing softly.

There was a dim light behind the kitchen door; she didn't know where the basement was, but Kenny had gone around the front, so she was sure she'd have at least a few minutes alone. She pushed open the swinging door, stepped toward the metal wall rack, looking at the staggered time cards. Adams . . . Delaporta . . . Dentin . . . she reached to grab them but misjudged the distance. The writing was going in and out of focus; she heard footsteps behind her, loud across the old oak floors. She backed into a waste can, knocked it over, spun, and fell as the door swung open.

The next thing she remembered was Kenny standing over her, helping her to her feet and leading her along the bar, which she used as a handrail. She fell onto a stool, wondering where she was; she began dabbing at her blouse with her hand as if she had spilled something, but there was nothing to spill in her hands.

What was going on? What was happening? she wondered.

"Cheese," Kenny said. She saw a white flash, blinding her. A camera flash. He was taking a picture of her.

"Who? Oh, shit," she said, laughing, "I spilled by, no, I spilled *my* . . . oh, shit, is that fummy?"

She took a deep breath and swayed in her seat.

Kenny took another picture, then another.

Pictures, she thought dreamily, like pictures on the wall, like pictures of those he killed. Killed?

She needed to go home. She needed to get into her

car and go home, but that wasn't right. That wasn't all that was wrong. There was something else that was wrong, something missing.

A hand moved to her hip, but nothing was there. No gun in her holster, no gun, that was what was wrong, no gun.

"I need air." She lurched from her stool and took a step toward the door.

And she saw the floor and then nothing.

16

Waterdrum, Pennsylvania

The roof was missing on top of the silo. She could look straight up through the trees and above the leaves to the blue sky. The walls were old and made of huge yellow ceramic blocks, covered with creeping moss and brown cords of ivy. Tiny purple flowers grew out of the yeasty-smelling silage that had solidified over the decades. The only way in and out was a small trapdoor on the wall of the silo a dozen feet above her. He had pulled up the ladder after he'd thrown her into it.

You could scream your lungs out and hear nothing but echoes. Even the world was silent about her; she could not hear a bird chirp, not a squirrel in the trees, not a car, not a plane, not a siren, nothing.

The silence was killing her as much as the anticipation of her fate. It was nearly torturous and she had taken to humming, talking to herself.

Ketamine, called Special K on the club scene, three milligrams dissolved in her drink would have been enough to knock her out for a whole night. She was here when she woke up, still dressed. She'd wet her pants, she knew that much. Probably whatever was going to happen to her was yet to come.

She knew who Kenny was now. She knew she was going to die. And the worst thing about it was, like the women in Cumberland, it would be years before anyone found her. Someone could be standing on the other side of the silo and never hear her screams. The only way anyone would find her would be to go through that trapdoor above her head, and she didn't doubt it was concealed from the inside.

Even after he killed her he could cover her with hay and a bucket of lime. No one would find her until these walls came tumbling down. She'd be bones and rotting shoes, an empty fucking holster, by then. How the fuck could she have been so stupid?

If only she had called Palmer and told him where she was staying; at least she'd had the sense to leave him a note. He'd trace her to the last gas station she'd filled up at in Somerset. Thank God she'd used a credit card.

Maybe they'd talk to the waitress at the restaurant where she'd ordered the hamburger near Laurel Mountain Park. She'd told people there she was going to Waterdrum.

Eventually he'd talk to Nestor. Palmer'd end up at the Trail's End Inn and show her picture around. Eventually . . . was that hours or days or weeks to come?

Kenny the bartender would have undoubtedly cleaned out her room and hidden her car, erased the room charges. He couldn't erase memories, though. She had talked to Jean. The other bartender, Walter. Sooner or later someone was going to remember that she had been at the tavern and it was late, figured she must have had a room. Kenny would be the last person who saw her. And then . . .

She thought about Jean. Jean would be back in Pittsburgh soon, long past wondering why she hadn't shown for a breakfast date. She might ask Kenny tonight what happened to her. Or maybe Kenny wasn't going back to work. Maybe he would kill her and move on, now that he knew the police were so close.

He couldn't use her cell phone; a cop's cell phone would be GPS-enabled. He "borrowed" three from the lost and found basket behind the bar, along with a page of the hotel registration he'd razored from the book. It wouldn't be long before they figured she was here. He'd already run her room charge through

American Express when she checked in. Clearing the charge wouldn't take it out of the system. In fact, it might look even more suspicious to someone going through her records.

Her belongings from the room he put in the trunk of her car. The car, along with his own, he parked in the barn.

They would use airplanes to look for a cop, but no one would see her from the air. It was black in that silo, all of it in shadow and covered by trees. There were only thirty or forty minutes a day that the sun was directly overhead.

In time they would put people into the woods, and then dogs, but it would all be over by then. It would be much too late to do anything about him.

He knew they'd have his fingerprints soon, and then they'd match him by a driver's license to Utah, use his picture to put him in Kansas and Missouri and then Cumberland. He laughed. He'd save them the trouble. They wouldn't need to bother with any of that. Not after this morning.

They'd know everything they ever needed to know about him the next time he called Sherry Moore.

It wasn't quite ten. George Thorpe would be wondering why he wasn't at work. It would be the first day he'd ever missed. George would have one of the waitresses mix drinks, probably Shelly. He wouldn't be angry until noon, then he'd start to second-guess the scheduling.

No one would be seriously concerned about his whereabouts until Walter came in for the evening shift and by then it wouldn't matter.

He dialed Sherry's number.

"It's me."

"Go ahead," she said.

"No good morning, hi, how are you?"

Palmer was running upstairs to his office in Harrisburg. He had just been notified of the call going through to Sherry's residence in Philadelphia.

There was a trooper waiting for him, pointing at the headphones and looking grimly at a map spread on a desk that detailed southwestern Pennsylvania.

He had been trying to get Corporal Hastings on the phone all morning. He looked at his desk, but there were still no messages. No recordings on his voice mail.

"I didn't realize how close you were getting," the voice said to Sherry Moore.

"Meaning what?" Sherry said plainly.

"I didn't plan on the policewoman."

Palmer looked at the trooper. He shrugged.

Sherry wasn't sure what the caller was talking about either. Apparently he suspected the police were getting close. Maybe the FBI?

"You want to talk to me, don't you?"

"Yes."

"Then you will have to make some concessions."

"I don't have to do anything, Sherry. You're the one who has to do things. I'm the one with Corporal Hastings."

Sherry grimaced.

Back in the state capital Palmer felt like he'd been hit in the stomach with a hammer.

He sat down hard and looked at Mary's last note to him, in the in box on his desk.

"Your policewoman. Ask your police friends listening in. They're missing someone, aren't they?"

Palmer put his head back against the chair. It was every cop's worst nightmare. One of their own in the hands of a monster.

"I'm listening," Sherry said. She was wondering what was going on. Hastings was one of Palmer's people. A state police officer. How had they gotten to him so quickly?

"Norwich, Connecticut."

Now it was Sherry who felt like she'd been struck.

"Things come full circle, don't they?"

Sherry found herself unable to speak.

Palmer was off the earphones, trying to reach the colonel.

"I read about it in a magazine recently. I didn't know you'd been to Norwich while I was away. I grew up there in Norwich. They said that you blew those schoolyard murders. That you led the cops on a wild goose chase."

Sherry had many regrets in her life, but none affected her more than Norwich. In the end it wasn't her fault, she'd learned that only later, but the fact remained she'd caused the mistake. She'd caused the police to divert precious manpower to search in the wrong place for the missing children. And then they all died. It was difficult not to feel guilt over that.

"Let's talk about now," Sherry said.

"No, let's talk about Norwich. Let's talk about what you see after death," he said. "You told the police those children were near a beach by a lifeguard stand. That little girl that died in your arms, how old was she? Seven? Eight? You must have been devastated. I know what it's like to watch someone die. You must have tried so hard to see what she saw, and yet when you couldn't, you just sent the police on a chase, far away from where they were, far from the basement of that old school to the beaches of Long Island Sound. They said there would have been enough air in that old air raid shelter to last them another day. If only they had looked in the children's own neighborhood instead of listening to you. Instead of looking at a beach when it turned out that little girl had never even been to a beach. Not in her whole short life."

Sherry bit her lip.

"Why were you wrong, Sherry? How could you blow something so important? Did you make it all up? Is that what you're doing with me, just making it all up?"

Sherry couldn't go on. She knew she was supposed

to keep him talking about Corporal Hastings, but she couldn't continue.

Norwich, the beginning of the nightmares, the very first time Sherry noticed the monsters in her zoo. It was ironic that she had just been thinking about it. Norwich had been the first of the things that Sherry had not dealt with, not handled well. John had often told her she needed to put Norwich to rest. She had forgotten about the terrible headaches, the sleepless nights, and then so many things happened so quickly last summer. And Norwich was still there at the bottom of the pile.

She remembered the emotion of the moment. A child ran into the street and was hit by a car; she was in and out of consciousness, then came the shocking news that she was one of the missing children from a small neighborhood in Norwich. Somehow she had escaped her captor. She must be able to tell where the other children were being held.

Sherry Moore was called immediately. There was little hope, the doctors thought, of saving her. Would Sherry please come to the hospital? The little girl's parents had read about her. They thought Sherry could save the other children's lives, if the worst were to happen.

The girl did die, it was exceedingly sad, and yet when Sherry took the little girl's hand, she felt elation that so strong a memory persisted in her final seconds of life. It never left her, not once in eighteen seconds.

She had been so excited about the prospect of finding all those children, she had never considered a child's way of thinking.

Later, after the children were found dead in an old school—a local sex offender, not registered, was keeping them in an old air raid shelter—she was assailed by the press, the parents of the dead children, the police, the clergy, everyone.

She'd never defended herself. She never later said that she believed what she saw was true. She took the criticism in silence as partial sentence for the role she played in their deaths.

She was told it wasn't her fault that the little girl who had gotten away from her kidnapper only to run into the path of a cab had died thinking of the calmest place she knew. The place she felt most safe, most loved, most happy. She had been thinking about her bed and a picture that hung on the wall over her head, of a lifeguard stand on a beach.

"Listen up, everybody. You cops listening in, get your pens out. There is a cemetery in Norwich. It's called Yantic, just above Hollyhock Island. The plot is 7873. Her name was Mary, just like your cop friend, Mary Hastings. You've done this before, so you'll all know what to do. Exhume her and we'll talk again."

"I can't do that," Sherry said.

"My name is Kenny Dentin," he said abruptly. "I've never changed it. You'll find out all about me soon enough. I want you—"

"I really can't do it," Sherry said. "There are legalities—"

"I don't give a damn about legalities, Miss Moore. I am giving you one opportunity to save this cop's life. I want to know what my mother was thinking about when she died. I want you to tell me word for word. Do you hear me? I have your cop. I want my mother exhumed. That's it." His voice was loud, he was losing control.

Sherry waited a moment, to let him calm.

"What if I could, Kenny? How would I tell you? What would happen next? I mean, you know you can't get away now, Kenny. And if you hurt Officer Hastings, things will be so much worse."

"Worse." He laughed. "Worse! Worse than being me, Sherry?" He was yelling again. "There's something worse than being me? Please, dear God, tell me what could be worse than that?"

He sighed loudly. "I will call you in a day. In exactly twenty-four hours. I will listen to what you have to say, and if you lie to me, I will kill Hastings while you are still on the phone. I will know if you are lying, Sherry. I will know. Do you want to know what I'll do to her? You've seen my work. I will put a noose around her neck and hang her from a hook."

"Kenny," Sherry said. "Just let her go. I'll do everything you want, but let her go. These things take time. I have some influence—"

"Liar," he screamed.

"No, Kenny, I'm not lying. I can do this. I can see your mother, just give me some time. Just let Officer Hastings go."

"You have a lot of traveling to do. I would suggest you tell your friends to get on the road. Twenty-four hours. You need to be there and then I want you back. No cell phones, no cop tricks, just you and me and whoever listens in on our conversations. I will call you and I will have questions and you had better answer them right."

Sherry was silent.

"You wouldn't want to miss my call. You wouldn't want to miss Officer Hastings's last words, would you?"

"Why don't—"

The phone went dead.

17

HARRISBURG, PENNSYLVANIA

The computers kicked out the name Kenny Dentin with a criminal history. The address he was using at the time was 33 Iroquois Drive. It was in the town of Confluence, on the river south of Waterdrum, one of the towns on Mary's list of places to visit.

Palmer had calls in to Connecticut, where they

were trying to unravel juvenile records for a Kenneth George Dentin of School Street in Norwich with the same date of birth.

He had messages in to the investigators who handled Dentin's assault charge. The victim had a record of prostitution; there might be a story there, but for now Palmer was on the phone with Phoenix Drug and Rehabilitation Center, Allegheny Department of Human Services.

"Kenneth George Dentin," Palmer barked into the phone. "D-E-N-T-I-N," he spelled out. "When did you last see him?"

The counselor hesitated. "I know that I'm not supposed—"

"Listen to me carefully," Palmer interrupted. "I'm going to hang up and you're going to get a call from a federal judge in Harrisburg. If you aren't on the phone talking to me five minutes later, I will come and I will take your files and I will place you under arrest for obstruction of justice and I will not care by then if you talk to me or not. Dentin is not under court-ordered care and you may not claim privilege to questions about his whereabouts. Are you beginning to understand me? You are a witness and that is all you are. And you do not want to become a hostile witness delaying the capture of a murderer. Believe me, you do not. Not with me."

Palmer had his answer in less than ten minutes. Dentin had gone to group therapy the day after the bodies were discovered in Cumberland. He had given an address in a trailer park in the town of Confluence eleven miles south of Waterdrum on the Youghiogheny River.

The counselor said he had shown up one night out of the blue and seemed distant in group, quiet, but that wasn't unusual. She had the impression he was working at a tourist bar. That's all. He drove an old green car, but she didn't know much about cars; it was kind of big or maybe medium.

There was a vehicle registration in the name of Kenneth G. Dentin; the address was the same trailer park, 33 Iroquois Drive. Troopers were amassing outside the place now. Palmer didn't think Dentin'd be stupid enough to still be there, but there were simply no rules when it came to this kind of thing.

They tried to locate Hastings's telephone; it was loaded with GPS but emitting no signal. Police had a broadcast to look out for her motor-pool car, and a description was given of Dentin, urging extreme caution.

Palmer thought of the women who had been assaulted by Dentin, stripped and strangled and brought back to life repeatedly. He tried not to imagine what Mary was going through now.

If only she had told him where she was going; was she working a plan, or was she stopping randomly at hotels and restaurants? He'd seen a copy of Nestor's list; he knew she'd be around the state parks and towns with river rafts and kayak rentals. But where in three counties had she been when she disappeared off the face of the earth?

Then it came, more bad news from Confluence, Pennsylvania. Kenny Dentin had not lived in that trailer park for more than a year. The man who owned it, Larry Whidden, said he'd moved out two or three tenants ago; he didn't keep real good records, but it wouldn't have mattered. Dentin always paid with cash.

The state police had effectively sealed off the north and south ends of Route 211 that split Fayette County. The murder of Karen Nestor and the two girls in Black Moshannon took place no more than a hundred miles from Confluence, where Kenny was last known to live.

He could be living anywhere in between. But somewhere in Hastings's travels, she had encountered him.

He picked up the phone. "Palmer."

It was Evelyn. The colonel was returning his call.

"Sir, we have to get Sherry to Norwich, sir."

"Dan, we have another problem." The colonel spoke softly, evenly.

"Sir?"

"The FBI was also intercepting Sherry Moore's calls."

"They were listening in on us?"

"They know all about Kenneth Dentin. The mother,

Mary, committed suicide in 1984. Kenneth's father moved them to Kansas. The boy was twelve at the time."

"Colonel . . ."

"Dan, I know what you're going to say. Just listen a moment, okay? Agent Springer has been leading a task force tracking a serial killer through the Midwest and Southwest for the past several years. They followed him back east in 2005—"

"To Cumberland," Palmer whispered angrily.

"They started looking into the Teng woman found hanging in Nemacolin. They think he might also be responsible for three hikers gone missing from the Laurel Highlands over the last two years."

"You want me to back off?" Palmer said angrily.

"They're already in Norwich, Dan. They've been to the cemetery. They're arranging to disinter the body."

"We have Sherry Moore."

"Dan, it's not a game," Karpovich said tiredly. "He has Hastings. That's all that matters to us."

Palmer slumped back in his chair. The colonel was right. Whatever worked the fastest was the right answer.

"Tell me what to do."

"The FBI is going to put a helicopter on Sherry's lawn. Talk to her. Tell her what we know. See that she's on it. I have a cell number for Agent Springer. Call Springer and let her know you've contacted Sherry. Springer will arrange to have an agent remain with Sherry to intercept the phone call when she gets back."

"Where is Hastings, sir? Do they know?"

"Dentin was working in Waterdrum at a place called the Trail's End Inn, not far from the tower that handled his last call."

"How long have they known?"

"We'll talk about that later, Dan."

"Hastings went in there blind. They could have warned us."

"Dan, when it's over. We wait until it's over," Karpovich said sternly.

Palmer's hands balled into fists.

"They have a satellite reserved for a six-hour window. The moment he calls, they'll lock onto him. Ten minutes later, we'll surround him. Ten minutes, Dan. It doesn't get any better than that."

Palmer knew what the colonel was saying. The state police could access digital information from cell phone providers, they all could; an Act of Congress known as CALEA required cell phone companies to assist law enforcement in locating or monitoring customer devices. But information to locate a single unit needed to be triangulated from three towers. There were things that could go wrong. If they lost the signal from any of the towers, they would get only part of the picture.

The FBI could do much better. One of their Echelon satellites could locate signals through global positioning, nailing its signal to within a hundred feet.

If Dentin was in the Western Hemisphere when he called Sherry Moore, he could not hide.

"We get Echelon, we get their SWATs, and we get every available East Coast agent. We'll put everything we have around that mountain and we'll be all over him before he knows what's hit him."

"Yes, sir," Palmer said. He knew it was the best that could be done. The FBI's resources couldn't be matched on earth, but he wouldn't forgive the fact that they could have prevented Hastings from being kidnapped in the first place.

No one was saying it, but everyone was wondering what Hastings was going through even now. Palmer knew you didn't want to be alone with this man, not for thirty hours, not for thirty minutes. No one could predict what kind of shape Mary would come back in, but Palmer kept thinking it didn't matter a hoot, as long as she came back. He would see they fixed her, no matter what.

"I'll call Sherry now and tell her what we need."

"Thanks." The colonel hung up.

Palmer picked up the phone, air conditioning tickling the sweat building up on the back of his neck. This wasn't happening, he told himself. This just can't be happening.

He looked at the wall clock. The FBI had just under twenty-four hours in which to disinter the remains of Mary Dentin, fly Sherry Moore to a helipad at Backus Hospital in Norwich, Connecticut, allow her to spend time with the remains, and get her home to intercept Dentin's call.

The FBI did not accept Sergeant Palmer's offer to accompany Sherry. In fact, the only thing they left for him to do was make the call to Mary Hastings's parents to tell them she was missing and that a manhunt was in progress to locate her.

Palmer wondered what he should do after that call. He thought about going to Philadelphia to await Sherry Moore's return, but there was going to be an FBI agent with her once she returned from Connecticut, so there was little he could do but wonder what was happening around Waterdrum.

If he went to Waterdrum, he'd have no influence over the FBI net around the town. Maybe he should go just to be there when Hastings was found. Hastings would need a friendly face. Hastings, if she was still alive, would need all the help she could get.

Sherry Moore's helicopter flew over Yantic Cemetery on its way to Backus Hospital in Norwich. The pilot, talking to her through her headphones, described the large white-and-yellow tent covering a portion of the tombstones by the railroad tracks. Black FBI Suburbans and minivans surrounded the area, he said.

The whole thing reminded her of the Norwich schoolyard murders in 2003—the air temperature, the heavy whopping percussion of the blades as they descended on evening rush hour. You never knew what was going to happen when you did these things. Never knew what you would be thinking as you flew away from a place like this. It would be for most people like feeling for a light switch in a dark room, not knowing what was inside. Both excited and afraid by what you might see.

She had been surprised on occasion with indescribable elation, and she had been saddened to the point of devastation, unable to think of much else for days afterward, at least until she had the time to put things in perspective.

Such a gift, but at such a price.

She didn't feel cheated; that was all of life, she thought. You didn't need to have eyes to see that there were no free rides. Not for anyone. You took the bad with the good and the older you got, the more you appreciated the difference.

You learned to be thankful for smaller things, thankful even for the joys you once had lost. At least you had them . . . At least I had him, Sherry thought, feeling John Payne's presence in the cabin.

"Thank God I knew you," she whispered.

"Ma'am?" The pilot turned to look over his shoulder.

"Mumbling," she said, smiling out the window, feeling sunshine radiating across her arm and her knee.

The FBI agent, a female who was quite young, took her arm when the helicopter landed and rushed her across the tarmac to a door.

The interior of the building was cold; she heard the muted sounds of an emergency center, but they moved away from it through the halls to an elevator. More people were waiting there and got on with them. The car went down several floors. The doors opened. "Ms. Moore?" a man said. "My name is Agent Samuels." He didn't bother to reach for the blind woman's hand. "Right this way, please."

Their footsteps fell in noisy discord. There were four of them now and they slowed for the whoosh of a glass door.

"Take her in," Samuels instructed.

The female agent, still unnamed, led Sherry by the arm into the morgue. The ceramic walls hurled echoes back and forth. She sensed a large glass window to her right. There were softer things, a plastic curtain, perhaps, in front of her. Sherry thought she detected wood, cabinets most likely.

"Do you need some kind of equipment? Masks or gloves or anything?" the agent asked. She must have drawn the short straw, or more likely she was junior to the rest and had no choice but to take Sherry into the morgue.

"I need you to get me to her side and help me locate her hand. That's all," Sherry said pleasantly.

She could block out the repellent odors and images of what the corpse might have looked like. The part of her that held a hand operated on a completely mechanical level, like a surgeon who works on burn patients: the sights and smells lost relevance, the endeavor was purely clinical, detached.

There was something in front of her, a light green wall, a picture of something, blurry, too unfocused to discern. Something was over her face; she could see down, her body was bare, feet bare, she was naked, something on the floor below her, something broken, something not right?

She saw the vague image of a toilet, an open door . . . a baby in a blanket . . . she saw an old man, his face creased, there were large blackheads all over his nose and the bottom half of his right ear was missing. His breath was rancid, his teeth unclean, he had his hand over her mouth as he licked her forehead.

There was a goldfish in a bowl, a ceramic angel on a clapboard dresser. She saw these things sideways, head on a bed, yellowed, stained sheets; the room smelled of cats and unwashed laundry.

She saw a cake, candles, someone's birthday . . . she was carrying something . . .

Ceiling blurred, glass lightbulbs, blood, a sandy-haired boy, and a shiny bicycle.

Something in her hands, dark, black, a hood, no, a mask with holes for eyes and a long hose to breath through.

There was a piece of construction paper in her hand, folded, there were pictures drawn in crayon . . . she was handing it to the wrinkled man with half an ear.

He took it and pulled her into his lap and yanked her by the hair, forcing her to look up at him. "No," she mouthed. "Daddy, no . . ."

The FBI's helicopter dropped onto Sherry's lawn and she was taken by the arm and pulled away from the rotor wash. She could hear the machine rising vertically over the seawall, then banking south over the Delaware River. Someone yelled in the background; a car engine started. The young female agent was still with her; she was going to remain with her while she took the call and Agent Samuels would fly back to Pittsburgh, where an army was amassing to assault the hills surrounding Waterdrum.

The phone call made her nervous. There was no way to know what Dentin wanted to hear or what questions he would ask her, and she knew that Mary Hastings's life depended on her now.

She thought about that for a moment. What did Dentin want to hear? The way things were or the way he wanted them to be?

In less than an hour it was going to be over. One way or another it was going to be over for Mary Hastings.

18

WATERDRUM, PENNSYLVANIA

The FBI and the Pennsylvania state police command buses were parked in two adjoining parking lots overlooking the falls in Waterdrum. Springer was in the back of one, talking on the phone with Agent Samuels. A pair of technicians was in a portion of the bus ready to intercept the call. Springer was in command of operations. She would be the first to hear the location where Dentin was holding his hostage. She would dispatch the SWAT teams first—they were waiting in a large black Sikorsky helicopter outside her door, ready to drop and to assault whatever coordinates she gave them.

The town, usually busy this time of year, had been easily emptied because the lots and grounds along the river were property of the National Park Service. A paved clearing afforded a helipad for their staging. There was no more need to be secretive. The logistics would dictate that they shut the mountain down, and as a matter of course, the town nestled within.

The FBI knew which tower he had been transmitting through and they knew that his signal strength put him within twenty-five miles of a particular longitude and latitude, so they were focusing on a circle of just under 2,000 square miles. Most of that was uninhabited forest, but several hundred rural homes and farms were scattered around the mountain. Any one of them could be Dentin's hiding place.

As long as he didn't change locations, which didn't seem likely with a hostage in tow, he was contained. The police and the FBI had started locking down the perimeter around him within an hour of his call to Sherry Moore. There were barricades on every road surrounding Waterdrum. Everyone had a description of the two wanted cars. Everyone was searching outgoing vehicles, including the backs of vans and trucks. Nothing was getting out of the area surrounding Waterdrum without inspection.

He was trapped as surely as Hastings.

Sherry Moore thought about the things she had learned in Norwich from Agent Samuels. He told her that Dentin's father had worked part-time jobs and was rarely at home when the boy was growing up. His mother, Mary, was never a stable source of affection. Mary wasn't altogether there, the family and neighbors said. Mary saw psychiatrists.

Norwich detectives had long suspected Mary Dentin's was an autoerotic death. There were scars and bruises from old wounds around her neck. There was no suicide note. Her nylon stockings had been put on backward, seams to the front of her legs, which told the investigators the obvious. The scene had been cleansed before they arrived and there was no one else at home to do it but the twelve-year-old child.

There seemed little reason to make it worse on the family, the prosecutor agreed. Suicide, intentional or accidental, was suicide. There was little point in embarrassing the family further or highlighting what the boy had witnessed. The kid was probably going to be affected enough by what he'd witnessed.

What a shame, they'd said. It was the eve of his birthday. There was to have been a party next door. He was expecting a bicycle, the neighbor boy said.

What must he have thought when he found his mother?

Kenny stretched his legs, cramped from sitting for the past four hours. That's when he first entered the property, just after he'd seen the helicopter taking Sherry Moore to Connecticut rise above the trees and peel off to the east. He came in through a neighbor's lawn; none of them would pay any mind to a nicely dressed man wearing Corporal Hastings's gold shield on his belt. The neighbors would be insensible to the comings and goings of cops by now. He need only appear confident as always.

Once he was in the perimeter, he circled the house until he found an open window into a walk-in pantry. The house would be alarmed. He wouldn't dare pass a hand through the screen until she was home again, but then he would have a chance. People never alarmed their homes when they were inside during the daylight hours.

Meanwhile he found a small outbuilding used to store tools and a lawn tractor with an unlocked door. He maneuvered his shoulders between the slender opening and carried away spiderwebs that stuck to his face and shirt. It was damp inside the shed; windows had been left open to dry the place out.

He took a folded mat of canvas and laid it out on the floor, then lay down and slept. It was the first sleep he'd had since meeting Corporal Hastings.

Five hours later an SUV pulled into the driveway. Almost immediately he could hear the whopping blades of the returning helicopter.

He peeked through the windows as the craft settled on the lawn. Sherry stepped out and agents took her around the front of the house. Not long afterward the SUV left, absent the female agent. Sherry was inside with a guard.

He crossed the lawn under trees to the open window, pried the screen out, and hoisted himself through the opening.

The pantry shelves were filled with canned goods. In one corner there hung winter coats, boots, and gloves paired and set out neatly on a rack.

He had Hastings's gun and a syringe full of Darkene. The pantry door was open a crack. He could see across the kitchen to the foyer.

He kicked off his shoes and waited. Entering the house into the pantry was his good fortune. Sooner or later, one of them would come into the kitchen. That was almost a certainty and from where he stood he could see them and not be seen.

He would not need to search the house for them. He would wait for his opportunity. Then the balance of power would change.

Sherry excused herself once they were inside and allowed Agent Ross to make herself at home. Ross paced the kitchen, opened the double stainless doors of the refrigerator, ran a finger across the expensive marble counter. The place was fucking huge, she thought, bigger than any kitchen she had ever been in before. And that view of the river from the backyard, what a fucking waste on a blind lady. You could rock till the sun came up on that patio and all your friends could tie their boats to that dock. Jesus, she'd love to have a pad like this. Maybe she should take up palm-reading on the side, she thought dryly.

She slapped the back of her arm, spun to swat whatever stung her, and saw a man's face come in and out of focus before she hit the ground.

"Sleep," Kenny whispered.

The cat padded into the kitchen, rubbed its whiskers over the agent's nose, then circled through Kenny's feet before sauntering away, back in the direction of the living room.

He followed it in stocking feet, looking around corners, seeing nothing but the cat, which continued down a hall, ignoring rooms to its right and left, slowly but surely bending corners toward a distant wing of the house.

He followed quietly, at last seeing the cat turn under an archway and pass between double doors pinned open on their hinges.

There was music playing in the room. He walked slowly toward the doors, careful not to make any noise. She was sitting in a chair, facing a wall of glass that overlooked the river.

"Agent Ross?"

"No. It's me, Sherry."

She sighed out loud.

The chair swiveled and she turned to face him.

He wiped the sweat from his lip. "I suppose everyone's on the edge of their seat. Fifteen minutes to showtime. I'll bet they're running around Waterdrum like an army of ants. Ready to rush in and kill me; they only need to know which direction to go."

"Is Agent Ross going to be all right?"

"Ross, yes. Agent Ross will come around in a few hours."

Sherry nodded. "And Corporal Hastings?"

"Hastings is fine, Miss Moore. I wanted you instead."

"You want to know about your mother?"

"I want to get close to you first, Sherry."

"You're talking nonsense. Why don't we talk about your mother, that's the real reason you're here."

"I used to love her, did you gather that?" He looked around the room. "But of course you probably twist that in some sick way. You probably think I'm a pervert."

"I don't think anything."

"And I don't mean it like that."

"It's normal to love your mother," Sherry said.

"All mothers aren't the same, you know. You didn't know mine. No one did. I'm not killing her when I kill. You probably think that too; everyone probably thinks that." He wiped his eyes with the heel of his hand, taking a step closer to her.

"Why don't you tell me where Corporal Hastings is?" Sherry stood to face him.

She heard the hammer snap back on the gun. It was an automatic, no sound of a revolver's cylinder rotating, probably Hastings's weapon, a ten-shot .40 caliber, she guessed.

"I've read all about you, Sherry. You so much as lift a foot from the ground and I'll kill you."

"I'm hardly a threat to you." She laughed.

"And I'm hardly an idiot." He dropped his bag to the floor, knelt, removed handcuffs, and slid them across the floor. "Put them on your ankles."

"Put what on?"

"You know goddamn well what. Kneel, pick them up, and put them on."

"I thought you came to talk."

"I came to do what I please, now put them on or we walk to the kitchen and I put a bullet in Agent Ross's head."

Sherry knelt slowly, gauging the distance, thinking he'd get two shots off before she could reach his legs. She picked up the handcuffs and snapped one over her ankle.

"Do the other."

She did.

"Now tighten them. I want to see you tighten them."

Sherry ratcheted the cuffs tight against her skin.

"Now sit. On the floor."

Sherry sat. "I'm not going to tell you anything if you harm me."

He reached in his bag and slid a second set of cuffs across the floor. "Snap it over your wrist."

"Don't do this. Don't make things any worse."

"Do it!" he screamed.

Sherry picked up the cuffs and snapped one side over her left wrist.

"Now turn, just slide around so I can see the hands behind your back. Put your hands behind your back."

Sherry wondered if he knew how to use the gun, if she'd have a second chance if he fired and missed the first time. It wouldn't take much to hit her, though; even panicked, he was close enough to get lucky.

She spun slowly around, wondering what the police would do if the call didn't come through on time. Knowing they would wait ten minutes and then ten more. If anything, the FBI might become concerned if Agent Ross didn't check in. She wondered if the agent had to maintain contact at prearranged times, but then decided not. Everyone was on pins and needles about the phone call. They would all want to maintain silence until that connection was made to her phone and its signal bounced off a satellite six hundred miles up.

"Put it over your other wrist and push them tight. I want to hear it."

Sherry complied.

He relaxed. He laid the pistol on the glass table and knelt to reach in his bag again.

"I wanted those women to be enough, to be the last," he said, removing a gas mask from the bag. "They didn't know me and they didn't care about me at first. But the longer they were with me, the more they liked me and realized it was me that mattered, no one but me."

"When you were strangling them, when you were playing with their life's breath, you honestly believe they were thinking about you?" she asked, unmoved.

Silence.

"Love," Sherry said. "You know the difference, don't you, between love and fear?"

"It wasn't fear. It was more than fear."

He was moving, to her left, circling her. He wasn't

wearing shoes, but she could hear him nonetheless. She followed the sound, and when there was no sound, she listened to the returning echoes of her voice. Echoes that would tell her what kinds of things were surrounding her; glass, metal, wood, human. Even more important, distance.

"You always knew that, though," she told him. "That they feared you, not loved you. They didn't even respect you. I think that's part of the reason you couldn't look at their faces. You were afraid to see their disgust. You only wanted to see their eyes."

Silence.

"That's why you put the mask on them, wasn't it? You wanted to see how their eyes reacted to you. Were they terrified, pleading, silently suppliant? You wanted to interpret that as love. You wanted that to be love. And then you got addicted. You couldn't stop yourself, because you couldn't remember anymore—"

"Have you ever tried it?" he yelled. "Have you never cut your finger and held it dripping over a sink a minute longer than necessary, mesmerized by the sound of your own blood dripping, leaving your body, knowing you are a drop closer to death with each second, wondering how many more it would take, five hundred, five thousand? Have you never held your breath to see how long you could deprive the brain of oxygen?"

"Curiosity is not the same as control," Sherry said.

"I'm talking about seduction, Sherry. Death is seduction, is it not? I've seen the ministers and mail carriers out there, the nurses and accountants and lawyers and teachers. They come to the red-light districts at night. They want to be beaten. They want to be humiliated. They want to be violated by strangers in the night. You know why? Because they want to feel something and the only way they can feel is to risk losing control of their life."

"You want to believe that. You want to believe that you're no different than anyone else."

"Everyone has their little things, Sherry, even you. What are your little things? What are your fantasies?"

"No," Sherry said. "Not everyone kills. Not everyone thinks like you."

He was moving now, getting closer, still circling her.

"But then not everyone saw what you saw when you were just a boy."

He stopped, made a noise, not a word, but more guttural. "What did you see?" His voice had a tremor to it. He was moving fast around her again.

"I saw everything," Sherry said. She spun on her behind, following his voice, but now only approximately, never looking straight at him, wanting to appear confused about precisely where he was in the room. At last she stared at a place just off to his left.

"Did you see me in her memory? Did you ever see me in any of those women's memories, Sherry?"

"You told me you would let Hastings go if I told you about your mother. Tell me where she is. Let them send help to her."

"I'll tell you once you've told me what I want to know."

"Want to know or want to hear, Kenny. You just want me to say that she was thinking about you. You needed to hear that more than anything else in the world."

"I want to know it all. I want to know what you saw. That way I'll know if you're lying," he hissed.

He wouldn't kill me, she thought. He wouldn't kill me until he heard me out.

She planted her feet and began to rise.

"Get down," he hissed again. "Get down."

Sherry continued to rise until she was standing tall, still looking at a place just off to his left.

She thought about his mother, about Mary Dentin's last seconds of life. She thought about what Agent Samuels had told her in Norwich.

"You found her hanging."

"She killed herself," he sobbed. "She was sick and she was depressed and she killed herself."

"She didn't want to kill herself, Kenny. Did she?"

Silence.

"She wouldn't have wanted you to find her like that."

"Stop," Kenny gasped. "I want you to put on the mask."

"My eyes are dead, Kenny. What is it you want to hide? You can't look truth in the face, can you? You keep seeing your mother and you can't find the truth in her."

"She committed suicide."

"No, Kenny. She didn't want to die. There was a part of her that just didn't want to remember. Just like there is a part of you that doesn't want to remember."

He was crying.

"She was naked. She was wearing the mask, wasn't she. She didn't want to die, she wanted to live. She wanted to feel something. You said it yourself. The idea of risk was seductive. Better than the shame she carried, better than the confusion over not being able to feel love."

"She wanted to die," he sobbed. "She always wanted to die, because she didn't love me, because she didn't love anything but herself. She would have killed me, if she had the chance. She knew I'd be just like her."

"No, Kenny, she needed the mask to pretend she was not the little girl in her memories. The child who was abused. She wanted to feel love, but the closest she would ever come was sex."

"You lie, you lie," he bawled. "She wasn't like that at all."

"Who was the man with half an ear?"

He looked at her. "Grandpa?" he sniffed.

There was a very long moment of silence. Sherry could only imagine his confusion, then realization, and a long mournful moan came from him.

"Grandpa?" he said incredulously.

"He abused your mother."

Sherry backed away from him toward the glass table, feet shuffling silently.

"Don't," she heard him say; he was following her, getting closer.

"What was she thinking, when she died?"

Sherry knew it had come down to just this. Since he was twelve years old, this question had germinated in his mind like a seed, finally taking root, growing, changing, searching for light with each woman he killed.

Lie or tell the truth? she wondered. Which one meant life for her and which one meant death?

"Your birthday," she said, still shuffling her feet, backing away from him toward the door. "She was thinking about a bicycle."

Sherry had moved a quarter of the way across the room when she stopped and stood perfectly erect. Then she fell backward as if she were standing on the edge of a cliff, just let herself go, dead weight dropping, hands behind midback, forearms striking the glass table, which exploded into shards and splinters that rained across the floor.

He ran toward her but by then she had already found the gun and was rolling onto her stomach.

Facedown with the Glock in hands cuffed behind her back, she fired three times as he dove upon her. When he landed, his weight slammed her face and body to the floor.

A clock in the opposite wing of the house began to chime, distant at first but then growing louder like a morning's dream coming to surface. The gun in Sherry's hand was pinned between their bodies, wrist bent awkwardly to one side.

There was no skill in firing a gun from behind your back; the closer the target, the better chance you had of hitting it, that was all that she had in her favor. Consequently there was no way to know what damage she had done to him.

She opened her mouth to speak and a bolt of searing pain shot between her jaw and temple. Her tongue found a three-inch sliver of glass that had penetrated her cheek.

"Corporal Hastings," she croaked, drooling the metallic-tasting blood from the corner of her mouth. "Tell me where she is."

A warm sensation spread across her shoulder, down the back of her arm to her elbow where it pooled between her blouse and the body on top of her, blood from the gunshot or other punctures or lacerations from the broken glass? His blood, her blood, there was no way to know.

She wondered if Agent Ross was dead or if, as he said, she would come to in a matter of hours.

Transferring weight to her hip, she attempted to roll his body from her back. It took a minute, but she succeeded, his body landed hard on the broken glass to her side. She let the gun slip out of her hand, rolled and extended her cuffed hands to reach the dead man, trying to find his own hand, wanting to know if he was thinking about Hastings in the end. She found it and squeezed and waited and there was nothing. She saw nothing!

The panic started in the base of her stomach, adrenaline rushing from two small glands by the kidneys, flooding her bloodstream in seconds. She dropped his hand and rolled about frantically searching for the gun.

There was movement, a scraping noise; then a hand seized her hair and yanked it back, rubber of the gas mask cupping her chin, snapping off the sliver of glass that was protruding from her cheek, he roughly pulled the mask over her face and across the back of her head to complete the hooding.

She thought in those last seconds before the mask completely covered her ears that she'd heard a wet gurgling sound, but all was muted now, all but the sound of her own breathing. She remembered the long tube from the face of the mask that she had seen in some of his victims' memories. Soon he would be stuffing that tube, blocking it off to rob her of oxygen. Soon he would begin playing the game of give and take.

She filled her lungs as he began to roll her on her back, straddling her, grabbing the end of the respirator hose. She could feel the rubber collapsing as he covered the opening.

The mask steamed inside. She held her breath as long as she could, releasing it slowly into the vacuum of space, waiting, waiting, at last instinctively trying to take a breath that wasn't there.

She fought the mask, fought the knees pinning her shoulders to the floor. She sliced her tongue on the sliver of glass that had punctured her cheek. A field of stars filled her vision and a voice called out to her, a voice so familiar, so gentle, so far removed in time.

"Mom," she mouthed the word as a rush of unexpected air touched her lips, pain excruciating as the man's knee drove forcefully into her left shoulder. He was shifting that way, from right to left, transferring all his weight in that direction when suddenly he toppled over, the top of his body striking the floor.

Sherry filled her lungs with the rushing hollow sound of air drawn through the respirator tube. She lay there gasping like that, spitting blood to clear her throat. His right leg was still lying across her torso and she rolled to the right until it too fell to the floor. Then she rolled back toward him, pushing her handcuffed wrists away from her body, fingers opening and closing, clutching to find his belt, his elbow, a wrist, at last a hand that she squeezed and saw *bloody hands grasping a black tube from the front of a rubber mask, her eyes behind the windows looking back, a man in a rocking chair, a dilapidated barn with a yellow brick silo, a trapdoor, a woman lying in a circle of brown and yellow grain, an old man with half an ear, a pretty dark-haired woman in a green dress, a hallway, a closed door, same dark-haired woman hanging from a light fixture, she was naked and masked, her brown eyes looking down through the glass windows, pleading, begging... comprehending.*

There were muffled sounds from deep in the house, vibrations of running feet, voices shouting.

People were entering the room, hands were grabbing her shoulders.

"Sherry," Palmer panted. Someone else was yelling orders to get handcuff keys. "Sherry, are you all right? Sherry?" He gently lifted the mask, starting with the sleeve around her throat, peeling it carefully off her chin, her face, across the top of her head and away from her wet hair.

Her voice was barely a whisper, hoarse, measured, sounding foreign to her own ears.

"She's in a silo, Dan. A pale yellow silo made of brick."

Acknowledgments

As always I thank Paul Fedorko, my agent and wizard behind the screen. To Colin Fox, senior editor, and the countless people at Simon & Schuster who work so enthusiastically on my behalf. To Cindy Collins—my first reader—for sound advice and punctuation, a faculty that has escaped me all my life.

1

Denali
Alaska

Raw winds hailed lacerating ice, stinging earlobes and ruddy cheeks beneath the climber's black snow goggles. The storm had an undergrowl that suggested it was both alive and malevolent.

It came out of nowhere as polar storms do, the clockwise rotation of Pacific highs meeting counterclockwise Siberian lows, fusing to form a cyclone in ancient cauldrons of granite and glacier. Mountains the size of Denali virtually produce their own weather.

Allison Metcalf descended the headwall below the summit clipped to a fixed line, testing the ice with crampons on the toes of her boots. The well-trod western approach was quickly vanishing under their feet, transmuting into an alien environment of wind-sculpted ice. She took another step and then another, trying to quell the rise of panic. Only three hours ago they had stood on top of the Western Hemisphere. Now they were in a race for their lives to get beneath it.

The spatial world was no more. There were no more ups and downs, no rights or lefts. One could reach out an arm and not see the glove beyond the wrist. If any of the climbers were to unclip from the fixed line, even for a moment, it was doubtful they would find it again; more likely they would wander off the side of the mountain or fall into one of the hundreds of bottomless crevices of prehistoric ice.

"You okay?" Sergio's voice caught faintly on the wind. He was below her, but still close, only a dozen feet away. *Was he straggling to look out for her?*

"Okay," she yelled, but the words evaporated on a blast of chilled air. She tugged gently on the line tethered between them and a moment later she felt his acknowledgment. It felt good, this tangible connection to another human being.

If they could descend at least to high camp at 17,000 feet, they might survive the night in the uppermost cradle of the summit. The poor buggers above Archdeacon's Tower had yet to negotiate an exposed knife-edged ridge. They would not be so lucky, would not last an hour when the sun dropped below the horizon and wind chills plummeted below minus sixty degrees. Allison could not imagine a night of terror in subzero hurricane winds, tethered to four other people in the open, any of whom might panic and make a fatal error for all of them.

Allison had only met two of the other climbers from the teams still up at the summit, both of them women from British Columbia. They'd shared stories of climbs in the Canadian Rockies and a stove for soup this morning as the sun began to rise. One of them was also named Allison. They'd laughed about the chances of that, but now she found that face etched upon her mind, could not dispel it.

Suddenly Allison's feet went out from under her and she began to backslide, frantically grabbing for the ice ax on her belt. Just before she went head over heels, she wielded the ax two-handed, driving its pick into the side of the mountain to break her fall. She hung there a moment on her side, both arms extended, hanging on to the handle, but then the ax let loose and she began to spiral away, headfirst, chin raking the ice-sheathed granite until she struck something solid and her legs came around and were pinned beneath her.

She tried to blink away the snow that covered her eyes, to see through the hail of white wind, and there was Sergio's purple snowsuit. He wrapped his arms around her waist and put his face to hers and it was cold.

"You okay?"

She tried to speak, but the words wouldn't come. Her mouth was filling with warm blood, her eyes welling with tears.

He helped her to stand; neither was able to see the other's expression through the dark lenses of their goggles. She put a gloved hand over his heart and held it there and he nodded. Then he gave her his ice ax, turned and pointed down and grabbed the line, descending into the whiteout. Allison nodded as he disappeared. There was no time to reflect.

But Allison did reflect. She had spent last night in Sergio's sleeping bag. It was the first and only time since they had met—eight days before in the village of Talkeetna where solo climbers come to buddy-up with summiting teams—that he had even spoken more than a dozen words to her. Allison thought him arrogant at first, one of those handsome playboy types with infinite time and money on his hands. She had even goaded him about it on the mountain—trying to provoke a reaction until an unguarded moment in their tent she saw an unmistakable look of despair on his face. It was then she realized there was more to Sergio than met the eye. He hadn't come to Denali to conquer the mountain. He had come here to run away. But from what: a lost love, a failed marriage, some deep incomprehensible disappointment in his life?

They never got to talk about it and perhaps, she thought, they never would.

She remembered his lips pressed to the side of her neck in the cocoon of that sleeping bag last night. He had actually cried after they made love. He did not want to leave the mountain, he'd told her. His warm tears were wet on her neck, he told her he did not want to return to who he was.

DENALI NATIONAL PARK
FIVE DAYS LATER

Harsh sunlight glinted off the big blades of the HH-60 Pave Hawk, creating strobe-like effects inside the helicopter's cargo bay. Captain Metcalf, sitting opposite Sherry Moore, shielded his eyes from the rapid-fire bars of white light deflecting off her snow goggles.

"Glaciers." He leaned toward the edge of her helmet. "We're almost there."

Sherry nodded, her stomach queasy as the craft began to tilt on it side, darting toward the tallest mountain in the Western Hemisphere. Sherry was no stranger to helicopters. She'd spent much of her life being whisked from one place to another, knew the crew seats of the big corporate Bells and Hueys and Sikorskys, even the fleet of luxury VH-3Ds designated *Marine One* when the President of the United States was on board. But the Pave Hawk was like nothing she had experienced before; it was like the difference between riding a flea and a bumblebee.

"Is it clear? The summit?" she asked.

"Blue skies. Hard to take your eyes away," Metcalf said absently. She felt him looking at her just then, knowing he was regretting the offhanded reference to sight.

Her own images of the mountain were formed from books she'd listened to on tape or disk, of blinding white snow and black granite walls, of ice blue glaciers and bottomless crevices.

"I can imagine," she said softly.

The Alaskans called the mountain by its Indian name, Denali, meaning the "great one," though U.S. geological maps still call it Mount McKinley. It towered four miles above five glaciers, with more vertical face than Mount Everest, high enough to be seen from Anchorage, a hundred thirty miles away, on a good day.

There were no climbers on the summit of Denali today. No colorful string of snowsuits negotiating the Denali pass or the notorious ridge or the turn called Windy Corner.

All of the climbers known to survive the storm had been found below 14,000 feet, near basin camp, where National Guard Chinooks were evacuating as fast as they could assemble.

Above 14,000 feet, conditions were simply indescribable, or, as one Denali ranger told reporters, a wasteland of flash-frozen cornices. Of valleys pitted with hidden fissures wide enough to swallow rescue teams or helicopters.

The storm was the result of a low-pressure system that had inserted itself on the mountain last Sunday, generating what was known as a polar cyclone. The system laid upon Denali for five days, producing a dozen feet of new snow in gusts of wind exceeding 100 miles per hour. The storm virtually resculpted the upper third of the mountain.

Now it was Friday and twelve people were still missing above basin camp. One expedition of four had summited the morning of the storm and was making their way back to high camp when the storm hit. Their last FRS radio transmission before the communications system went down due to the storm was from the Denali pass, 800 feet above high camp. They had every chance of making it then, but five days later they could not be reached and it was impossible to know where they had finally dug in to weather the storm. It was also unlikely their supplies were sufficient to sustain them.

Other expeditions, one from Thailand and one from British Columbia, were only nearing the summit when the storm suddenly developed. Their last reports indicated they were going forward, only a few hundred feet to the top, before they would turn around.

The cyclone hadn't been predicted, but that was the nature of Denali. Any beautiful morning could end with an afternoon storm and a climbing disaster.

Meteorologists, as always, wasted no time getting their warning out, but those on the upper third of the mountain needed days not hours to make their descent, and that was under optimal conditions. Anyone above basin camp last Friday was there to stay.

From the television on board the private jet taking Sherry to Alaska, Sherry learned there was little hope for climbers above 16,000 feet. Teams attempting the summit would have cached much of their equipment and food below, leaving them light for the final two-day ascent to the top of the mountain. Which meant that time was their greatest enemy. Even if they managed to reach their last cache of survival gear, there would be little food and fuel for heat, certainly not five days' worth.

The park rangers set up triage in the permanent medical station on basin camp, doctors from Anchorage and Fairbanks dividing their attention between cases of frostbite and acute mountain sickness. There was no small number of broken bones too, and a tent was set aside for bodies retrieved from a rescue in the gully below the vertical headwall under Camp 6. Three had fallen to their deaths there.

A fourth body, photographed by search planes, was dangling off that headwall by a line wrapped around his boot. He was hanging just below the 16,000-foot mark and his jacket, once bright purple, showed faint lavender under a sheath of heavy ice. Perhaps a carabiner or ascender broke, releasing him to the gale-force winds. Perhaps the winds themselves upended him and tangled the rope around his boot? Whatever the case, exposed to the elements as he was, he managed to make a signal mark with luminescent paint on the granite wall. The mark appeared to look like an arrow pointing upward with a circle on top. He was obviously trying to leave a message. To show rescuers there were survivors above the ledge. By altitude, he could only have been one of the team of four who had radioed they were trying to reach high camp the day the storm set in on the summit of Denali. Apparently they had descended to Camp 6 over the next two days, where they would have had to dig a snow cave, but where above the ledge and under all that new snow should they look? Any original sign of a cave would have disappeared an hour after it was built and finding it now, under new snow, was fairly impossible.

A spokesperson for the National Park Service announced they would not be committing teams to a random search above basin camp. It would pose too great a risk for the people and equipment it would take to get them there. More than a hundred people were on Denali when it hit, all but fifteen having had time to descend to the ranger station at basin camp, or they were already below it. But even this group suffered countless casualties.

Landing zones above basin camp could no longer be presumed safe. Also, it was late in the climbing season and glaciers were beginning to fracture under the snow and form bottomless crevices, some already as wide as a house. New snow above them presented the constant threat of avalanche and last, but hardly least, another storm was forming off the Bering Strait that would be upon them by midnight, obliterating the mountain in yet another whiteout. Rescue teams made it clear they would make no attempt to search the upper third of the mountain without clear evidence of life. The endeavor was not only risky but would divert badly needed personnel and helicopters already committed to evacuating known survivors. As for the body hanging from the ridge, his team was probably already dead. The marking he had made on the side of the mountain was not a sign of life, they reminded. It was only a sign, and how many days old?

It was all a little hard to digest, Sherry thought. She'd been following news of the disaster on Denali throughout the week. There was a sad recap of the story every evening as the storm prevented rescuers from getting to the mountain. But a mountain in Alaska was far removed in place and time from her living room in Philadelphia. She could not imagine a relationship to it.

Then, this morning, Garland Brigham, her neighbor and best friend knocked on her door. It was 6 A.M. He had been awakened by a call from Washington State senator Metcalf. The senator's only daughter, Allison, had been with the team of four believed to have survived the first day of the storm.

There had been a break in the weather. Rescuers were gearing up to reach the survivors. Metcalf wanted to know if Brigham's famous friend would fly to the mountain and attempt to learn if there had been any radio contact between the survivors and his daughter's team before the communications systems went down. Sherry, he said, would be given access to the bodies of the fallen climbers. Could any of them have seen his daughter descending when the storm hit? He was grabbing at straws, Brigham said, and the senator well knew it. Still, it was only 2 A.M. in Alaska. She could be on Denali before noon if she left right away.

Sherry Moore would do anything for Garland Brigham, even if it were to make a demonstration of compassion. By 6:30 A.M. she was in a military police car speeding for Philadelphia International. At 6:50 she climbed the carpeted stairs of a luxury Gulfstream jet and was handed a mug of coffee. She was the only passenger flying at .885 Mach across the country.

She knew from what Brigham had told her that the rescuers had daylight in their favor. The Alaskan sun wouldn't set until midnight, providing nineteen hours of light. She also knew that the senator's son, U.S. Navy SEAL Captain Brian Metcalf, would be meeting her in Anchorage, where she would transfer to a privately contracted helicopter from Washington State that would take them to Denali National Park and basin camp.

Sherry had dozed on and off during the flight, listened to cable news on satellite television, and spoken with Brigham by phone several times. He told her that Captain Metcalf had contacted him and wanted to know if she might attempt, with him, to reach a body hanging from a headwall. Metcalf was convinced it was a member of his sister's team. The man had apparently been trying to leave a message with signal dye on the side of the mountain when he died.

It wasn't a request and it didn't require an answer. Brigham was only warning Sherry what to expect when she arrived in Anchorage. But there must have been a conversation between the two men about her physical capabilities. Metcalf would not have raised the possibility of descending a mountainside with a blind woman unless he knew she was in that kind of shape. Brigham wouldn't have told Sherry what he thought she should do—he never tried to lead her one way or the other—but he might have considered it a real option.

One thing she knew with all certainty: he wouldn't let her do anything that might compromise her safety. She knew that as surely as she knew her own name. If Brigham even raised the possibility of such a thing, he had complete confidence in Metcalf's abilities. As for the biological side of it, all Sherry needed was a body intact, with the remnants of a neurological system and an inactive brain, to see a corpse's final seconds of memory.

Sherry felt the helicopter getting buffeted in the wind. She knew something about the Pave Hawk. It was a modified version of the army's Black Hawk, seventeen million dollars' worth of technology refitted for rescue work in hostile terrain. It was used not only in the mountainous extremes of Afghanistan but also in civilian rescues like Typhoon Chanchu and the Indian Ocean tsunami and Katrina in New Orleans.

There were three other men in the chopper, all navy SEALS, she'd been told, and they were strapped in harnesses on the benches to her right. Sherry's toe struck the duffel bag between them. It would be orange or red or yellow, filled with morphine and oxygen, heat packs and adrenaline syringes, and there would be CO_2 charged splints and neck braces and of course disposable body bags. Metcalf might have come to perform a rescue mission, but all rescuers knew that such undertakings often turned into a recovery. She knew Metcalf was thinking about that. Thinking about his sister.

She couldn't quite say how it had happened. One moment she was heading for the relative safety of basin camp to see the bodies of three dead climbers. The next she was listening to Metcalf's argument for reaching the dead man, donning heavy snow gear to descend the side of a mountain.

Metcalf was not a man of many words, but he was nonetheless convincing. She felt confident in his presence and it was contagious. She knew now why Brigham had let it get this far. You didn't always need eyes to size up a man. The perception of presence was not exclusive to people with sight, nor were qualities such as competence and confidence. He was a navy SEAL and that presumed certain abilities, but there was far more to Metcalf than ability.

The plan was extraordinarily simple, he told her. The pilot of the Pave Hawk would drop them above the headwall at 16,200 feet. Then they would belay off fixed lines—already attached to the side of the mountain—and rappel 400 feet to where the body was hanging. Recovering the dead climber's body was not an option—there was no time for rescue baskets and Metcalf could hardly divide his attention between a blind woman and a dead man once they were down there. But if the dead man had been part of Allison Metcalf's team, Metcalf might be able to make clear the meaning of the message the climber had been trying to write on the side of the wall. If they could decipher it, Metcalf could radio the information to his men up above and they could focus their search accordingly.

Sherry often went into these kinds of situations feeling doubtful. What a person was thinking about in their last few seconds of life was not always what her clients wanted to hear. No one knows the precise moment they will expire and what random thoughts might occupy their short-term memory when they did. This was especially true when death is inevitable but protracted. People preparing themselves for death run the gamut of emotions, all the while searching the mind for visual references of their journey through life.

The man hanging from his boot had surely frozen to death. He was probably thinking about loved ones in the end, most people did, but he might also have been occupied by the technical problems of his situation, how to regain the fixed line on the side of the mountain, how to right himself again.

Even if he could still focus on the message he was trying to leave, Sherry couldn't imagine him producing a mental image that might help them locate a team of climbers buried in a snow cave above them. In fact, she could not imagine how he had hoped to find his own way back in a storm of the magnitude that had been described.

It occurred to her that he might never have had an intention of returning. That he might have known he was not coming back, that his message on the wall was an act of extreme selflessness.

"Kahiltna Glacier," the pilot's tinny voice came over the headphones. Metcalf tapped the side of her helmet and Sherry nodded to acknowledge that she'd heard. That her equipment was operating.

She pulled the microphone away from her mouth to speak to Metcalf privately. "You know the Admiral?" Brigham had never mentioned Senator Metcalf before. She was aware that Brigham had friends on Capitol Hill, had even overheard a woman at one of those rare gatherings at Brigham's house comment on a birthday card with the presidential seal.

"Mostly by reputation, ma'am."

"Reputation?" she repeated lightly. Sherry had never thought of Brigham in terms of having a reputation. . . .